She bent her head and kissed him, and he didn't have the good sense to end it.

She had been to the bakeshop! The lingering flavor of vanilla invaded his senses. With a twist and a swoop, he shifted her body down. Now he was the one on top, the one directing the kiss.

In a second the aroma of baked goods was gone, leaving in its place the heady scent of a woman.

He shoved back her bonnet, loosened a pin from her hair. Soft locks tumbled over his hands, tangled in his fingers.

Why was it he felt triumphant and guilty at the same time? The woman was his wife, dash it! He deserved more than kisses. Judging by the way her shapely bottom shifted against him, she wanted more.

Author Note

Thank you for picking up *The Rancher's Inconvenient Bride*. In the hustle and bustle of everyday life I'm happy that you have chosen to slow down and spend a few hours with Agatha Magee.

If you have read *The Cowboy's Cinderella*, you will know that Agatha is nothing like her twin sister, Ivy. They are like sunshine and shadow, with Ivy being confident and outgoing and Agatha being timid and fearful.

But that's not all there is to our bruised Agatha. As she struggles to find her way from helplessness to independence, she discovers the courageous woman inside her. She goes after the life that she wants for herself even when she still wants to hide away.

I believe we can all feel some kinship for Agatha. Every day we face challenges that we would like to run from but cannot—the car breaks down, the bills are past due, the computer crashes or your sweet toddler raises the roof while you wait in a checkout line.

Some days we need to call upon our inner lioness, go out and claim life's joy. And some days we need to find a quiet place and let it all pass.

I hope you find a bit of escape and a bit of cheer in Agatha's journey.

CAROL ARENS

—

The Rancher's Inconvenient Bride

HARLEQUIN® HISTORICAL

Recycling programs
for this product may
not exist in your area.

ISBN-13: 978-0-373-29955-3

The Rancher's Inconvenient Bride

Printed in U.S.A.

Carol Arens delights in tossing fictional characters into hot water, watching them steam and then giving them a happily-ever-after. When she is not writing, she enjoys spending time with her family, beach camping or lounging about a mountain cabin. At home, she enjoys playing with her grandchildren and gardening. During rare spare moments, you will find her snuggled up with a good book. Carol enjoys hearing from readers at carolarens@yahoo.com or on Facebook.

Visit the Author Profile page at Harlequin.com.

Written in loving memory of my mother,
Catherine Alene Ebert.
Love cannot be separated.

Chapter One

Tanners Ridge, Wyoming, July 1883

"The Devil Wind is blowing and it's going to make all those circus folks go mad."

William English pressed his hat to his head. The wind was blowing devilishly, but he doubted it was going to push anyone over the brink of sanity. Unless, maybe it was the elderly woman leaning on her cane and frowning intently up at him.

"I'm sure they're no more likely to go mad than anyone else, Mrs. Peabody."

"If you'd seen the things I have, Mayor English, you would be running for the hills." She pounded her cane on the boardwalk in front of Tanners Ridge Community Bank. Twice. No doubt the extra thump was to make sure he was paying attention.

A third thump might have been in order, given that he really was paying more attention to keeping his dearly priced bowler hat on his head than to her unrealistic fears.

"I'm sure you've seen some interesting things——"

"The skeleton of a three-headed dog," the woman declared, cutting off his attempt to ease her fear. "And a man swallowing a sword—a flaming sword—and a fellow putting his head in the mouth of a lion! And that happened without the wind blowing. Who knows what might happen tonight."

"Everyone will have a fine time. Just you wait and see."

"What I'm waiting for, is for you to hire Tanners Ridge a sheriff."

William smiled, his lips pressed tight. As mayor—and hopefully future governor—of Wyoming, it would not do to let his emotions show.

The fact that Tanners Ridge had no sheriff was no one's fault but the good folks living here. He had presented no less than four candidates and they had all been voted down or refused the job because of low pay.

"Will you be at the meeting this afternoon? I've another candidate to introduce for the job."

"Of course—unless I'm murdered by a fat woman with a beard who has gone raving."

"Would you feel better if I went down to take a look at things?"

"Why, that would be a good idea." Mrs. Peabody's smile brought out the charming wrinkles in her cheeks. Her look of relief made the trip down the hill to where the circus was camped seem worth the effort.

He tipped his hat to her, nodded. "I'll see you this afternoon at the meeting, then."

"Be careful," she warbled after him.

Chances were, the only danger in going down had to do with walking the steep, rocky path, not circus folks gone wind-mad.

A quarter of a mile down the path the ground leveled out, giving the traveling circus plenty of room to set up their big tent.

Even buffeted by wind, the huge structure barely moved. Still, it couldn't hurt to have a look around and make sure folks would be safe inside tonight.

A fair distance from the tent there was a circle of colorfully painted wagons. He supposed this was where the performers and other employees lived.

The scent of baking pastries and simmering stew came from one of them. Had to be the chuck wagon, or the circus version of it.

On the way to the big tent, he passed by a circle of large, wheeled cages. A dozing leopard lifted one eye when William passed. In another of them, dogs of all shapes and sizes barked at him. Other dogs roamed freely about, so he imagined the ones who were confined were not pets but performers.

Within the circle of cages, a pair of elephants were tethered to a pole.

This was something he'd never seen! True-to-life elephants. All he could do was stare in amazement while dust swirled around their big feet and their swaying trunks.

Because he wasn't paying attention, his bowler blew off. It rolled over the ground toward the big tent.

On a run, he snatched it up. He secured it to his head with a thump, straightened his bow tie, then brushed off his lapels before stepping inside the canvas tent.

It was an impressive space. For all its size, it didn't sway overmuch in the wind. Perhaps if the roustabouts who raised the tent had used a few more ropes it wouldn't sway at all. If William had been in charge of things, he would have—

Done nothing different. Even though his mother lived twenty-five miles away and he hadn't seen her in months, her narrowed eyes and firmed lips appeared in his mind.

Her voice whispered as clearly as if she had been standing beside him.

"William Byron English, you do not need to be in charge of everything."

Maybe not, but still he wondered if heavier wood should have been used on the risers where folks would sit.

Letting go of control was a lesson he'd been trying to learn since the time he was a boy and had decided that the fire in the hearth would be better with six logs rather than the two the butler had put in.

It had taken a week before his mother would smile at him and a week after that before the stench of smoke cleared out of the house.

Gazing at the two brightly painted rings used for performing, William couldn't think of a way to improve them. That was a relief, and good enough to send his mother's voice home to Cheyenne where it belonged.

He'd heard that P.T. Barnum had three performing rings, but Tanners Ridge was not a big enough town to attract that man's attention.

Hell, it wasn't even big enough to attract a reliable sheriff.

"Halloo!" came a voice from the far side of the tent.

He turned toward the voice to see a short man, his belly round as a ball, step from behind a curtain. The fellow waved his arm, indicating that William should cross to where he was.

The crossing took some time because the tent was large.

While this circus production was not as grand as some, it was the most exciting thing to come to Tanners Ridge in a long time, so he'd been told. Having only been mayor here for six months, there was much he was still learning about his new home.

"Halloo to you, sir." The man extended his pudgy hand. "I'm Frenchie Brown, owner of this fine production."

"William English." He shook Frenchie Brown's hand, surprised to find so much strength in that soft-looking fist.

"Ah, the mayor!" The man nodded vigorously. He had no hair and the smooth skin of his head glistened in a ray of sunshine that cut through a gap in the tent. "I ought to have known who you were by the fine cut of your clothes. Welcome, Mr. Mayor."

Back home in Cheyenne no one ever remarked on his wardrobe. Gentleman ranchers of the area dressed the same way.

"I just came down to see how you folks were faring in the wind. It's blowing like the devil outside."

"We've held up fine in worse than this." His grin was wide, exposing a gold front tooth. The stench of strong cologne trying to mask the scent of cigars and clothes that hadn't been washed in some time made William back up a step. "Come, I've something special to show you. Tonight, folks will have to pay to see her but being that you are the mayor—well I'll give you a peek at her for free."

A free peek at a woman was not something that William figured he really wanted. But in case the lady was in need of help, he followed Frenchie around the curtain.

"Meet Gloria." Frenchie stroked the curve of a huge gray hip. William backed up several paces. "The only taxidermized pachyderm known to the civilized world."

The creature's trunk was lifted high as though she were trumpeting, her tail was also lifted, forever proud.

"During her lifetime this good old girl earned me plenty of money." With what appeared to be a loving embrace, Frenchie stroked her ivory tusk. "Couldn't see any reason that should change."

"No…" William glanced about, wondering if the skeleton of a three-headed dog would come bounding by chased by a sword-swallower, his foil aflame. "I imagine not."

Agatha noticed the spider in its web a second before it saw her.

The startled bug scrambled across the delicate threads it had spun between the spindles of the porch of the trailer that she shared with Laura Lee. The small arachnid disappeared nearly as fast as she spotted it.

How she envied that quick little creature. Spiders were not required to face the world beyond the shadows.

Agatha closed her eyes, took a deep breath, feeling the wind buffet her hair, tug at her hat.

As much as it frightened her, she did have to face the world. She had spent most of her life shut away. Not by choice—far from it. She hadn't even known that she had a choice.

"Good day to you, Miss Agatha," greeted Hugo Fin as he passed by carrying a ladder.

Hugo was the boss canvas man in charge of raising the big top and keeping order among those who worked for him. As rowdy a bunch as the roustabouts were, no one dared step out of line with Mr. Fin's leveled stare upon him.

A frizzle of apprehension shot up her neck but she forced a smile and returned his greeting.

After he rounded the corner of the next trailer, she wrapped an imaginary cloak of confidence about her shoulders and walked down the stairs. In her mind she tugged it tight.

Without thinking she turned toward the path leading to the chuck wagon. It would be less traveled. She stopped so suddenly that a cloud of dust puffed about the toes of her shoes.

She was behaving like the spider when she needed to act like Leroy. The circus lion was always assured of his status as king of the beasts.

Spinning about, she strode purposefully along the more populated path.

Several yards ahead of her three women, two of them brave aerialists, had stopped to talk. Their skirts blew madly and they held their hats to their heads.

Instead of walking wide around them like her feet itched to do, she approached them.

"Good afternoon," she greeted, noticing that her hand had broken into a sweat. What must they think of her just marching up and boldly beginning a conversation.

"You're our new kitchen girl!" the youngest of the three declared.

"Agatha, isn't that right?" asked the one who was known as the Fat Lady. "I hope you are more talented than the last girl we had. Her cooking was so bad that I began to waste away. You'd think butter and sugar were short of supply. Lands of glory, I was close to losing my job."

"I hope I am more talented, too, ma'am." She surely did. She did know for a fact that there was plenty of butter and sugar in the larder.

Too bad it was Laura Lee who was the cook. Her friend had worked in the kitchen back home on the Lucky Clover under Mrs. Morgan's skillful guidance. Laura Lee was the one who had been given the job. Agatha only helped as best she could.

Agatha's talent for food was to consume it. For most of

her twenty-three years, she hadn't known what a pleasure eating could be. Her ever-watchful nurse, Hilda Brunne, had insisted that anything with the smallest amount of spice would ruin her charge's health.

After all the years of deprivation, she was still too thin, but she was slowly gaining.

Agatha nodded goodbye to the three ladies then continued on her way, leaning into the wind.

That hadn't been so bad. In fact she felt proud, buoyant of step, even. Only a week ago she would never have approached them.

The choice to leave the only home she had ever known had been a good one. Very hard and frightening, to be sure, but it was what she had to do.

If she was ever going to be an independent woman who could stand on her own, she needed to face a fear that had been planted bone-deep in her.

It hadn't been an easy thing to do, leaving her twin sister, Ivy, and her husband, Travis, and kissing their baby daughter goodbye. Truly, all she'd wanted was to sit in the shadow of her balcony and be safe.

What she had to remind herself, each and every hour it seemed, was that by hiding in her suite back at the Lucky Clover, she was not living life.

Life with all its tension and thrill, was what she needed—wanted—desperately.

With renewed purpose in her step, Agatha continued along the way to the cook trailer. It circled around outside of the circus settlement, the backyard, as Hugo Fin called it.

There had been a time, and not long ago, when Agatha could not even walk. For her own twisted reasons, her nurse had made sure to keep her helpless.

Now, if she had to march twenty miles a day to build her strength that was what she would do.

"Lady," came a voice from between two trailers. "Can you help me?"

Agatha stepped into the shadow between the trailers to see a woman sitting on the ground, her back propped up by the wheel behind her.

A young coochie girl, by the looks of her. Agatha had heard enough gossip to know that the dancing girls who worked for Frenchie Brown did far more scandalous things than dance without their clothes.

What had happened to her in her young life to make her a slave to prostitution and addiction?

Poor thing. Agatha understood more than most people did, that life could take a person in a direction she would not have chosen.

She scanned the ground near the sallow-skinned woman, looking for a bottle. Yes, there it was, just under her hand.

"I've run out of laudanum." The woman gazed up at her with unfocused eyes, her mouth slack. "Go into my trailer and fetch me another bottle, won't you?"

Something dark, fearful, raised its head inside of Agatha, snarled its claws about her. As clearly as she heard the wind rustle the brush, she heard its seductive voice.

She backed away without answering the prostrate woman.

Even though her hands grew damp and her stomach nauseous, she was not going to pick up the laudanum. If she did, she feared she would find a dim corner and drink it down.

It was time for a visit to the elephant. She cut across the yard, rushing past the bull hand who guarded the huge pachyderms against curious townsfolk.

It was not those elephants she sought. It was the one inside the big top that drew her.

Pausing beside the entrance, she glanced behind her. In the distance she spotted a man making his way up the stony path toward town. Something about him, the way he moved, seemed familiar—reassuring.

That was odd since she could see nothing of him but the back of his coat as he huddled against the wind. Odder still, that a stranger could give her a sense of comfort.

Agatha hurried across the floor of the Big Top. Glancing about, she ducked behind the canvas where Gloria stood still and majestic even in death.

She wouldn't visit for long. Mr. Brown did not like people near his elephant unless it was by a personal invitation or purchased ticket.

This was a rule that Agatha had ignored from the first moment she saw the beast.

"I'm not you," she whispered to the hulking gray corpse.

But she had been. Under the influence of the laudanum that Hilda Brunne had kept her subdued with, she had been as lifeless as this elephant.

Dead inside, gray and still outside, appearing to have life but with no spark of animation.

Some people might think it strange that she likened her past to this petrified creature—she even thought so sometimes. But other times, when she was afraid, when simply giving a stranger the time of day made her want to hide away—she needed to be reminded that she was alive—to vow that she would never again be a slave to laudanum.

She feared this great hulking creature that seemed to represent life in death.

She feared herself, what she might have become without the help of William English.

Yes, Ivy had been the one to help her overcome her addiction, but it had been William who kept her from going back to it when, fearing her sister had died, she wanted to find oblivion again.

On that wicked stormy night, he'd placed a book in her hands and made her read it out loud to him. It hadn't been easy to do, given that she was mightily distracted by the masculine scent of him, by the warmth of his arm and the lean muscle of his thigh touching hers while they sat on the couch waiting.

Of course, she'd had a crush on him for years. But whenever her young heart would begin to flutter, Nurse Brunne would point out that she was not fit for any man, especially not one like William English.

She'd been right about that. William was a prince and she had been—dead—like this poor elephant.

But she would not be again.

Today she was breathing, alive and getting stronger. No one, or nothing in a beguiling little bottle would take that new freedom from her.

The stew was not thickening as it should. No matter how long it cooked, it remained broth and not gravy.

The Fat Lady would hate it.

"I don't know what's wrong, Laura Lee." The Fat Lady was not the only one who was going to be displeased. "Frenchie Brown will be angry."

"I'm homesick," Laura Lee stated as though Agatha had not spoken.

"He's going to bellow at us if his food isn't correct."

"It's been two months and I miss the Lucky Clover to my bones. I'm going home, tomorrow." Laura Lee turned to look at Agatha, moisture glittering in her eyes. "Did you add flour?"

"Going home!"

She couldn't go home! The two of them had come on this adventure together. Why, Ivy and Travis would never have allowed her to come if Laura Lee hadn't accompanied her.

Especially had they ever dreamed the adventure would lead to this cook trailer.

As far as anyone back home knew, she and Laura Lee were working in the kitchen of a fancy hotel in Cheyenne.

Before Agatha had even become skilled at peeling potatoes, the hotel closed for good. Within a couple of days, Laura Lee had secured them this job.

Maybe she ought to have gone home then, let her friend go on alone, but she had set out to find independence. What could be more daring than living among circus folks?

"I've got to go. You know how I was sweet on Johnny Ruiz?"

How could she not know? At only five miles from home Laura Lee had begun to sigh over him and hadn't quit.

"We've been writing to each other every day. He's coming for me and we're going back home to be married."

"But you haven't finished teaching me to cook."

What a cowardly thing to say! Agatha regretted it the instant the words left her mouth.

"You came here—joined a circus for mercy's sake—in order to learn to stand on your own."

Yes—it was true that she had. Still, she hadn't learned nearly enough about cooking to do it on her own and she'd discovered that circus people did enjoy their meals.

"You should go, Laura Lee!" She really should. "Go home and have lots of sweet little babies with Johnny."

Dropping the wooden spoon into the large pot of watery stew, Agatha wrapped her arms around her friend. With luck she would believe the tears on her cheeks were tears of joy, and they were for the most part.

But it couldn't be denied that she was indulging in a big dose of self-pity. She hadn't a doubt in the world that once Ivy knew where she was, she would send someone to fetch her home.

Ivy would not come herself. She had a newborn to care for, and a ranch to run. But someone would come and she was not nearly ready.

"Don't look so worried, Agatha." Laura Lee let go of her and scooped up a cup of flour, mixed it with water. "I know you're concerned about being forced to go home. But I'll assure your sister and Travis that you are thriving and the circus people are watching over you like they would their own kin."

Someone was. Mr. Frenchie Brown. She felt his eyes on her back whenever she ventured from the cook trailer.

In her opinion, his attention was not so protective. He frowned at her often, shook his head. Given the chance he would dismiss her.

Agatha watched Laura Lee stir flour mixed with water into the pot. "Look at that! It's stew. Nice thick stew."

"Here's the secret to cooking, although Mrs. Morgan would paddle me for saying so."

Laura Lee winked. Mischief made her eyes sparkle.

One day Agatha hoped her own eyes would sparkle. They didn't now, but one day they would. As much as her friends' did, as much as Ivy's did. And Ivy's eyes always sparkled.

"If a dish isn't right add butter, lots and lots of butter. If it needs to be thicker, flour, and if it's dessert lots of sugar, and butter, butter, butter—a good dose of cream doesn't hurt, either."

Chapter Two

The door slammed behind the current, and fifth, man that William had presented for sheriff. It was hard to tell if the wind had to do with it or if the fellow was hopping mad to have traveled a hundred miles only to be judged unworthy for the position.

William frowned at the citizens sitting in the chairs facing the council table. The way they were going, they would never agree on a lawman.

"I'm glad to see the back of that one," uttered Mr. Henry Beal. Henry sat beside William at the long council table drumming his fingertips on the polished wood. His vocation of blacksmith showed in the soot rimming his fingernails. "Too prissy to be sheriff if you ask me."

"And small," declared a middle-aged woman perched on the edge of her chair. "We need a larger man."

"Yes, a much larger man." This from the younger lady sitting beside the woman.

William glanced away quickly when she winked at him and nudged her companion in the ribs.

The wood legs of his chair scraped across the floor when he stood up. He made eye contact—frowned more to the point—at the four men seated with him at the table.

"I understand that you want the best person for the job. We all do. But that man was qualified and willing to accept the pay you offered. He may have been short, but he came highly respected. You read his letters of recommendation."

"Still too small." A man stood up from his chair near the front door of the Tanners Ridge Library where town meetings were held, shrugged his shoulders. "I think we all agree on that."

"He might be married," came a muffled voice from the back of the room. Just not muffled enough so that folks didn't hear the comment.

"Really, Aimee." The woman's seat neighbor whispered too loudly. "Why do you care? The most eligible bachelor of them all is standing right in front of you. Forget about winning a sheriff."

"He's not married." William pursed his lips.

This was supposed to be a serious meeting, not a matchmaking fest. He ought to be used to that kind of attention by now. Every unmarried woman and her mother knew he was rich, ambitious and needed a wife.

But the matter at hand was to appoint a sheriff. Surely they understood how urgent the need was.

"We're running out of time, folks," he pointed out. The man most concerned about the size of the fellow who'd just stormed angrily out of the library sat down. Feminine giggles stopped abruptly. "You know that Pete Lydle will be here soon. Do you really want him opening up a saloon like the one he had in Luminary?"

"I wouldn't mind having a nice place to play a game of cards," Henry stood up to say.

"It wouldn't be a nice place. Pete's Palace was a hellhole. Drinking, gambling, prostitution—it attracted a lot of unsavory folks."

"You been there? How do you know?" Henry spread his arms.

"I'm the mayor. It's my business to know."

As soon as the old Bascomb Hotel had been sold and rumors of a saloon surfaced, he'd made sure to find out what he could about the new owner. He'd discovered Pete Lydle to be an objectionable fellow who would do anything to earn a dollar. Didn't matter if the thing was legal or not.

"There are decent watering holes. This town could use one if you ask me," said a man near the back of the room.

"Maybe Lydle's gone respectable," said Henry. "Otherwise why would he come here? Why would old man Bascomb have sold out to him?"

"It wasn't him who sold out!" Henry's wife stood to glare at her husband. "It was those next of kin in New York City, did that. And don't think you will be going to the Bascomb come an evening. Mark my words!"

"Just so!" agreed another woman, coming to her feet and wagging her finger.

"Folks change. You women are seeing the boogeyman when you might not need to."

"Are you willing to risk the town's safety on that? You need to hire a sheriff and you need to do it now," William declared, trying to drive his point home. "What do you think will happen without a lawman to protect you?"

"Maybe that fellow wasn't so short after all," Mrs. Peabody declared from her place in the front row. "He did have a hard look in his eye."

The glare had been because they insulted his stature and questioned his ability, William figured.

"Who else have you got for us?"

"Who else?" Did they think lawmen just wandered by seeking employment every day? "No one."

"But we need protection!" Mrs. Peabody stood up to speak her mind. She shook her cane to make her point. "We'll be murdered in our beds when the saloon gets here—if the circus folks haven't got to us first."

"We've got more'n a month." Roy Backley, the banker, stood up beside Mrs. Peabody and placed a hand upon her shoulder. "Don't you worry. The mayor will find us someone by then. For now, I say we all enjoy the circus tonight. Forget about that saloon for a while."

"I second that," added the blacksmith. "No need to worry now when it might turn out to be a fine establishment. It's hard to imagine the Bascomb Hotel turning tawdry."

The owner of the livery, sitting on the right side of William, stood up. "I third that notion and declare this meeting over. See you all at the circus."

William had lost count of the times he half regretted accepting the position of mayor of Tanners Ridge, but he had to begin his public service somewhere. He'd hoped to get his start as an appointee to the Territorial Legislature of Wyoming, but it hadn't happened.

The men who made legislative appointments had voted him down because he was not a married man. In their opinion, married men were more stable of character. In William's opinion, it was their wives wanting other women to socialize with, hold balls and galas and the like.

The loss had been a great disappointment. Especially since he had planned to be married. He'd made an arrangement with Ivy Magee. His money to save the Lucky Clover from ruin in exchange for her hand in marriage. The union would have given him the prestige that the highly respected Lucky Clover had to offer.

In the end she'd turned him down and married Travis Murphy instead.

She was right to have done so. For all that she would have suited his needs, she was a woman who deserved being loved. And Travis loved her to his bones.

The problem with having befriended Ivy was that it complicated his bride hunt. Eligible ladies who would suit his needs in every way threw themselves in his path daily.

An availability of suitable woman was not the trouble.

The trouble was knowing how Ivy loved her man. Having seen it with his own eyes, well—he wanted that now. Or at least something close to it.

He wanted a woman who sparkled for him. But he also wanted to be governor one day. For that he would need a wife and, God willing, children.

Little girls to bounce upon his knee and little boys to play ball with. He wanted them, governorship or not.

"I'd have voted for your man, Mayor English." William gazed down into the face of a pretty young woman who smiled up at him with a winking dimple. "May I call you William?"

One day he hoped to be as lucky as Travis Murphy.

Gazing down at the woman preening beside him, he doubted it would be today.

Agatha reread the first three lines of the book on her lap, unable to concentrate. Here in camp, all was peaceful, although the wind swayed the trailer like a cradle.

Everything added up for a cozy evening in the company of fictional characters whom she knew quite well, having read the book four times already.

But just there, beyond the solitude of the nearly abandoned camp, she could hear a crowd of voices raised in merriment.

A part of her longed to be out there, laughing and enjoying the thrills. But the nightly customers were loud and lively—there were just so many people.

She ought to force herself to go out, she knew that, but the adventures of Miss Maudie O'Hurley would do for tonight. Indeed, the beleaguered Maudie was about to be carried off by her true love. What could be more thrilling than that?

Being carried off by her own true love, of course.

"You aren't going to meet him sitting here," she mumbled.

Still, it was windy outside.

"What if the man of your dreams is visiting the circus at this moment?"

What if the man of her dreams was walking about out there with his dark hair glinting in the torchlight that illuminated the shadowed paths? What if his blue eyes…she'd long known them to be the color of the sky just before sunrise…were sparkling with pleasure at all he was seeing?

What if William was here and she missed him because she was sitting in her safe chair reliving Maudie's happiness…once again.

Now there was a silly thought. William here? If she was going to indulge in daydreams she might just as soon dwell on something that really happened.

She could at the very least relive the time that William had danced with her at a party hosted at the Lucky Clover. He had only asked her to dance because she was Ivy's sister, she was certain, but nonetheless it had been magical—the stuff of her dreams.

At the time she hadn't even had strength enough to

stand on her own so that handsome man—that prince—
had taken her hand, lifted her with an arm around her
back and supported her through a very brief dance.

Nothing that Maudie O'Hurely had experienced came
close to that!

Agatha snapped the book closed then crossed the small
space to stare out the window. Moonlight cast shadows
of tree branches on the roof of the trailer across from
hers. They looked like malevolent fingers all twisted and
spooky.

"Idiot," she murmured. "They are shadows and you
need to go out."

Not to find her prince, but to find her strength. The
very last thing she needed at the moment was to find a
royal protector—or the Wyoming equivalent.

One day that would be a fine thing. Loving a man and
having him watch over her, while she in turn watched
over him.

At the moment, finding that companion was the very
last thing she needed to do. If she fell into a life of being
protected, it might be akin to seeking relief in a small
blue bottle of laudanum. She would gain strength by
standing on her own two feet and no other way.

Plucking her wrap from its hook on the wall, she
tugged it tight about her. If she was to become a woman
whom men would respect, she had to be a woman that
she respected first.

Surely she could be as brave as Ivy's pet mouse. That
sweet creature ventured out nightly.

The moment she stepped outside a small shaggy dog
met her at the bottom of the steps.

"Where were you at feeding time, Miss Valentine?"
A short time ago the dog had been star of the show,
well-groomed and pampered. Now that she was begin-

ning to show her age she'd been cast off, left to fend for herself or die.

As far as Agatha could tell, no one cared about her fate one way or another. It was the same for the other mutts Agatha fed with the scraps left over from dinner.

"Come along. We'll stop by the chuck wagon and see what's left."

Valentine wagged her curly tail and limped along after Agatha. The poor creature hadn't been limping yesterday. Perhaps that was why she didn't show up with the other dogs to be fed.

Bending low, she scooped Valentine up. "It's a crime how they tossed you out. Why, if you were earning them money I reckon they would have the veterinarian look at your foot right off."

The distance to the cook trailer was not so far, maybe a couple of hundred yards. But the path was dark, isolated and a bit unnerving. The shifting light cast by the torches seemed creepy rather than reassuring.

This was a challenge, nothing more. The shadows at her back didn't really cry her name. The rush of leaves across the ground was only that. It was her imagination turning them into light, quick footsteps pursuing her.

Hilda Brunne was dead. Everyone believed it. There was no reason not to. Because her body hadn't been found, Ivy and Travis had hired the Pinkerton agency to search for her.

Even the professionals presumed Hilda was dead. The moaning presence pursuing her was nothing but a dark, emotionless wind.

Agatha no longer needed to fear her. What she did need to fear was what her nurse had tried to make her. A girl afraid of everyone—believing she could only trust one, twisted woman.

Until she became be strong enough to live among strangers, she would never be free of Hilda Brunne's ominous ghost.

All at once the shadows gave way to bright light, crowds and laughing people.

Tattooed Joe stood on a stage flexing the tiger emblazoned on his back. Near him, Sword-Swallowing Smithy consumed red-hot flames.

From inside a tent Agatha heard the guffaws of the Fat Lady.

Couples strolled arm in arm, gazing more at each other than the bizarre things happening around them. Parents covered their children's eyes at every turn while their own eyes popped wide open.

Over to the right, a group of young men gathered around a painting of three-breasted Josie. It seemed they could not hand over their quarters fast enough for the chance to see the oddity. They were, of course, being duped. Josie was as two-breasted as any other woman. But the fool boys would see what they expected to see in the dim light of the tent.

Valentine wriggled in Agatha's arms, trying to lick her face.

The distraction nearly caused her to slam into the back of a tall gentleman who had stopped at the fortune-teller's stall. A finely dressed woman clung to his arm.

"I see your future, young people." Leah Madrigal, the fortune-teller, tapped her red fingernail on a glass globe filled with colored water. "For a penny, I'll share it with you."

"Oh, yes—please do tell." The lady clapped her hands. "Mr. English, do you have a penny?"

Mr. English!

Agatha stumbled backward. It couldn't be—but yes—

it was! She knew that silhouette! Indeed, she'd half recognized him earlier in the day when he'd been climbing
the hill toward town. The sense of familiarity she'd felt
had not been misplaced.

"Come now, Mayor!" The woman fairly bounced on
her toes. "I know you have a penny!"

William—her very own William was here! He was
mayor?

She wanted nothing more than to hug him about the ribs
and feel safe. He'd made her feel that way once before—
safe and protected on that awful afternoon when no one
knew what her sister's fate might be. If not for William
standing between her and an evil blue bottle she might
have succumbed to it.

Leah noticed her cowering in the shadow, nodded and
winked.

She prayed that William would not see her! How
would she act? What would she say? No doubt she'd
trip over her words. It had been some time since she'd
seen him. He hadn't been to the ranch since Ivy turned
him down.

What if he didn't remember her?

The bouncing woman snatched the penny out of William's fingers then dropped it on the fortune-teller's
brightly decorated table.

"What do you see for us?" The eager miss clung to
William's hand. His fingers had to be going numb, her
grip looked that tight.

Leah caressed her glass ball, made a show of staring
into it. All at once her brows arched, her lips curved.
She leaned sideways to peer around William and his
lady. Her puzzled-looking gaze held Agatha's for five
full seconds before she returned her attention to her
customers.

"I see marriage—for you both. But not to each other. You, my dear girl, will make a lovely match that will make your parents proud and your friends jealous. But you must be patient. This will not happen in a moment."

The lady started to protest because clearly she wanted William and she wanted him now.

Dismissing her, Leah turned her gaze on William. She smiled at him, then oddly, she winked one more time at Agatha.

"Now you, my handsome one, you will marry sooner than you think. It will come as quite a surprise to you— and to your bride. Oh, I see you are worried, but this will be a long marriage blessed with many children."

"I don't believe her!" the woman exclaimed. "You don't, either, do you, William?"

It was an odd reading. Agatha had heard a few of Leah's fortunes and they all ended with happily-ever-after for the hopeful lovers who paid their pennies.

"I believe I was entertained," William said. Agatha imagined he was smiling, although she could only see the back of his head. "Thank you, ma'am."

With that, he placed another penny on the table and walked away with the woman who, very clearly, had not been entertained.

With a crook of her finger, Leah motioned for Agatha to come out from the shadow.

"Most of the time, this is no more than a ball of water—but once in a while it does see things."

"How do you know the difference?"

The fortune-teller tapped her chest with her crimson fingernails. "It's in here."

"How lovely for Mr. English, then." He did want a horde of children. Ivy had told her that about him.

"Go on your way, Miss Agatha. Enjoy your evening."

Yes, but first she needed to feed scrawny Miss Valentine. It was distressing to feel her ribs, so sharp and angular under her fur.

While walking away, she heard Leah's throaty laugh, then seconds later, "I see your future young ones. For a penny I'll tell you what it is."

Sitting on the steps of the chuck wagon, Agatha listened to the distant wail of the pipe organ.

Miss Valentine had finished her second plate of stew and was nosing about in the dirt for fallen scraps.

Agatha drummed her fingers on her knees and wondered if William was going to marry the bouncing woman or the one who would bear him many children.

She sighed. She had never truly considered the possibility that she would ever be William's bride. Although she could hardly control her nightly dreams. But the light-of-day truth was, she was not at all the woman he needed.

That was why, when the Lucky Clover had been threatened with financial ruin, Travis had gone in search of Agatha's missing sister and brought her back to marry William.

Everyone knew Agatha would never be a suitable match for their wealthy neighbor. She didn't have the stamina; she was too shy.

Sadly, her father had been informed by the doctor that she should never have children, being much too frail for the stress. Over the years Nurse Brunne made sure Agatha understood that she was not fit for any man because of it.

"I don't care if you think you're in the family way!" Frenchie Brown's voice slammed the wall of the food trailer, bounced off and echoed down the dim pathway.

"I will not be shot out of the cannon!" came the outraged reply.

"I have a signed contract, Mrs. Otis. You have no choice."

Agatha stood up and peered three trailers down.

Frenchie Brown's big fist was clamped about the pregnant human cannonball's arm. No wonder the woman was struggling to get free. This was a dangerous act—even when the wind was not blowing.

"Put the costume on or take it up with my lawyer."

The red-sequined outfit lay on the ground glinting in lamplight—flaunting its indecency. Why, the wicked garment didn't even have a skirt. It was no more than a pair of fancy long johns.

"Take it up with God!"

"Around here, I am God." Now his voice was low, but unmistakably growling.

What a terrible situation! No one was in the area who might help Mrs. Otis.

No one but—

Agatha stepped into a wavering beam of torchlight. "I'll run for help!"

Frenchie Brown let go of Mrs. Otis. She dashed away into the darkness.

"You! Girl! Come here."

In spite of the fact that she had been willing to go get help, she was not good at dashing. No, she doubted she could do it if she tried.

She approached her boss, who apparently believed he was equal to the Almighty, with her heart beating madly against her ribs.

He studied her silently, walked around her in a slow circle.

"You'll do." He snatched up the costume from the dirt and tossed it at her. "Put it on."

"I couldn't." She really could not. It was a comfort that Miss Valentine had trotted up to stand beside her.

"Do not try my patience. Folks paid good money to see a woman get shot out of a cannon. The reputation of this company depends on you."

"No, it does not. My contract is to feed you." Be bold, be bold be bold! "It's far too windy for that stunt, anyway."

"Danger is what it is all about! Folks like to get all het up inside. Gives them a real thrill."

"I must decline," she said while he tried to shove the costume at her. "Most firmly."

"You leave me no choice, then."

With a grunt, Frenchie squatted down.

Really, folks might pay to see that feat.

He snatched up Miss Valentine. "Put it on or I'll break the mongrel's neck."

She did believe that. No doubt he would stuff the dog and mount her high on the elephant's trunk.

"Very well."

Agatha snatched the long johns and marched into the cook house. She would put the awful thing on, act like she was going to comply, then when the dog was safe, she would run. She would make a dash for it—as best she could. Clearly she would need cunning as well as speed.

Her plan fell apart when Frenchie's fist anchored about her arm before he dropped Miss Valentine in the dirt.

He yanked her toward the cannon exhibit. She dug in her heels.

"I won't do it!"

He grabbed her around the waist and lifted her off the ground.

She wriggled and pounded his arm, tried to peel his fingers off.

"Put me down!" she shouted. "I will not do this!"

"Take it up with your lawyer later—if you are able. It is a blustery night. Anything can happen."

Chapter Three

The thing William regretted most about the evening was the encounter with the fortune-teller.

Somehow Aimee Peller had convinced herself that the seer intended to say that they would be married soon. For the past half hour she had clung to him, pride of conquest clear in her smile. He'd lost count of how many times she'd stared at her hand, at the finger a wedding ring would circle.

While it was true that Aimee would be an appropriate wife—she was beautiful and socially accomplished—he would never marry her.

He'd been cursed with knowing what could be between a husband and wife. He'd seen it in Ivy's eyes whenever she looked at Travis.

Hang it, but he wanted to see that look in the eyes of the woman he married.

All he would see in Aimee's eyes was triumph over her social position.

Maybe he ought to have married Ivy's sister last year like he'd considered doing after Ivy turned him down.

But no. Marriage to Agatha was out of the question. While she was a sweet and docile girl who touched his heart with her shy smile, she would never be able to stand up to the rigors of political life.

It had been a good while since he'd seen her. He had not visited the Lucky Clover since Ivy turned down his marriage proposal.

He did wonder about Agatha from time to time. What had become of her? He hoped that Ivy had managed to restore her to health. He prayed that she had not become addicted to laudanum again.

Had life treated her differently, she might have been as bright and sparkling as her twin sister. That night he'd carried Agatha about the dance floor, he'd seen a spark of joy in her eyes.

Somehow, that brief encounter had left him feeling tender toward her. She had gazed up at him as if he were her hero. It could not be denied that he'd looked down at her, warming to the role.

"If we were to marry, William," Aimee began again. He did not recall encouraging her to call him by his given name. "When do you think it would be?"

In a hundred years was what popped into his mind, but he needed to be careful not to say something to alienate her, or the votes her family might cast for him when he at last ran for governor.

A noise interrupted his thoughts.

"What was that?"

"We were discussing our wedding date?"

"I thought I heard a scream."

"Well, my dear, this is a circus after all."

"I'm sorry, Aimee. You've gotten the wrong idea about—that was a scream."

Very clearly a woman was in distress. The trouble sounded like it came from the area where the cannon was.

The cannon that was due to spew a human being out of it.

That was one circus act he would ban when he had the power to do so.

He ought to bid Aimee farewell and send her back to her friends, but the cry was becoming more urgent.

Surely others would arrive to help before he got there, but regardless, he turned his back on Aimee and ran full out.

A few men had arrived before him. Judging by their manner of dress, they were employees of the circus. Unbelievably they shifted from foot to foot, watching silently while Frenchie Brown tried to stuff a small woman down the mouth of the cannon.

A dog latched its teeth into the leg of Mr. Brown's pants. Luckily the critter was agile and avoided the circus owner's attempt to stomp on it.

But the woman was not faring as well. She was no match for the brute strength being forced upon her.

While she cursed at Brown, he caught the back of her long red hair, wound it around his fist, then yanked downward, forcing her further into the cannon.

"Mr. Brown!" William shouted. "The lady is unwilling!"

"This is circus business, Mayor. You have no say-so here."

"When I catch you trying to force a woman, it damn well is my business."

"Boys?" Frenchie Brown stared at his men. "The show will go on. Escort the mayor to an appropriate area."

"Where's Mrs. Otis?" one of the fellows asked.

"Packing her bags as you'll be doing if you don't obey me."

"I don't think this here tiny lady will survive being blown out of Old Bessie," the youngest of the men said.

All of a sudden Frenchie yelped. Blood welled from his fat hand.

It seemed the tiny lady in the cannon had taken that moment of distraction to bite him.

He lifted his bleeding fist, balled it up. William caught it on the downswing and shoved him backward.

The woman scrambled out of the cannon then crumpled on the ground, shaking.

"William?" her voice quavered under the fall of red hair that hid her face.

She knew him? There was something familiar about her voice—he couldn't place—

"Help me up, William." She lifted her hand toward him. Her pale fingers trembled.

He squatted beside her, drew the hair from her face.

"Agatha Magee? Is that you?"

"He's on the ground, boys! Get him."

Feet shuffled in the dirt. Glancing up, he gathered Agatha closer to his chest.

Two of the roustabouts were walking away, but the other two advanced, bulging arm muscles glistening, flexing.

"Oh, my word!" A woman's gasp drew Frenchie Brown's attention to the shadows.

William recognized her and her young fellow when they stepped into the lantern light. They had both attended today's meeting.

"Nothing to be alarmed at folks. All a part of the cannon act." Frenchie Brown's voice was suddenly friendly as a slice of peach pie. "Naturally the lady was fearful, it being her first flight. But this act is widely known to be safe."

Hell, the man lied as easily as most of William's fellow politicians.

William stood up, keeping Agatha close to him. She was breathing too hard. Reminded him of a small bird he'd rescued once.

Scooping her up, he backed away.

"Take my girl and you'll hear from my lawyers!"

"She's no longer your girl." He'd never had reason to growl, but now he thought he did it as well as the circus owner.

Frenchie Brown made a motion to run his hand through his hair, but given that he was bald, he only slapped his scalp.

"Fetch me another girl," he said to the single remaining roustabout.

"Shut down the cannon attraction," William ordered.

"You have no rights here!" Frenchie Brown insisted, his belly jiggling in outrage.

Maybe he did not, but he wasn't going to take Agatha away only to have some other unfortunate girl take her place.

"Find Mrs. Peabody," he said to the young couple. "Tell her the circus folks have gone mad in the wind. Let her know to spread the word to everyone that they should seek the shelter of their homes."

If there were no customers, no one would be shot out of the cannon.

He strode away, hugging Ivy's sister tight, hoping that she was strong enough to withstand what she had been through, that she would not lapse into some sort of malady or seek escape in a drug.

"Wait!" Her voice was hoarse, no doubt raw with all the screaming she had done. "Miss Valentine. I can't leave without her."

"We've got to get out of here now, honey."

She blinked up at him. Her green eyes were prettier than he recalled them being.

"Frenchie will kill that little dog if I don't bring her along."

William glanced over his shoulder. Agatha was right. The wicked round man had picked up a piece of lumber and begun to swing it at the dog.

"Can you stand?"

"Of course."

He was not convinced and set her down with care.

"Hold on to this rope." It was one of the cables on the outside of the tent.

He dashed back, ripped the plank out of Brown's fingers and tossed it away. He scooped up the dog, cursing at the circus owner and not bothering to do it under his breath.

Sprinting back to Agatha he found her still standing. Judging by the way her fingers looked bloodless while gripping the rope, he figured it took all her effort to remain upright.

Placing the bedraggled mound of fur in Agatha's arms, he scooped her up again, charging quickly through the crowd.

Must have been a sight to see. The mayor of Tanners Ridge carrying a woman dressed in glittering, skintight long johns in his arms.

Sure enough, folks were staring. Especially Aimee Peller and her group of friends. Poor Aimee looked like she'd been run through.

Charging ahead, he carried Agatha around the animal trailers then started up the hill. It was a good thing she didn't weigh more than a dime.

Glancing back, he noticed people beginning to leave

the circus. Whether they believed the circus folks had gone mad, or just wanted to see what he was up to, he had no way of telling.

At least Agatha's breathing was no longer as quick as a trapped dove's.

First thing in the morning he was going to wire Ivy and Travis to come and fetch her.

"Mrs. Bronson!" William called, being propelled into his house by a gust of wind. "Mrs. Feather!"

His housekeeper and his cook had not gone to the circus, claiming a dislike for such nonsense.

The events of the evening had proved their wisdom.

Pushing the door closed with his backside, he called again.

"Surprised they ventured out in the wind," he murmured more to himself than to Agatha. Was she even conscious after the rough treatment she had been through? She'd been silent all the way up the hill and the walk across town to the Mayor's Mansion, as the folks of Tanners Ridge took pride in calling it. "Sure hope that tent holds up."

"I'd give it only even odds." Agatha wriggled in his arms indicating that he should put her down. "Mr. Brown does take shortcuts."

"Let me take you to the parlor. The divan is quite comfortable."

"I'd rather walk."

"Can you?"

Could she? Last time he'd seen her she could only manage a few steps without help.

Something about her did seem different, though. She was frail as a waif—he knew that because he'd carried her up the hill and to his house without much exertion. The difference was in her expression. Where she'd once looked wounded, cautious, she now gazed up at him with confidence. Somehow the mix of fragility and pluck touched his heart. Made him regret having to put her down right away.

"You've been through an ordeal."

Why had she been through an ordeal? What was she doing so far from home and at, of all things, the circus? Perhaps she had been kidnapped! He'd always assumed she would remain at the Lucky Clover where Ivy and Travis could watch over her.

Ivy was not older by much. Truth be told it was only by moments since Agatha and Ivy were twins. But the sisters were not alike in any way.

In his mind, Agatha had seemed quite a bit younger.

"I can walk."

Maybe so. "I'd feel better setting you safely on the couch."

So he did, in spite of her protests.

"I'll hunt up Mrs. Bronson to prepare your room for the night. As soon as I find Mrs. Feather I'll have her bring you some soup. Would you like that?"

"I'm not hungry."

"Nevertheless, you shall eat."

Why was she frowning at him? He wasn't sure he'd ever seen that expression on her sweet face.

"Mrs. Bronson! Miss Feather!" he called, rushing out of the parlor and into the grand entry. The sooner Agatha was settled into a warm bed the better he would feel. "Mildred? Ida?"

As soon as William left the room in search of his employees, Agatha eased up from the couch.

She was a bit wobbly and overwhelmed by what she

had been through. Defending oneself took more energy than she could have imagined—could she have imagined that she would ever be called upon to do so.

But William was wrong in his assumption that she was an invalid. She could easily have extracted herself from his big wonderful arms, had she the mind to.

"I didn't, though," she murmured to Miss Valentine. "And how are you, you sweet girl? I'm so proud of how you avoided getting kicked, even with your hurt foot."

Agatha bent over, felt light-headed. She traced the line of white that shot through the tan on the dog's forehead.

Miss Valentine turned her head, pressing her face against Agatha's shin.

"What a sweet hug. I'll get William to call a veterinarian to look at your foot."

From upstairs she could hear him shouting for Mrs. Bronson and Mrs. Feather.

While she listened, purely enjoying hearing the sound of his voice, she glanced around the parlor.

Opulent was the best word she could think of to describe it.

Not a cozy place like the Lucky Clover. The ranch was grand, to be sure, but for all its grandness, it never felt stuffy or overdone.

Did William feel comfortable with all this fuss and frippery? She did not—although he was right about the divan, it was a nice place to sink into.

Heavy brocade drapes hung on every window. Regal paintings adorned the walls.

She wondered if his ranch near Cheyenne had this royal look.

It sure was noisy outside, with the wind slapping the walls. It wasn't hard to imagine the sound being Frenchie Brown's fist pounding out his anger.

She wanted to cower in a corner remembering the way that hand had looked like death coming upon her, dripping blood and wrath.

Straightening, she stiffened her back, pictured energy and strength pulsing through her muscles. Even if William had not stopped Frenchie's blow, the worst she would have been was bruised, or maybe had a bone broken.

Compared to other things she had been through in her life, a bruise was insignificant. Nothing could be worse than helplessly opening her mouth and allowing Mrs. Brunne to pour laudanum down her throat.

There had been a time, before Ivy came home, when she had called that woman Mother. Nothing, she now knew, could be further from the truth. All Agatha ever was to her was a replacement for her own lost daughter. There were times when her nurse did not know the difference between Agatha and the kidnapped Maggie.

In the end, Hilda Brunne's perception of what was past and what was present had become blurred and driven the woman insane.

Something smacked the window hard, might even have cracked it. Crossing the room, she drew the heavy curtain aside.

The night was dark. Dirt and sand blew everywhere. By the light of the lanterns lining the sidewalk, she saw folks hurrying along, bent against the wind and blocking grit from their faces with lifted arms.

A group of young ladies crossed through a beam of light, all of them looking well-to-do.

One of them stopped to stare at her. She recognized her even though she'd only seen the woman from behind while she clung to William hoping for the fortune-teller's blessing.

The lady pointed her finger. Her companions gawked, nudging each other in the ribs.

It was understandable. Who would not stare at someone dressed the way she was? Indecent was how she looked.

"Oh, my!" It suddenly occurred to her that everything she owned was in her trailer back at the circus encampment.

She was not going back there! Elephants could not drag her back down that hill. Which meant this was all she had to wear.

When the women on the sidewalk did not move on, but continued to look at her as though she were a sideshow attraction, she let go of the curtain.

All of a sudden her arms ached, and her legs. The altercation with Frenchie must have taken more out of her than she first thought.

With some effort, she returned to the couch. Lying down, she motioned for Miss Valentine to join her. It would be polite to ask William if dogs were allowed on his furniture, but that would mean hunting up her prince.

She hadn't the strength for that.

One day she would, though. One day she would run for a mile and not become winded.

For tonight, she was going to sink into this couch, close her eyes and find comfort in the small but solid weight of Miss Valentine pressing into the curve of her belly.

Impossible!

William paced the upstairs hall, crushing the note in his hand.

He stopped, pressed it open one more time. Even reading it for the fifth time did not change the words.

Mrs. Bronson and Mrs. Feather had been called away to tend their ailing mother. In the future, he would have to remember not to hire sisters.

They had written that the situation was urgent, and a wire had arrived to summon them home. They'd given an address for him to send their wages, which left him wondering if they would return at all.

"Impossible!"

He had carried a woman dressed in glittering, morality-defying underwear into his house. Many of the folks in town had seen him do it.

And now there was no chaperone when he had expected there to be two.

Unless he wanted his reputation smeared, his career ruined, there was only one thing to do.

Going down the stairs, he tried not to think of everything all at once. If he did he'd be overwhelmed.

He could only be in control of one thing at a time.

Coming into the parlor with the note pinched in his fingers, he found Agatha asleep on the divan.

The dog's head was resting on her ribs but it wasn't sleeping. Its brown eyes tracked his progress while he crossed the room, built up a fire in the hearth then settled into a chair facing the couch.

The last thing he wanted to do was wake her. Someone as tender as she was would need to regain her strength, maybe shut out the ordeal she had been through for a time.

The poor thing looked a proper mess with dirt on her nose, twigs and leaves in her hair—and just there on her chin, a faint smear of Frenchie Brown's blood from when she had bit him.

Even with it all, she didn't seem as gaunt as he recalled she'd been the last time he'd seen her. She'd filled out some, with curves in womanly places—

Curse it! Why was he looking there?

Because where else was he to look? The girl was wearing something that looked like sin, designed to draw a man's attention.

But why was she? What was she even doing in Tanners Ridge? It was twenty-five miles from home.

In the end it didn't matter why she was here, how she had ended up in a circus and was being forced into the mouth of a cannon. Here she was, under *his* protection. The details would sort themselves out later.

"Agatha," he whispered. "Honey?"

Not an eyelash stirred.

"Hey, dog. Lick her face, do something to wake her up."

Without the household staff present, he didn't dare even touch her shoulder to shake her awake.

The dog sighed deeply and closed its eyes.

"Agatha! Wake up!"

She sat up suddenly, eyes blinking in confusion. The parts of her that had filled out, which he should not be seeing the outline of but could not help it, jiggled.

The dog moved to the far side of the couch. After he settled the situation between them he would tell Agatha dogs were not allowed on the furniture...or in the house for that matter.

"William?" She looked confused, as though she did not recall that he'd carried her here.

"You're safe, honey. Don't worry, we'll be married as soon as this wind lets up and the preacher can get here."

Chapter Four

"William Byron English!" Agatha stood up, used the arm of the couch for balance since all of a sudden the world had gone tipsy. "What makes you think I would marry you?"

She felt a blush throb in her chest. It crept up her throat to her cheeks because it occurred to her that he might think it odd that she knew his middle name.

Please don't let him guess that she used to sit in her chair repeating it over and over in her mind until Mother Brunne would reprimand her for smiling.

"I didn't know you knew my full name."

"Ivy told me—it just slipped out." What a bald-faced lie! "I don't dwell on your name—in fact, I rarely dwell on you at all."

Rarely! Now he knew that she did occasionally dwell upon him.

"That's neither here nor there. Once we are wed you can use my full name, dwell on me or don't."

How utterly mortifying! No doubt she was red as flame.

"I can't imagine the woman who would not swoon at such a marriage proposal, as absurd as the notion is."

He mumbled something—Aimee Peller—she thought

it was. His ladylove no doubt, the woman who had stared at her from the sidewalk earlier, the very one who had tossed down a penny wishing for the proposal Agatha was getting.

No, probably not this proposal quite.

"We have no choice about it. People saw me carry you into the house. They'll know we spent time alone."

"There's your staff. We are hardly alone."

"There's only two of them who live in the mansion. They aren't here. An emergency came up with their mother and they left. I have no idea when or if they are coming back."

"I imagine our reputations can survive until the weather lets up," she said, knowing it was not true. Both of their reputations would be gleefully danced upon.

He looked her up and down, his gaze lingering on parts of her body where a man's gaze had never lingered.

Why, in the upheaval, she had nearly forgotten that she was dressed like a harlot!

People would think he had carried a coochie girl into his house!

This was a mess—but marriage? Surely there was another way?

"It'll be morning before I can get you to a boarding house. Besides, you can't go outside in that."

Not if her life depended upon it! But, she had nothing else.

"Folks have short memories." Hopefully she sounded confident, convincing. But folks also had long memories. Some old-timers at the Lucky Clover still gossiped about Agatha's mother, how she had divorced Papa and taken only one of her twins with her. "This won't be much of a scandal a few weeks from now. Oh, you've got a cracked window, by the way."

He stared at her in silence for so long it became uncomfortable.

His eyes used to have the most appealing twinkle. It was not evident at the moment.

Honestly, he could not want to marry her any more than she wanted to marry him.

"I'm running for governor one day. You know that. I'll have enemies who will go looking for any way to discredit me."

"That's still many years away. New scandals will come along. No one will recall this."

"I wish that were true, Agatha. But politics is an ugly game. People will remember and in the nastiest way."

She pressed her fingers to her temples to try and lasso her stampeding thoughts. He was right, wicked-minded folks would remember—remember and talk.

It made her sick to her stomach to think he might lose his dream because he came to her aid.

"If it's such an ugly game, why not forget about running for governor. Go home and care for your ranch."

"The ranch doesn't need me. My mother runs it better than any man." A punching wind blew something over outside. She heard it tumble across the yard. "And why aren't you at home? What were you doing involved with the circus?"

"That's a talk for another time. Right now we are discussing why you want to be involved in such dirty business."

He shrugged one shoulder, tipped his head. "I see injustice and I want to make it right. It's like an itch in my bones, righting things while crooked politicians act on things that only benefit them."

Suddenly she suspected that lamplight was reflecting

on the crimson sequins of her costume in a way that did not protect her modesty.

Agatha picked up the dog, positioned the furry little thing over her breasts. Too bad the tip of her wagging tail would not be hiding anything, but accentuating it.

Marry William? No! She could not possibly marry him—the very man she had dreamed of since she knew how to dream.

He was far too safe. Why, she could live in his house and never have to worry about anything for the rest of her life. She could sit in a chair by the window and watch the world go by—just like she used to do.

"I don't know, William. You might make a difficult husband. You are just plain bossy."

He laughed, low in his chest, and there in the corner of one eye, the mysterious twinkle flashed.

"You and my mother will like each other."

"And you are assuming I have accepted your proposal." The weak-kneed child inside of her wanted to— urged her to—crawl up into her prince's arms where life would never hurt her. Where shadows would never chase her down and threaten her. "I have not."

Speaking her mind in such a forceful way was not what she was used to. She would become used to it, though, once she spent enough time on her own.

William walked to the window and drew back the curtain. He traced his finger over the crack in the glass. With a curse, he let the drape fall into place.

"Is the wind worse?" She set Miss Valentine gently on the floor, exposing herself once again. It was not as though she could take back anything he had already seen.

"It's worse, but not so bad as to keep half a dozen people across the street from ogling their mayor's front door."

"I don't wish to marry. I'm sorry, William, but I don't."

Except, that maybe she did.

"It wasn't what I woke up wanting, either."

Without warning, Leah Madrigal's wink flashed in her mind. The fortune-teller said that sometimes the glass ball saw things. No—that could not be. More likely the perceptive woman had seen the look of longing on Agatha's face while she had been staring at William's back.

"You, at least had a bit of warning." She must be getting desperate to even bring this nonsense up. "I heard the fortune-teller tell you that you would soon marry."

"She also said it would be a long, happy marriage."

"With lots of children." Leah had said that, too. "It can't be me you are supposed to marry."

William's gaze dropped away. He jabbed fingers through his hair.

He glanced back up suddenly, stealing her breath with the determined set of his eyes.

"Also a subject for another time. I believe in facing one problem at a time."

Even though she was not going to marry him, she did wish he had not called the proposal a problem. It felt like a tiny dagger twisting in her heart to hear it put that way. No matter that she completely agreed.

"If I did give in to this insanity, the issue would have to be faced at one time or another."

"Another, then." He strode forward so that they stood toe to toe. He cupped her cheeks in his long fingers, looked her steadily in the eyes. "I like you, Agatha. I always have. I've seen you fight things that wanted to enslave you. I am not one of them. Please don't fight me."

"It's not so simple as that. I like you, too. But I need to stand on my own. Make my own decisions and live with the consequences."

Dratted consequences! The result of William rescuing her might cost him his dream—the ambition of a lifetime.

Ruined reputations were not easily overcome.

Yes, she might keep her independence at the cost of her reputation—all on her own become the strong person she was learning to be. But in the end others would still see her as pitiful.

Worse, they would see William as unworthy of their trust. How could she live with herself knowing he lost everything for her sake?

She stepped away from him because she wanted to lean into him, feel his arms fold about her and deflect the ugly words that were bound to be spoken about her.

"You would want to be in control of me."

"Only insofar as it's for your own good."

"Do you understand that it's up to me to decide what is for my own good? I spent my whole life trusting Hilda Brunne to know what was best for me. I won't allow anyone to have that power over me again."

"That was evil power, honey." He caught both of her hands in one of his, pressed them against his chest. The steady beat of his heart thumped against her palms. "I would never treat you that way."

"I know that, William, but—"

"What if I declare, in the wedding vows, to try not to be overbearing, excessively protective. Even though it would be my duty as your husband to do so."

How could she not laugh? He looked so sincere about saying vows that he did not agree with.

She could not let herself be swayed by that consideration, though. William English was a man who wanted control. He might be ever so sweet about it, but it didn't change anything.

Freedom to grow was what she needed. For as much as he might not want to tell her what to do and when to do it, such behavior was in his nature.

A test. She would give him a test to see if he could really let go of control.

Sliding her hand down his shirt, she felt the firm ridges of his chest. She yanked her hand away then slowly, deliberately, picked up Miss Valentine and set her on the expensive divan.

The dog scratched the fabric then circled searching for a comfortable position. After finding the cushion to her liking, she settled in to lick her injured paw. A damp circle darkened the fabric.

Agatha watched William frown. Purse his lips.

As she suspected, he did not want animals in the house.

"I believe that dogs belong—" he closed his eyes, shook his head "—where their mistress says they belong."

My word. She had not expected that.

"She needs to be taken to the veterinarian. No doubt he will agree that she must have a soft place to recover."

"I'll have him look at her tomorrow. I'll put her back on the couch, myself."

"I'm grateful, William." More than he could guess. "She's a brave little soul."

"Now will you marry me?"

She could not possibly marry him. With her gaze fastened on his eyes, she slowly shook her head.

"Please don't turn me down. For both of our sakes, you've got to become my wife—tonight."

"I suppose we could marry then divorce after the risk of scandal has passed," she suggested even though it was not what she had ever dreamed she would say to this man.

He shook his head. Reflected light from the flames in the hearth danced in his hair. If she did agree to marry him, maybe one day she would be bold enough to run her fingers through those dark locks.

"There will be no divorce." Funny how she was relieved to hear that. "If you choose not to live with me, I will support you financially. But a divorce will not do."

"I suppose I could make a very long visit to the Lucky Clover."

"I would permit that." He was far too handsome, flashing that teasing smile. "Will you marry me now?"

"I would go home to the ranch according to what I decide. Not what you will permit. You must understand that I need to make my own choices."

"I'll do my best, Agatha. I swear it." He did look sincere. "Do you choose to marry me?"

Did she? He'd saved her future that awful night when he'd kept her from turning to laudanum for comfort. He'd sat down beside her, put a book in her hands and become the comfort.

Now, his future depended upon her.

"I can't. I have nothing to wear."

"Step right up close to me, honey."

She did. He measured her height with the flat of his hand. She was as tall as the button on his collar. Next he cupped her waist with his fingers, seeming to judge its size.

The last thing he did before he stepped away from her was to kiss top of her top of her head, pluck a dried leaf out of the tangled mass. From the corner of her eye she saw it drift to the floor.

"Will you marry me if I show up here with a preacher and a wedding gown?"

"And a witness. Don't forget a witness."

* * *

It had been a couple of hours before that William had decided that a tornado was not poised at the edge of town ready to rush in and blow everyone away.

The dressmaker had not been pleased to be awoken at four in the morning, but she hadn't minded being paid triple the amount for the three gowns he'd purchased.

Her expression had been miles beyond curious so he'd simply told her the truth—nearly the truth, that they were for his wife.

No one need know that the preacher had not crossed his threshold until nearly five o'clock. That the man's good wife had found Agatha reading a book on the couch in the parlor and hustled her upstairs to dress her in the wedding gown draped over his arm.

The dress had been intended for a bride in Cheyenne, but given what he was willing to pay, the seamstress said she could make another.

The promise of more business had apparently been enough to keep her from asking questions and simply extend her good wishes.

With any luck this marriage would be accepted without a great deal of unwholesome talk.

He'd lose votes for sure if anyone spread lies about Agatha's virtue.

No one voted for a candidate who punched them in the nose—which he might do if anyone maligned sweet Agatha.

He'd been so caught up in his thoughts and staring at the dust he'd forgotten to wipe from his boots, that he failed to hear the rustle of fabric at the head of the stairs until the preacher nudged him in the ribs.

"Your bride awaits, young man."

Glancing up, William had to catch his heart. It felt

like it had escaped his chest and gone running up the steps to embrace her.

Agatha Marigold Magee was captivating! Out of the blue, without warning, she enchanted him.

Dawn light shone through the window onto the landing, igniting the flame color of her hair and reflecting fairylike sparkles in the crystals bordering her lace collar. Her eyes glittered bright green, but not by any trick of early sunlight.

How had this dazzling creature been his neighbor for so many years without him noticing how lovely she was?

Because she had not always been dazzling. Before Ivy came home, Agatha had been a wraith hiding in shadows and seldom seen in public.

With one hand on the bannister, she descended to the foot of the stairs. When she placed her pale, slender fingers in his hand, he was struck by the enormity of what he was about to do.

In moments this fragile woman would become his—to protect for the rest of his life.

There was something about Agatha Magee that hit him deep in his heart. Ever since the night of the barbecue at the Lucky Clover, he'd felt touched by her.

There had been a storm that night, and seeing her sitting in a corner of the parlor watching the dancers whirl by, he'd been moved in an unexpected way. Not with pity, exactly, but something akin to it. Compassion for her plight, maybe?

Yes, she was the sister of the woman he had hoped to marry, but his attention toward her had not been only for Ivy's sake.

He'd been overcome with a strong urge to make her smile, to whirl her about the dance floor until she did.

Of course, she could not whirl about the dance floor.

He'd had to support her, lead her with slow precision. He could not help but wonder what would she have been like that night had she not spent years as the captive of her nurse?

He liked Ivy, but had Agatha been the healthy one—?

It didn't matter, because at that time, she hadn't been.

Before Agatha's father died, when he had approached William about a marriage deal—his wealth to save the Lucky Clover in exchange for the social prestige the ranch would give him—he had been assured that Agatha was too weak to ever suit his needs. Bearing a child would kill her, so the doctor had said.

So it had been arranged that he would marry Ivy—just as soon as she could be located.

Now here he was, marrying Agatha after all.

It was true that he needed this marriage to safeguard his reputation for his political future, but that was not the whole of it. He wanted to protect Agatha's reputation as well.

Looking at her now, she did not quite seem the forlorn girl he remembered. For one thing, it was apparent that she was not a girl, but a woman.

A strong-minded woman, but one who was still far too thin, too frail.

Something about her made him want to stand in front of her, arms spread to deflect every stressful thing life might place in her path.

As her husband, he could. Although, apparently with great discretion.

Clearly, his hovering presence would be no more welcome than Hilda Brunne's had been.

With the four of them gathered in front of the grand fireplace in the parlor, the preacher went through the vows. They were the typical, sacred ones that brides and grooms recited.

Amazingly, Agatha held his gaze through them all. She did not shy away, look frightened or even resentful, as she might have.

Preacher Wilson asked if he would love, honor and cherish her. Yes, he would. Perhaps in some small way he already did cherish her. In a short moment she would share his name—become his family.

Next, the preacher asked Agatha if she would love, honor and obey him.

She blinked, frowned then slid her attention to Mr. Wilson.

"I imagine I might come to love him—in time, sir. Perhaps honor him as well. But obey? In truth I cannot vow to do that, as Mr. English well knows."

"Oh! Well said, my dear," Mrs. Wilson gasped. "It's as though you have been married for ten years already."

"Mr. English, shall I proceed or do you wish to—"

"Agatha, honey, I vow to you that I will do my best not to interfere with your free will—as best I can. You may continue, Mr. Wilson, if my bride is willing."

Seconds ticked by. Agatha cocked her head, studying William this way and that.

"Yes," she said when he was good and sure his heart had quit beating. "And I do promise to obey you—as best I can. Please do carry on, Mr. Wilson. I wish to—"

Agatha took a long slow breath, held William's gaze. What was it she wished? He only hoped it was something he could give her.

"I wish to kiss my groom."

There! She'd spoken what was on her mind! It hadn't been easy. The girl she had been all her life wanted to run upstairs and hide under a blanket.

But the woman she hoped to become wanted to kiss

her husband—to feel his arms curl around her, lift her off her toes and make her feel—wanted.

Now, there it was. Spoken for all to know. She wanted William to want her.

Apparently the preacher did not know what to make of the unconventional vows. He blinked at her, his mouth half-open on a stalled comment.

"Hurry up, Herbert. Let the youngsters have their first kiss."

"Oh, my—well—by the power invested in me by God and the territory of Wyoming, I now pronounce that you are man and wife. Please do kiss your bride, Mr. English."

She wasn't sure what she was expecting but it was not the briefest graze of his lips across hers. Why, she barely felt the warmth of them.

In her many dreams, kissing William had always felt warm and exciting, holding the promise of the commitment of a lifetime.

While she was suddenly committed for a lifetime, the warm excitement was lacking.

By six thirty, Mr. and Mrs. Wilson had departed, leaving Agatha alone with her groom.

She didn't know what to do—barely knew what to say. This time yesterday she had been wiping sleep from her eyes while helping Laura Lee make fried potatoes and eggs. Less than twelve hours ago she had been living the adventure of a book character.

"You must be hungry," she said, taking note of how her wedding gown swirled about her when she turned. How it caught the first rays of dawn streaming through the window.

She had never worn anything more lovely in her life.

Unable to help herself she twirled again just to watch it

shimmer. If Mother Brunne was watching from the great beyond, it would be with much disapproval.

"I'll fix us something to eat after I change out of the gown."

"I'm sorry, there's no one here to help."

"I'll manage. Just yesterday I was helping Laura Lee fix breakfast for a hundred people."

"I meant with the buttons on the back of the gown. You can't reach them."

Her breath caught. He was right. She could not. Either she could fry up potatoes in her wedding gown and risk a splatter, or she could allow him to help her take it off.

Then what? Put on the red costume again because she did not care if eggs exploded on it? Be humiliated? Or flip eggs wearing her corset and petticoats? Cooking in her underwear would still be humiliating but it would also be prettier.

There were two more dresses upstairs, but she would not risk ruining them, either.

"How hungry are you, William?"

He spun her about and opened two pearly buttons at her nape. The heat of his breathing brushed her skin. "Hungrier than I thought."

"Are there eggs and bacon in the kitchen? Bread for toast?"

"I assume so—but it's been a long day. Let's think about food tomorrow."

"But you said you were hungry."

His breath skimmed the back of her neck, his fingers clenched briefly on her shoulders. "Very—but I'm also tired."

"Let's sleep, then." At least she didn't have to risk ruining anything lovely by cooking in it.

Cool air touched her back when two more buttons

fell open, which reminded her. "What happened to my wedding kiss?"

Why was it that, around William, she blurted out what was on her mind so readily?

"I can't tell you how grateful I am that you married me."

Three buttons popped free all at one time.

"And I'm grateful that you kept me from being blown out of a cannon."

The hall clock ticked away a long silence. Outside, the wind didn't sound loud as it had.

With a quick flick of his fingers, William freed the button at the small of her spine. The front of the gown sagged so she grabbed it close to her chest.

"Can you manage the stairs?" he asked, taking a deep breath, then several steps away from her. "If it's too trying I can give you a downstairs bedroom."

Ivy and Travis shared a bedroom.

"I managed them fine a short while ago." It would not be a hardship to share a bed with William. "I'm no longer an invalid. You don't need to fear for my health."

"I owe you, Agatha." Dragging his fingers through his hair, he frowned at the floor then looked up at her. "I'll take care to make sure no harm comes to you."

"Really, I don't know why it would. I believe that I've proved that I can take care of myself—unless someone is forcing me into a cannon and I doubt that will happen again."

"I imagine not. But you are mine to protect, nonetheless."

The bodice of her dress flopped down when she balled her fists and anchored them at her waist, but she did not care at the moment.

"If a situation arises in which I do not feel comfortable, I will let you know—then you may protect me to your heart's content." She wagged her finger at him, which was not quite polite but her temper was heating by the second. How odd was it that for most of her life she hadn't known she had a temper. It must have been drugged out of her. "But I must—and will deal with problems on my own."

"Of course."

He caught her hand, folded it up in his. "I was speaking of getting you with child."

An image of tangled bed sheets and entwined limbs flashed in her mind. Secret kisses and touches. Heat pulsed in every nerve of her body, especially—

"I won't endanger you that way."

What? She yanked her hand free, remembered that her bodice was dangling about her waist and decided to let it remain there.

"I might have something to say about that, William."

Outside the creak and rattle of a wagon passing by filled a long silence between them. A dog barked. Tanners Ridge was coming to life.

So was Agatha Marigold English.

Chapter Five

"Mighty glad the wind has stopped."

Walking down the boardwalk toward Hamilton London's Steak House and looking forward to a late lunch, William patted Agatha's hand where it nestled in the crook of his arm.

He liked the way it fit. While not even twelve hours into marriage, he thought his union with Agatha might be a success, for all that it was unanticipated.

Agatha sure did look fetching in the green gown he'd purchased in the wee hours of the morning. With her red hair and green eyes—there was no denying that Mrs. William English was a beautiful woman.

Funny how he'd never noticed that. In his eyes she had always been Foster Magee's sickly girl.

For all her loveliness, she did seem nervous.

And why wouldn't she be? He was nervous and he was accustomed to speaking with people. He would have to take care not to overtax her with social events. Although there would be some she would need to attend.

Or perhaps her agitation had nothing to do with facing society's challenges.

It could be that her nervousness had to do with him.

No doubt she was uneasy about so suddenly becoming a wife. He could hardly blame her for that.

Last night, he'd tried to assure her that she had nothing to fear from him, that he would never force his husbandly attentions upon her, but that conversation had only left her looking even more distressed.

It hadn't felt right bringing up such an intimate topic with an innocent—but it had been necessary. In most cases, sexual intimacy was at the heart of a marriage.

But not this marriage.

Had he married Ivy or Aimee, even, things would be different. They were healthy women and his husbandly attentions would not put them at such a great risk.

His wife was not like them—although it seemed as though she thought she might be.

Unfortunately for him, each hour he spent with his bride tempted him to wonder what it would be like to share the marriage bed with her.

Fantasizing was as far as he would take it, though, because the line between fantasy and nightmare could be a narrow one.

If he thought otherwise all he had to do was remember being a child, recall the joy he anticipated over the birth of his baby sister, then the crushing sorrow of holding her lifeless newborn body.

Giving birth was hard enough on a strong woman. Putting Agatha in that situation was out of the question.

He grunted under his breath, forcing his thoughts in another direction—toward lunch because he was ravenous.

Near the door of the restaurant, Agatha stopped suddenly. She glanced behind, squeezing his arm.

"What is it, honey?"

"Nothing—just a shadow." She smiled up at him a bit too brightly. "And a chill."

A chill on a July afternoon! "Are you well?"

"Of course. Although, I wish people were not staring at us as if we'd just tumbled from the moon."

"They'll get used to it," he said, leading her to his favorite table in a bay window overlooking the street. "All they need is a little time."

"Like us, I suppose."

He pulled out her chair. After she was seated he took the one across from her.

"I hope it wasn't fear of me that gave you a chill, Agatha. You have no need to fear me."

She removed her gloves slowly, one then the other while she held his gaze. "It wasn't you."

Probably not. A woman who was uneasy in his presence would not look at him so steadfastly.

"There was a shadow. It shifted suddenly and reminded me of my nurse, Hilda Brunne."

Shadow was a good way of describing Brunne. He'd only seen her a couple of times and only once close up, but he knew her to be a dark soul.

"I imagine, given time I won't see her lurking in dim places."

"It's a shame they never found her body. It might be easier for you if they had."

"I suppose when I come to the point that I find her body inside of me, lay her to rest in my soul, I guess I mean, then it will be all right."

"Did you get any sleep this morning?"

"Strangely, yes. I slept quite well." For some reason that made her blush. "How did you sleep?"

His wife looked pretty with a pink tint in her cheeks. It made her eyes look greener, her hair a more vibrant red.

"Not well, I'll confess. There was a something gnawing at me and I couldn't let it go."

"Life has dealt us a change. It's no wonder you were restless."

"It's not that. I think we'll make a go of it." He reached across the table, traced the lines of her palm, then squeezed her hand in reassurance. Of course he wasn't sure which of them he was reassuring. "What were you doing working for the circus, Agatha? Last time I saw you, you could barely walk. Does your sister know where you are? I can scarce believe she allowed you to leave home alone."

"You need not have lost sleep over that, William. First of all, even though I was dressed the part, I am not a coochie girl or anything of the sort. I worked in the chuck wagon helping to prepare meals. Second, as you see, I can walk. And as for Ivy allowing me? She is my sister, not my keeper." She folded her hands in front of her, leaned forward. "I'll admit, she wasn't happy about my choice. But I didn't come alone. Laura Lee, one of the kitchen girls at the Lucky Clover, came with me."

"But the circus?" He shook his head. "Why not do something safe in Cheyenne?"

"Oh, we didn't begin at the circus. We started out somewhere else."

A waitress set two steaming cups of rich brown coffee on the table even though they had not yet ordered. It was how he usually began his meal at the steak house and he figured the woman was eager for a close look at his bride.

"It was for the best, I think," she said with a nod.

Agatha blew her coffee before she sipped it. Her mouth formed an intriguing—no it did not! Even if it did he would not look at it.

"Safe is not what I needed, but it is where I have ended up, I suppose." She arched a brow at him.

He was glad that she considered him safe. He was her husband now and it was his God-given duty to protect her.

The challenge was going to be watching over her without letting her know that he was doing it.

But in his defense— "I could hardly let you be shot out of a cannon."

"And I could hardly let your reputation be ruined."

"So here we are for better or worse."

"Till death do us part."

Thank the Good Lord that she was smiling when she said it because she was also lightly drumming her fingertips on the table.

A hum of lunchtime activity went on all around while he sipped his coffee and wondered what sort of marriage this would be.

"I did not believe it!" From the tone of Aimee Peller's voice, the lady still did not.

There was nothing for it but to dive in and set the rumors to rest.

"Miss Peller." William stood up. He extended his hand in a formal greeting, which the young lady ignored. "I'd like to introduce my wife, Agatha English."

"That strumpet in the red underwear?" she hissed quietly. "After the fortune-teller said that we were to be together for the rest of our lives, you went off and married a stranger!"

She never should have ventured out in public!

There was no reason that Aimee Peller should not believe she was an immoral woman, that she was not fit for the likes of William English.

A belief that Hilda Brunne had recited time and time again.

"Won't you sit with us, Aimee? Have a cup of tea?" William asked in a congenial voice as though the woman had not just insulted her.

How she wished he had not invited Miss Peller to sit! She never wanted to lift her gaze from her lap again but—

Fabric shifted as the jilted woman took a chair beside William.

"Agatha." William's voice sounded warm…loving even when he said her name. "Won't you meet my constituent, Miss Peller?"

Agatha glanced at her husband. She understood what he had just done. Given her the chance to stand on her own. To act the woman she claimed she wanted to be.

Indeed, he could have sent his constituent off with a tongue-lashing for her rudeness, but instead he had left it for Agatha.

She shifted her gaze to the woman and added a smile. Hopefully the gesture did not look as timid as it felt.

"How lovely to meet you, Miss Peller."

Judging by the slash of her brows, the scorned one did not feel the same.

"Actually, Mr. English and I are not strangers. We have been acquainted for some time." She took a good long breath. "And while it may have appeared last night that I was a strumpet, indeed I am not."

"Why the hasty marriage then?" Aimee pointed the question at William.

He answered by reaching across the table, running his thumb along the ridges of Agatha's knuckles. A twinkle danced in the corner of his eye. "What man would not be in a hurry to wed this beautiful lady?"

Why, he made her feel like she was the only woman on earth worth looking at. He might be saying that only for Aimee's sake, but still, her heart skittered about in her chest.

All of a sudden there was a loud tapping on the window glass.

They all turned to see Laura Lee with Johnny Ruiz peering over her shoulder.

Her friend looked like she had bees in her corset. She mouthed something then flailed her hands in exasperation.

A second later she was steaming her way through the dining room, Johnny looking like a dinghy bobbing in her wake.

"I turn my back for one night! A few hours only, and you get married?"

"Would you like to sit?" William asked, indicating the free chair, and briefly introducing Miss Peller.

Her friend plunked down, leaving Johnny to stand behind her looking nervous.

"So, Mr. Mayor." Normally, Laura Lee had a sweet voice, but it wasn't evident at the moment. "What game are you up to? Is it the Lucky Clover you still want? You'll do anything to have it, I've got to wonder!"

"The Lucky Clover Ranch?" Aimee's eyebrows shot to fine points in her forehead. "She has to do with the Lucky Clover!" Aimee stood up looking quite offended. "Now I understand why you tossed me away—all for greed."

Laura Lee shot up so suddenly that she knocked Johnny Ruiz back three steps. Her friend was loyal to a fault.

"That isn't true! What a wicked thing to say!" With her anger refocused, Laura Lee stared in outrage at Aimee. She looked like she was about to utter a curse word. Agatha had never heard Laura Lee spew anything unkind before.

William spoke before Agatha had a chance to know if she would really do it.

"I did not toss you away, Miss Peller. You were never mine to toss. As for coveting the Lucky Clover? No, I do not. I married Agatha because I chose to marry her." William turned his attention from Miss Peller, settled it on Agatha. His fond expression made her feel that they were alone, his message meant for no one else. "I'm grateful that she accepted my proposal."

"We all saw how you were forced—"

"Miss Peller." Agatha cut her off. "I believe you have influence in the community. Please let everyone know they need not worry about us. I chose to marry Mr. English as well."

Luckily, the woman had the good sense to understand that she had been dismissed from company. She presented her back and was gone in a quick flick of her fashionable skirt.

Agatha tried not to sigh her relief too loudly, but it had taken all she had to put up that false bravado.

"I can't imagine what I'm going to tell your sister." Laura's Lee's frown shifted from Miss Peller's retreat to Agatha. "I was supposed to watch out for you."

"You can tell her that my reasons for marrying William are my own and I am content with what I have done."

"Tell Ivy and Travis that I'm satisfied as well and that I will watch over Agatha." His gaze slid her way. "In as much as she will allow it."

"At least someone is satisfied." Laura Lee's sigh was short but resigned as she sat slowly back down.

"The ones whose opinions count are." Agatha smiled, trying to put her friend's worry to rest because her fears were not unjustified. The marriage *had* been sudden. Even Agatha had fought it initially.

"Say, Laura Lee," Johnny declared. "You and me are getting hitched soon as we get home. Can't see how that's much different."

"You and I have been in love for six months."

Agatha watched her new husband in profile while Johnny grinned at Laura Lee.

She had been in love with William for far longer.

An hour later William took Agatha shopping. Tanners Ridge would have some of what she needed premade, but for the elegant gatherings she would be hostess of, the gowns would have to be sewn custom.

Apparently, Aimee had done her job, spreading the word, or gossiping more likely, that he was now a married man.

Folks on the street stopped to chat and wish them well. As far as he could see, the only people who weren't pleased were Aimee and her parents.

Evidently the whole family had set their cap for him—or rather, his position and his money.

"Really, William!" Agatha hoisted the pair of hatboxes she carried. "I can send home for my things."

He intended to do that, but she would need more than he suspected she had. Money at the Lucky Clover had been tight for a time.

"Indulge me, honey. I want to buy you things."

"I don't mind it, truth be told." She shot him a wink. The gesture nearly brought him to his knees. He was not used to this side of Agatha, hadn't known it existed. "So long as you don't treat me like your dress-up doll."

Agatha wouldn't know it, but her comment brought him up short. Because he had been thinking just that way. What she should wear to this event or that social gathering.

She had been so sheltered all her life—no, not sheltered but secluded—that he hadn't given her credit for knowing about current fashion.

"It's getting toward sundown and you must be weary. I reckon we ought to head home."

"Yes, well. There's that coat in the window two stores up. It would look fetching with the last four gowns you purchased."

He suspected it wasn't the coat she wanted so much as to prove to him that the stress of the day had not wearied her.

"Mayor! Mayor, wait!" Mrs. Peabody's call reached him from half a block behind.

He turned to watch her charging up the boardwalk. "Mrs. Peabody, have you met my wife?"

"Not face to face. But I did see you carry her off when the circus folks went mad. Lovely to meet you with your clothes on, my dear."

Agatha opened her mouth but no words came out. Mrs. Peabody didn't seem to notice.

"Mayor, there's a stranger over at the Bascomb. Didn't look a savory sort, if you ask me."

"Thank you, Mrs. Peabody. I'll look into it."

"The sooner the better. Gave me the shivers." She hurried on her way, no doubt to bolt her doors and windows.

He hoped the fellow was a product of the old woman's fear because if he wasn't he could be one of Lydle's men.

That didn't bear thinking. Pete Lydle and his bunch weren't due for another couple of months.

At least the circus had packed up and gone on to their next engagement. Word was that only half of the tent had blown down in the wind. Luckily, the same report said no one had been injured—unless one counted the stuffed elephant. It had been knocked over, its tail bent in the attempt to set the thing upright.

"I wonder why she came to you about it. It seems a job for the sheriff, not the mayor."

"One would think so. The truth is we don't have a sheriff." He took one of the boxes she carried and stuffed it under his arm. "Every time I present someone who wants the job, they turn him down."

"It sounded like that woman thought it was up to you to deal with the trouble."

That was exactly what she thought. It was what they all thought. The next man to apply for sheriff was going to be hired.

William's job was to deal with civic matters, not disorderly folks.

"Let's get that coat. It's been a long afternoon and I'm ready for the comforts of home."

"If you have butter and flour in the larder, I can fix up something for us to eat."

"You shouldn't have to. I'll hire a temporary cook and housekeeper tomorrow."

Two hours later, he sat at the table eating something. He was not certain what it was intended to be but it was thick and buttery with carrots in it.

Agatha had stood over the soup pot for an hour watching, waiting for the ingredients to turn into stew.

She had added more flour, more butter, another carrot. With any luck William noticed how fetching she looked in her new apron rather than how her brows knit together in puzzlement while she stared at the pot.

Now, with his dinner sitting before him on the table, she watched while he lifted the spoon from the bowl to his mouth. Nervously, she tugged the full, ruffled bow of the apron tied at her waist.

It was odd how the apron had all but called her name from its hook on the wall of the mercantile, because it had never been her dream to become the best chef in the land.

No, she thought the apron had more to do with the idea of making a home—for herself but even more for her husband. And what was more homey than an apron?

What could be more satisfying than seeing William enjoy a meal she had prepared with her own hands?

The soft voice of her conscience fluttered across her mind. "Giving him a child," it whispered.

The man had saved her from being shot from a cannon. He'd rescued her reputation from ruin by giving her his name. He'd promised to do his best not to be overbearing, which she suspected was not going to be an easy thing for him to do.

Now, above everything else, he smiled when he swallowed the stew, did not grimace when he dipped the spoon in the bowl for a second bite.

All of a sudden she wanted to hug him tight. He'd given her so much and she'd given him nothing, nothing at all.

Oh, he claimed that she'd salvaged his reputation as well and that was critical for his future plans. Still, he would not have been in a questionable situation had he not carried her away from danger—probably saving her life in the process.

She ought to be able to give him something he wanted. The thing he had given up when he married her.

A baby.

Any other woman he married would have been able to give him one.

She gripped the apron in her fists. It had been years

since the doctor pronounced her unfit to bear a child. Given the condition she had been in then, the diagnosis would have been correct. But she was no longer an invalid.

"Sit, Agatha. Eat your dinner."

Sitting down on the chair across from him she drummed her fingers on the table and stared at the lumpy brown "stew" in the delicate china bowl.

What if it was awful? She would rather go hungry than taste it and find it inedible.

"It won't hurt you." He raised his spoon to her. A glob plopped back into the bowl. "See?"

He placed the spoon in his mouth, swallowed then smiled.

If he could eat it, she had better.

"Well," she said once she had forced the swallow down. "I don't imagine it will make us sick. I'm better with bacon and eggs, though."

"You don't need to be good at cooking. I'll find someone who can begin right away."

They would be better off for it, she had to admit.

"Why the frown, honey? Do you want to do the cooking?"

"No! I enjoy eating good food. Please, do hire a cook. It's just that, really, William, I don't know what I bring to our marriage. You are wealthy, well-respected, kind and heroic. Everything a girl could dream of. I'm just—nothing."

"It's what you were led to believe." Standing, he walked around the table and sat down on the chair beside her.

"I believe there is someone very special, in here." He tapped her chest with one finger, just over her heart. "Fighting to find her way out."

It touched her deeply, knowing that he truly saw her.

That he understood how the person she used to be fought hard against the one who wanted to break out and be free.

"Other than Ivy, you are the only one—" she had ever let look so deeply into the heart of her.

She did not finish the thought out loud. Rather than ask her to, William leaned forward and kissed her forehead.

"Let's go to the library. I think we ought to send letters home. Gossip spreads uncannily fast. I'd rather our families heard of our marriage from us."

So would she. She only hoped the letter would get to the Lucky Clover before Laura Lee did. A message of this importance needed to be told from her own lips, or pen.

There were many rooms in the house she hadn't seen, the library being one of them.

While she gazed at the bookcases that stretched from floor to ceiling, William knelt beside the hearth and built up a fire.

This was a charming room with lots of polished wood and large windows. Since it was dark outside, she could not see what was beyond them, but she pictured a garden with flowers of every color.

William drew a chair to the desk and indicated that she should sit on it. He took a seat on one opposite. Opening a drawer, he withdrew paper, pens and an ink bottle.

"What are you going to say?" he asked while pushing paper and a pen across the desktop. He opened the ink bottle and set it between them.

"Oh, I suppose I'll say that your wealth backs the Lucky Clover after all." She set the pen to paper not knowing how she was really going to explain things. "What are you going to say?"

"I finally got the Lucky Clover's reputation to boost my career."

His eye twinkled. Her heart shifted.

Silence fell between them. William's high spirits seemed to dim.

"Are you sorry at all, Agatha?"

"It's not something I planned, but no. I do not believe that I am." She must have been pressing the pen hard. A blob of ink pooled on the paper. "What about you? Are you sorry, William?"

"I am. But only in that you had no choice in the matter. You should have had one. My plan was to marry soon anyway, I'll admit. I'm not sorry it turned out to be you. I meant it when I said it had nothing to do with the Lucky Clover."

All of a sudden the twinkle in his eye returned. She had to glance away.

"Dear Ivy and Travis," she mumbled as she wrote, then her mind went blank.

How was she to explain that she left home to find independence and found a husband instead? And that she was happy with the turn of events?

She could not explain this to herself let alone her sister.

"Finish up your letter, Agatha." William blew on the ink of his own letter to dry it. "I think we are both done in. It's time for bed."

Her pulse jumped when she realized she was ready to be his wife in every way. Only two days ago she would have sworn this to be impossible.

She jotted something down quick. Later she would write a longer letter.

At the bottom step he placed his hand under her elbow. He must believe she did not have the strength to go up on her own.

"I can manage." She tried to yank her elbow free but he only gripped it more firmly.

"No need to risk it."

"I would not attempt to climb the stairs if I thought there was a risk, William."

In spite of her insistence, it wasn't until her foot was planted securely on the landing that he set her free.

There were a pair of grandly ornamented doors at the end of the hall, but he stopped at the door to the room she had napped in after the wedding.

It was a cozy feminine space. She did not think it suited William in any way.

"Is this our room?"

"No, it's your room. Mine is right there." He indicated the fancy doors with a nod of his head.

"Isn't it appropriate for married people to sleep together?" Back home as soon as dinner was over Ivy and Travis fairly ran upstairs.

He took a deep breath, held it while he nodded.

"Many do, but I believe you understand why we cannot."

It felt like he had ripped the heart out of her and stomped on it. She was not going to cry. If it took all her will she was not going to weep because the man she had never had a hope of marrying had become hers, and now he was casting her off.

What a ninny she was. He could hardly be casting her off before he had even taken her. But it did feel like being cast off and her heart ached.

But to be fair, their marriage had been as much a surprise to him as it had been to her. The only one who had not been taken off guard was the fortune-teller.

"Agatha, honey…" He stroked his thumb across her cheek, dashing away a gull-durned tear. Why had her sister's turn of phrase come to mind? Probably because she had no strength of her own she was drawing on Ivy's.

"You think I don't want you with me but it's not true. I just won't put your life at risk by sharing a bed with you. What kind of man would I be?"

Oh, well, given what he believed about her—what the doctor had told her father, he would be—

"A selfish brute." Drat! She hadn't meant to mumble that out loud and it was not at all what she meant.

"I won't be that. You are a sweet girl. Please trust that you are safe with me."

"Good night." She stretched up on her toes, kissed his cheek lightly, then shut the door.

When she heard him go into his room, she sagged against the wood. The knob pressed into the small of her back.

He thought she was a sweet girl! Little did he know that the scrape of his beard stubble on her lips made her go all hot and cold at the same time. The sensations twirling in her belly were far from sweet—not a bit innocent.

Day by day she was going to make herself stronger, in body *and* spirit. One night soon, she was going to go into that bedroom, crawl into his bed and take her rightful place.

No matter what, she was going to give him the thing that only she could.

One fine day, she was going to place a squalling, lusty infant in his arms.

Chapter Six

Twelve deep gongs of the great clock downstairs vibrated through William while he blinked sleeplessly at the ceiling. He sat up, swung his legs over the edge of the bed and tapped his foot on the floor. He couldn't help but wonder if Agatha had been woken by the noise.

Hopefully, she had not been disturbed—roused from sleep to pace her room in the sheer nightgown he had purchased for her today—walking past the big window where the full moon would be shining in.

"Hell."

It was good to be alone where he could curse with no one to hear what he said. The public William could not express such a thought. He would lose votes.

But he was alone now and his bride was in the next room possibly pacing before a window that would illuminate her body with light and shadow.

"Hell and damn."

Once in a while he wished he had become a cowboy like his late father always wanted him to. Those hardy souls cussed hourly and no one thought a thing about it.

Life would be easier if he'd followed his father's plan for him. Cowboys applied for employment, got hired. A politician had to make sure folks liked and trusted him more than they did another politician. Even if they did elect him, the whole process of currying votes started again after a few years.

Although he'd been through these thoughts hundreds of times, he always realized in the end that he was, indeed, seeking the right career. The uncertainty of his political future was not what was keeping him awake.

It was Agatha Magee English.

At what point, in his mind, had she changed from a girl to a woman?

The way his body had reacted to the knowledge that she expected to share his room made it clear that his mind had changed.

This was a lot of thinking to do sitting at the edge of his bed.

Dressing quickly, he tiptoed down the stairs and left the house, closing the door quietly behind him.

Outside, the air was still and warm. It settled about him with the sensation of a friendly hand on his shoulder.

Up and down Main Street, lanterns had been snuffed. Moonlight cast everything in bright light and muffled shadow.

He stepped off the boardwalk because his shoes clicked harshly on the wood.

Down here on the dirt of the road, his progress was as quiet as a wraith's.

With the chirrup of crickets and the hoot of an owl for company, he hoped to think more clearly.

He was married.

Married to a woman whom only days ago he had thought of as a girl.

When he'd carried Agatha from the circus, she had

been Ivy's helpless sister. His intention had been to send her home at once.

Circumstance had certainly changed that intention. Indeed, had changed his life. And hers.

Had she really thought she would find what she needed by leaving home? Frenchie Brown's enterprise was a shady thing. Agatha had landed herself in a nest of vipers.

Marriage to him had to be better than that.

But when had she changed from a girl to a woman in his eyes? And not just his eyes, but his heart? He'd always held a fondness for her, had pitied the thin young lady watching the world go by from a chair on her balcony.

He'd felt something of a hero when he'd danced with her that night at the Lucky Clover, because that was the way she had made him feel as she gazed up at him.

What he felt tonight, watching his mooncast shadow stride before him, was not fondness or pity.

It was lust.

Perhaps the transformation in his attitude had happened when she'd stood before him in red underwear refusing to marry him. Or, during their vows when she'd refused to obey him.

Or more likely, when she'd demanded her wedding kiss. He'd not soon forget how her eyes looked in that moment. Her gaze was so vulnerable—but at the same time challenging. He'd spent a lot of time since then trying to figure out what was going on behind that deep emerald gaze.

One thing was certain in that moment, something stirred in a place he hadn't expected it to.

"Hell," he muttered but more quietly than he had in his bedroom. Now he was in a mess.

He wanted a woman he could never have. No matter that she bore his name, she could not bear his children.

There was only one thing to do. Set his mind on the marriage being one of deep friendship.

Many marriages were based on that.

And some were not. If he had held that hope for himself in his heart—and he had for a time—he must now put it away.

He kicked a dirt clod. It exploded on the toe of his boot and rained back on the road in a puff of brown.

Apparently, no matter how logically he thought about this, it didn't keep him from picturing Agatha English pacing in front of her window with moonlight stroking her skin.

He had no reason to think she was pacing. As far as he could tell, she was sweetly asleep. With any luck she was not facing the turmoil he was.

He was halfway to the Bascomb Hotel when he spotted something that should not be.

Light, as if from a dim lantern, moved from one window to the next on the second floor.

It seemed that Mrs. Peabody's concerns might not be unfounded.

There was no way of knowing unless someone checked. Since there was no sheriff to do it, he reckoned the job fell to him.

He'd expected the front door to be locked and it was, but luckily, the back door was not.

As he came in through the kitchen, all was quiet. Walking through the dark lobby, he dodged covered chairs and couches.

All was quiet here as well. He started to climb the stairs. The first one squeaked, the third one squealed.

Any chance he had of surprising the person carrying the lamp was gone.

Just as well, for he didn't really want to encounter anyone.

"Hello?" he called. "Anyone here?"

Something on the next level fell over, sounding like it clattered on the floor.

Dashing up the rest of the stairs, he saw a beam of light coming from under a door.

"Hello!" he called again as he eased the door open.

No one was inside, but a cane lay on the floor. No doubt it was what he had heard fall over. A rumpled black cloak was draped over the back of a chair.

Whoever it belonged to had clearly fled to another part of the hotel.

"I'm not going to chase you!" he called. "I'm Mayor English. Come to my office tomorrow and we'll find you a better place to stay."

Clearly this was not the demon Mrs. Peabody had feared but some poor soul down on their luck.

There was no response to his call.

"I'll see you tomorrow, then!"

Four days after her wedding, Agatha stared at the ornate doorknob on her front door.

The blamed thing was not going to turn itself and let her out. She actually had to touch it in order to leave the sanctuary of her new home.

"Don't forget your bonnet." Beatrice Holmes snatched it from the hall tree, placed it on Agatha's head then tied the ribbons in a neat bow under her chin. "Off with you now. Enjoy this bright sunny day."

"Thank you Mrs. Bea."

The housekeeper William had hired might be the single most cheerful person Agatha had ever met. It was true that she hadn't encountered all that many people in her sheltered life, but she was convinced that Mrs. Bea was the sunniest woman in Tanners Ridge if not all of Wyoming.

"Don't let that lovely fair skin of yours get freckled."

Agatha smiled, making sure not to promise that. After spending so much time indoors she did intend to let the sun shine down upon her.

Once she went out of the blamed door, she intended to walk all over town before her anticipated appointment with the dressmaker.

Having been dull for so many years, she now found that she loved bright and pretty things. In this she could not be more different than her twin. Whenever she could, Ivy left her corset behind in favor of pants, while Agatha loved the sound of fabric swishing about her knees and ankles.

Mrs. Bea reached behind her, turned the knob and flung the door wide.

"I'll have a nice spot of afternoon tea waiting for you when you return."

Out on the porch, with the door closed behind her, Agatha wanted to weep. She ought to have been able to open her front door on her own, to step out onto the porch with a smile and a nod for anyone who might be passing by.

Oh, she did, in fact, have a smile. She only wondered if the man who just tipped his hat to her noticed that it trembled at the corners.

What she wanted was to feel that smile coming from toe to bonnet.

"Good morning," she said then went down the stairs, her hand extended. It was what William would do, and now that she was his wife she represented him. "Isn't it a grand day?"

She felt much better about herself now, if only because she had done what anyone would do.

If the fellow had questions about her sudden marriage he kept them to himself and returned her greeting.

And it was a grand day. She had not made that up. It was early enough that the earth still held the coolness of the night, and the sun had not yet become blistering.

Walking west down Main Street, she eventually came to open land. Up here at the top of the ridge, one could see for miles all around. The area below where the circus had camped was now a vast field of grass stirring ever so slightly in the morning breeze.

Drawing in a lungful of fresh air, she held it as long as she could. This was a daily test she gave herself. In her mind, the longer she could withstand taking a breath the heartier she was becoming.

Eleven seconds! She hopped up and down like a child, clapped her hands. When she had begun this trial, three seconds would give her a coughing fit.

A blur in the distance caught her attention.

A herd of horses moved west, then south. Galloping closer, individual animals became defined. Sunlight glimmered on hides of black and brown. When they were nearly to the base of the ridge, she was able to see how their great muscles pulled and stretched as they raced along.

What if, every morning she came to this spot and ran? What if she pulled off her bonnet, lifted her face to the sunshine and dashed about with her arms spread wide?

She would become stronger. In time, perhaps she would not be judged unfit to give birth to a child.

Perhaps William would take her to his bed.

Since there was no better time than now to begin an endeavor she drew the bonnet off, gripped the ribbons in her fist.

She had tried to run once, but the attempt had been more like stumbling.

Anything worth doing took time, she reminded herself.

Time and baby steps. Twenty feet today, thirty tomorrow.

One day she would be strong, like those beautiful horses down in the valley.

An hour later she stood on the dressmaker's dais with yards of shimmering blue silk draped over her shoulder. She felt the effort of the exercise settle into her muscles. By bedtime she was bound to be one huge ache.

"It will take some time, Mrs. English," the dressmaker mumbled through a collection of pins held between her lips. "But when I'm finished with these dresses you will be the envy of every woman."

Walking in a circle around her, Mrs. Hoover plucked the pins from her mouth and studied Agatha's hips.

"No need to look dismayed, Mrs. English. While your husband was well sought after, you have no need to worry." She stopped, nodded and tapped Agatha's hip. "I think a drape of silk right here will be just the thing. Your husband is a fine man."

"Yes, he is." No doubt what she really wanted to know was more about how they came to be married.

"Of course, you already know that. Mr. English tells me that you have been acquainted for some time."

A flash at the window caught her attention. It came and went so quickly that it gave the impression of a black smear, but there had been the image of a face in it.

For some reason it sent a chill along her arms, up her thighs.

That only happened when she thought of Hilda Brunne. She had to get over this fear of a dead woman.

No, it was not the dead woman she feared, it was the person she had tried to turn Agatha into. Forever a girl afraid of shadows, believing she could only trust one twisted woman.

"I just remembered another appointment." Agatha yanked the silk off her shoulder and shoved it at Mrs. Hoover.

Stepping off the dais she hurried for the front door. It was too tempting to hide inside the dress shop where it was safe.

Out on the street she looked north, then south. Carriages rolled past, stirring up dust. Children chased each other laughing while their mothers warned them not to dirty their clothing. The scent of baking cinnamon came from the confectioner's shop.

As she knew deep down, Hilda Brunne was not a lurking shadow in the alley between the dress shop and the general store.

Since it wasn't yet time for the tea Mrs. Bea had promised, she decided to visit William in his office.

Over the last three days she hadn't seen much of him. He'd claimed to be busy, but she felt that he was avoiding her. Not outright, but subtly busy with work.

The fact was, she missed him. He was one of the few people she felt easy with. There was Mrs. Bea, of course. One could not help but feel easy around her new housekeeper.

But there was something else about William. While he did make her feel at ease, he also made her feel—twitchy. Yes, twitchy was just the word. At ease and twitchy, all at the same time.

The one and only thing she could think of that would help would be a kiss.

In the many books she read, a kiss always set things to right.

* * *

Henry Beal sat across from William at his desk, drumming his soot-stained fingers on the highly polished wood.

"Mrs. Peabody saw someone at the Bascomb. It's time to hire a sheriff."

Past time, he thought but refrained from saying so. Diplomacy was what he practiced even though wanted to shake the fellow by his lapels and remind him of every one of the men the council had turned away.

"It turned out to be just a poor soul down on her luck."

"Her?" The breath went out of Henry in a rush. "No need to be afraid of a woman, I reckon. You saw her? You sure it was a lady?"

"I didn't see her—it was only an impression." Henry looked too relieved. "That doesn't mean you aren't right about needing a sheriff. Pete Lydle is coming and he's no gentle lady. From what I've learned about the man, you won't like what he's bringing to town."

The front door opened. Sunshine and his wife swept inside.

"Good day, Mrs. English." Henry stood up, extended his hand. Agatha must have seen the dark condition of his fingers but she set what she was carrying on his desk and shook his hand anyway.

Perhaps she was a better match for his political ambitions than he could have hoped for. Aimee Peller would not have touched a dirty hand.

William stood to greet her, too, his heart warming over three times.

"I'll leave you newlyweds to your lunch." With a nod, Henry sauntered off.

Something delicious was under the covered tray that Agatha had set on the table.

Something delicious was in the smile on her face.

In order to better focus on the food, he gave Agatha a quick kiss on the cheek then sat down.

His feelings for Agatha were changing in a way he could never have expected. How could it be that only hours into the marriage he felt desire for her as a woman when for years she had been barely more than a girl in his eyes?

He watched her lift the napkin from the tray, the movement of her fingers graceful. He wondered what they would feel like if she touched—no he did not! He could not.

The vows had been to honor and cherish. He would obey those vows no matter the cost.

"It was kind of you to think of me, honey. I was getting hungry as a matter of fact."

She did not sit as he expected her to. She stood beside the desk gripping a box that she had carried in with the food.

"Sit down. Eat with me."

When she made no move to do so, he realized that his invitation sounded like a demand.

"Please, sit with me, Agatha. I would enjoy your company."

She cocked her head, her smile as shy as the first pink bud on an apple tree.

If the feelings simmering inside of him were to be believed, and they were, the biggest threat to Agatha's health might be her own husband.

"I've bought you a present."

A gift? For him? "Many thanks, Agatha."

With a wriggle of her fingers, she indicated that he should slide his chair away from the desk a bit.

"I've discovered that you have credit all over town."

"So do you."

"Yes, I've discovered that as well. Shop owners are most welcoming."

He reached for the box, but she set it on the desk then settled lightly onto his lap.

It felt like a feather had floated down upon him, except that it was warm and—forbidden!

In a million years he would not hurt her feelings by hoisting her off even if he wanted to, which he did not. The trouble was, she was not exactly sitting still and something was happening to him that she was too innocent to understand.

That was something to be grateful for at least.

"What is it?"

"I'm not quite sure but—" Her cheeks flushed, pink and pretty. Apparently she was a bit shy about giving him a gift. "I mean, open it and see."

He lifted the lid to find a dashing-looking bowler nestled in gauze. She dipped her head. Her cheek grazed his temple.

"It's to replace the one you lost at the circus."

Had she been in the bakeshop as well? She smelled like a cinnamon roll.

He settled the hat on his head, grinning.

"It's better than the one I lost!"

"Oh, good."

She touched his ear. Slowly, she drew her fingers along the line of is jaw, turned his face side to side, seeming to study the look.

She bent her head, kissed him and he didn't have the good sense to end it.

She had been to the bakeshop! The lingering flavor of vanilla invaded his senses. With a twist and a swoop, he shifted her shoulders down. Now he was the one on top, the one directing the kissing.

In a second the aroma of baked goods was gone, leaving in its place the heady scent of a woman.

He shoved back her bonnet, loosened a pin from her hair. Soft locks tumbled over his hands, tangled in his fingers.

Why was it he felt triumphant and guilty at the same time? The woman was his wife, dash it! He deserved more than kisses. Judging by the way her shapely bottom shifted against him, she wanted more.

Breaking the kiss, he breathed hard against her neck. How could an innocent like her even know what it was she wanted?

What he could never in good conscience give her— or himself.

Love and cherish—he'd vowed those things and already he felt them. Only a few days into the marriage and his heart was hers—but not—not ever his body.

"It's a wonderful hat, Agatha. I thank you for it. And now." He glanced about, grabbed a sheet of paper from the corner of the desk, wondering what it even was. "I have urgent work to finish."

She did not rise at once, but pinned her hair and put the bonnet on her head. Why did she have to jiggle so?

Of, course, she would have no idea how she was tormenting him.

He retied the ribbon under her chin.

At last she stood, gave him the oddest little smile. "I'll see you at dinner, William."

"I'm looking forward to it."

Funny how much he was. And it was not because of the amazing talent of Miss Fitz, the new cook he had hired.

Way down deep in his heart, he wanted to spend time with his wife. He only hoped he would behave with honor toward her.

If it meant keeping a table length between them, or inviting Mrs. Bea to dine with them, that was what he would do.

An image popped into his mind of crawling the length of the great dining table, drawing Agatha up with him, shoving chicken and mashed potatoes aside then feasting on what he wanted most.

To his discredit, he was enjoying the image too much to set it aside.

Chapter Seven

Chapter Seven

"It's clouding up. I predict we'll have a storm tonight. What is that you're reading, dearie?" Mrs. Bea hustled into the sunroom carrying a tray with tea and sweets balanced upon it.

Agatha slammed the book upside down on her lap, her cheeks burning. If only she wasn't so prone to blushing. Although, what she was studying would cause anyone to turn pink.

"Whatever it is, I hope it won't spoil your appetite. Miss Fitz has begun a crusade to put a few pounds on you and I quite agree."

Mrs. Morgan, the gifted cook back home at the Lucky Clover, had also tried.

Given that she was a different person then than now, she wondered if Miss Fitz might be able to give her a few curves. The gray-haired woman did have a wonderful way with food.

Agatha enjoyed indulging in it all. In the same way that she loved pretty clothes, she craved delicious food.

Why, until Ivy forced her to nibble a chocolate croissant, she hadn't known food could explode with flavor.

Mother Brunne had always forbidden her to eat anything sweet or flavorful, always insisting that it would ruin her health. In order to save Agatha all kinds of illness, she'd eaten the food herself.

Eating that croissant had been a revelation, although Brunne had considered it rebellion. The scolding had been worth it.

Thinking back on it, Agatha realized the punishment had been about Mother Brunne's fear of Agatha's growing bond with Ivy as much as anything else.

Luckily, Hilda Brunne was gone and Agatha was free to indulge in whatever delicious scent passed her nose.

"Increased it I would think, Mrs. Bea."

Unless she missed her guess, there were strawberries beneath the flaky tart crust.

When the housekeeper set the tray on the table, Agatha reached forward. The book slipped off her lap.

For all that she was round and lovely, Mrs. Bea was quick. She snatched it up.

Oh, no! Agatha's only hope was that besides being cheerful, Mrs. Bea was discreet.

There would be no end to scandal if people found out what the mayor's wife was reading. It was no wonder she had found the book tucked in a corner of the bookshelf behind a copy of the Bible and *The Common Man's Guide to Weeding*.

Had she not been searching so diligently for something romantic, the book might have gone undisturbed for years. Judging by the layer of dust on it, William did not know it was there.

"Why, aren't you the smart one, Mrs. English. Not all brides are curious about the fleshy side of marriage. Although if you ask me, they would be better off for it."

Did she trust Mrs. Bea enough to confide in her?

Considering her amiable smile, feeling comfortable at the wink she cast, yes, yes, she believed she might.

"I'm not all that smart. That's why I'm reading the book."

Mrs. Bea scanned a page, grunted then turned another.

"Rubbish," she muttered.

Agatha took a bite of sweet, strawberry tart, followed by a sip of tea. Whatever the housekeeper was reading at the moment made her lips purse, as though she were about to spew out a curse.

Hopefully, the private things that went on between a man and wife were not that dire.

"This was written by a man," she announced. "I do doubt that this one ever bedded a woman. If he did, I cannot imagine the poor woman was satisfied with the outcome."

"Satisfied?" Agatha sputtered on the second bite of tart. "There's an outcome?"

"There's an outcome to everything, dearie. The outcome of lovemaking should be to leave the lovers sated, breathless and extremely satisfied."

Agatha hardly knew what to say about this revelation so she held her tongue, hoping Mrs. Bea had more to reveal.

"It's hard to tell from the illustrations." Mrs. Bea tapped her finger on the book.

"Take this one for instance." She turned the book about for Agatha to see. "They are on the bed, which is fine, but other private places will suit as well, such as closets or arbors." Mrs. Bea sighed, seemed to look inward, then rousing herself, continued, "Do you see how the man is grinning while he does his business on top of her, and the woman has her arm flung over her eyes?"

"Should I not fling my arm over my eyes?"

"Indeed not! Nor should you have your sleeping gown drawn only to your hips."

"How far up is proper?" All the way to her neck? Was it wicked to hope so?

"Proper? Proper is for spinsters. The gown, should you be wearing one, ought to be torn from you and tossed upon the floor. Nothing at all should come between you and your husband."

She set the tart back on the plate. This was good news.

"No wonder my sister and her husband run upstairs every night right after dinner."

"Well." Mrs. Bea smiled brightly, dropped the book on the floor and stomped on it with her boot. "Where shall we begin? Tell me what you do know."

"I think I know what fits where in order to have a child."

"That's a start. May I ask where you gained this knowledge?"

"I grew up on a ranch. I saw things from my window."

"Horses and cows?" Mrs. Bea took her hand, patted it.

"Yes, but even then it was from a very great distance since I never left the house."

"Let's start at the beginning, shall we?" Mrs. Bea poured two cups of tea and helped herself to a tart. "With touching and kissing."

"I have been kissed! Just this noon!"

With Mrs. Bea's help she would learn the mystery of the bedroom.

If it all began with a kiss, she was on her way.

Sitting at a game table in front of the fireplace in the parlor, William watched his wife's frown while she gazed at the checkerboard.

He'd been avoiding her as much as he could. It was a cowardly thing to do, he understood that, but he'd needed some time to sort out his emotions.

They were confusing to the point that he could barely think straight.

"This is quite a storm," he said in order to make light conversation. "I think the last lightning bolt hit the garden."

"It shook the house," she answered without letting go of her frown. "I can't decide where to move my piece so you won't jump me."

Firelight reflected on her hair, cast her skin in a rosy flush.

He tapped his finger on the table to keep from reaching over and touching the faint throb of her pulse at her wrist.

Judging by the reaction of his body at being so close to her, he ought to have kept to himself tonight as well.

But one could not avoid one's wife indefinitely.

After the inappropriate, and completely absorbing, kiss in his office this afternoon, he figured sweet and fragile Agatha was not going to let herself be avoided.

Clearly he was going to have to be the one to do it. The question was—how?

The last thing he wanted to do was avoid her. He wanted to enjoy her company, see her smile, listen to her laugh.

Blast him, but he wanted to feel her desire for him— revel in the simmer of heat in his veins. He was shocked at how an innocent yet proactive gaze from those green eyes could bring his heart to heel.

Slowly, she slid her piece with the tip of her finger. He jumped her and she sighed, looked unhappily into his eyes.

Just when had those eyes gone from dull to sparkling. Even though she was frowning they were alight.

Who, exactly, had he married?

"One day I will get the best of you, William." The sight of her pink smiling lips made him nearly topple from his chair.

One day? Perhaps she already had, just not in the way she realized.

Her expression was nothing but sweet, but it spoke to his soul. It might be an easier thing to resist the charm of Agatha Magee English if his heart was not becoming as beguiled as his body.

Gazing back at the checkerboard, she tapped her lips with one finger. A gesture of deep thought? Or a reminder of what had sparked between them in his office chair?

As if he needed reminding. What he needed was forgetting.

This young woman might be his wife, but he could never know her in a carnal way.

As much as he might want to—hell, he did want to—his first duty was to protect her. Above all else he would see to her well-being.

Being a husband involved a whole lot more than sharing a bed.

Agatha hadn't wanted to marry him, but she had and saved his reputation and future dreams in doing so. The last thing he was going to do was betray her.

"I don't know why you look so distressed." As though deep in thought over her next move on the board, she tapped the delicate hollow on her throat. "You have me all but beaten."

"We need to talk about what happened this afternoon." Her shy smile sliced his heart. He would never do anything to hurt her feelings, damage the self-confidence she was fighting so hard to gain. "I reckon—"

A rustle of fabric in the hallway silenced him. The private matter he was about to discuss was not for the ears of the hired help.

Mrs. Bea popped into the room followed by Miss Fitz. She set a sweet-smelling pastry beside the chessboard.

"Miss Fitz and I are headed to our rooms. But first here's a pie for the two of you. A succulent cherry pie!"

She winked at Agatha. That was odd. Even more odd, the wink made Agatha blush.

"If you need anything, don't try and rouse us. We are so tired we will not be awakened even if you pound on our doors. Isn't that right, Miss Fitz?"

"Oh? Well, yes, I suppose I am rather weary." Funny that she didn't appear to know it until Mrs. Bea said so.

The ladies both went out the doorway at the same time. Their skirts mashed together, making them look like two people inside of one dress.

Mrs. Bea turned about suddenly, flashing him a spring day smile. It was a welcome thing to see on this stormy night.

"Your wife looks especially winsome tonight, don't you agree, Mr. English?" she said.

"I do." As if he needed reminding.

How could he not agree? He half wished she did not look so appealing. It was going to be hard enough to remind her that he would not consummate the marriage. The fact that the cherry pie was not the only thing in the room that was succulent made it that much more difficult.

He'd feel a lot more comfortable if Miss Fitz had baked a nut pie—or fig.

Outside, drooping hydrangeas became visible in a flash of stark white light. Thunder banged over the rooftop. Upstairs, he heard the distinct closing of doors.

"Pie sure smells delicious," he commented then looked at the board, planning the move that would crown him the winner of the game.

After making the victorious move with his piece, he glanced up.

Heaven help him! Agatha had unbuttoned her blouse down to the fifth button. Her fingers trembled upon the sixth.

"What are you doing, honey?" He knew what—of course he did. It was just that he could scarcely believe her boldness.

She stood up suddenly. Fanned her chest with her hand. "It's getting warm in here, don't you think. I'll get us some pie before we begin the next game."

Heat, or perhaps more a chill, frizzled along his neck. What game did she have in mind? He feared it was not checkers.

She set a plate with a huge slice of pie on it in front of him. The fork clinked when she laid it on the china. The small fire snapped and rain pattered on the window.

"It's a summer storm," he said. "We've got a fire going. It's understandable that it would be hot."

"It's hot because we are newlyweds and here we are..." She shrugged her slim shoulders. "All alone."

Taking one bite of pie, she stood then rounded the table and took him by the hand. There was a dash of red at the corner of her mouth, cherry juice.

He stood when she urged him up. He followed her like he was a man with no will—like his innocent bride had suddenly become a siren leading him to disaster on the rocks of self-indulgence.

The soft give of couch cushions hit his calves. With a gentle shove she pushed him and he fell quite willingly.

Her small body, angular in places and plush in others, settled down upon him.

He circled his arms about her back because he couldn't help it, drew his fingers along the ridge of her spine.

The small bumps reminded him that she was frail—that he was a cad.

"Honey, we can't do this," said a mouth that would rather be kissing.

"It wouldn't take much. Our lips are only a breath apart."

"I had no idea you were so bold."

"Nor did I," she said but lowered her mouth.

Her kiss was sweet, affectionate and playful. His body reacted as though she had been a seasoned seductress. What would happen when she learned something besides kissing?

He would be lost was what. His good intentions would come to nothing. In seeking his own satisfaction, he might kill her.

Even after twenty years, he remembered the face of his newborn sister, so white in death. She'd given one weak cry before she stopped breathing. The doctor had told them that Mama would die as well. Fear had kept William on his small knees for a whole week. It had kept the brandy bottle at his father's lips. One morning, his father announced that he was going on a winter hunting trip at a friend's lodge. He never returned. The friend claimed to know nothing about the trip.

He would not end up like his father.

Agatha would never look death in the eye the way his mother had.

He did not believe he could survive living through that hell again.

With a great, regretful sigh, he placed his hands at her waist and lifted her away.

"I know that you wanted to kiss me—and—more," she muttered, walking toward the window, then gazing out at the rainy night.

"How?"

"You don't know?" She tipped her forehead, touching it to the glass. "Mrs. Bea said that a man gets—"

"Mrs. Bea!" He bounded up from the couch, staring at the reflection of her face in the glass. "You are learning about intimacy from the housekeeper?"

"She said the book I found in the library gave wrong information. That if I followed the author's advice I would never have intimate satisfaction."

"A book? Mrs. Bea?" He plopped back down on the couch, held his face in his hands and spoke through his fingers. "Agatha, honey, I know I'm the one you should be learning from. It's my duty as your husband to teach you about that part of marriage, but you know what the doctor told your father."

"I was very ill then."

He looked up from his hands. "I can't risk your safety."

She remained silent for a time, drawing a squiggly line in the mist her breath formed on the window.

The room blanched with another bolt of lightning.

Agatha screamed.

She backed away from the window while he rushed for her.

He spun her about, cupped her face in his hands.

"What's wrong?"

"I saw a face in the window!"

"What? Who was it?"

She clung to him, trembling while he stroked his fingers down her back.

"I don't know—it was there and gone so fast."

"It was probably a trick of light. I reckon because of the rain on the glass, maybe because of the lightning flashing through it."

She shook her head. "I don't think so. I thought I saw the same thing earlier at the dress shop."

"Go to your room. I'll check the yard."

He watched her go up the stairs before he headed for the kitchen door.

Chances were, she was overwrought. What young lady would not be, finding herself a sudden bride—and yet not quite? Opening the back door, he was pretty sure he was going to find only dripping plants and sulfur-laden clouds.

He should have taken the time to put on a coat. Wind and rain blew at him, soaked him through. It was difficult to see with the backyard such a watery blur. He wiped his face with his open palm. If there was someone out here, he needed to know.

Crossing the yard, he hunched his shoulders, stared hard into obscured corners of the garden.

Coming to the window, he realized that with no curtain, anyone standing in the yard would have seen the pair of them, playing checkers, maybe even tangled up with each other on the couch.

The window was not visible from the street so what went on inside would be private, unless viewed by a prowler.

Standing outside, staring at the glass, he saw the print where Agatha's forehead had rested, the condensation left by her breathing.

But what was that? Another misting of breath, only inches above the sill—on the outside!

Stooping, he spotted a trail of footprints. Blades of grass were bent. The impression seemed to be caused by small shoes.

They led from the planter below the window to the gate banging open and closed in the wind.

He ran into the rear yard where a stream flowed through. After looking in both directions several times, he decided that whoever had been spying on them was gone.

Going back into the yard, he latched the gate behind him, shook it to make certain it was secure.

Coming back inside, he made sure the kitchen door was locked. It left him more than a bit unsettled to think someone had come into the yard—spied upon them.

He knew most everyone in town. Climbing the stairs to his room, water dripping off his clothes, he wondered which of them would do that.

Not a single soul came to mind except the squatter at the hotel. Still, just because someone was down on their luck did not mean they were up to no good.

He closed his bedroom doors then swiped the sopping shirt off over his head. He dropped it on the floor then stepped out of his pants and long johns.

A chill crept over his naked flesh. He couldn't be sure whether it was from the water on his skin or the unease of being secretly watched.

With a sigh, he closed his eyes and flopped backward onto the bed.

He heard breathing, felt warmth beside him. He turned his head, cracked open his eyes.

A foot away on the mattress, Agatha knelt with her hands folded in her lap, her eyes round and unblinking.

"I was too frightened to be in my own room."

Chapter Eight

And a lucky turn of events that turned out to be!

It was also lucky that William hadn't bothered to light the lamp on the bedside table. Because of the dark, and the fact that she had done her best to sit still as a marble statue, to even breathe like one, he hadn't noticed her.

During the seconds it took for him to rip off his clothing and fall back on the bed, she made a lovely discovery.

Her husband was quite a handsome man under his clothes. She had never seen a naked man before but she had a feeling this one was exceptional to look at.

The anxiety that sent her to his room instead of her own faded somewhat.

Instead of being shaken by a cold dread type of quiver, she shivered with a delicious flush that thrummed just below the surface of her skin.

It seemed to take him a moment to believe she was kneeling on his bed. He stared up at her as though he were struck dumb.

"You look chilled," she said for the need of something to say.

The observation must have brought him to the here

and now for he bolted upright then grabbed the edge of the comforter and yanked it across his waist.

According to Mrs. Bea, married people ought to see each other naked every day. Also according to Mrs. Bea, the part of himself that he was hiding from her view was nothing to be feared, but something to bring her pleasure.

Truthfully, she could not quite see how that would be possible. It was difficult to imagine how things would fit where they were supposed to.

Scooting, he backed to the far corner of the bed.

"Because I spent fifteen minutes in the yard looking for your intruder."

"That was brave of you." It truly was.

Shivering was an odd thing, she realized, when at the same moment in time one could be shivering hot and cold—dread and anticipation demanding her attention all at once.

"Did you find someone?"

"No. Not someone, but something."

Without thinking, she clasped the clover charm on her necklace. Rubbed the smooth gold between her fingers, seeking what courage could be found on the small solid surface.

"What you saw was a cat peering in the window. Must have been looking for a dry place."

A cat! All of a sudden she had to look away. She sent him into the rain because of a cat?

She was not becoming a stronger person at all! Until she could stop seeing Hilda Brunne in a feline's face she was not a person to be respected.

"I'm sorry." With regret, she got off the bed then walked toward the door.

"It was a very large cat, honey. Don't go quite yet."

He tossed the covers off and got up from the bed. This time she had the decency to stare at the floor.

When he touched her arm, she looked up to find him wearing a dressing gown.

"No wonder you think I'm weak and silly."

He frowned, looked like he was about to say something but only shook his head.

After a moment, he drew her into a hug and kissed the top of her head. "I do not think that."

Setting her aside, he went to a table beside a big stuffed chair and lit the lamp on it. The room suddenly flared in a warm yellow glow.

"Sit down." He pointed to the chair then dragged another, smaller one from the bedside. "There was something I wanted to discuss with you earlier, before the cat interrupted."

Rain pattered on the widow, emphasizing the fact that she did not know what to say to lessen the shame of seeing the boogeyman in the face of a feline.

"Maybe another time."

The very last thing she wanted to discuss was the thing he no doubt wanted to.

He was not willing to share his bed with her. No doubt the only time she would see her husband in the way a wife deserved to had passed a moment ago.

He placed his hands on her shoulders and gently pressed her into the chair. He sat down beside her with the window at their backs. She could not see the lightning moving off into the distance but the noise of it lessened as it pounded over the land.

"I've had a telegram from my mother," he announced.

Of all the things, that was not what she had expected him to say.

"How lovely." It was lovely. How lucky he was to have a mother to send him a telegram.

"You might not think so when you hear what she has to say."

"I did suspect she might not approve of me."

She clasped her hands in her lap, twisting her fingers, because she really had hoped that her mother-in-law would approve. How could she blame her, though? They had been neighbors. Mrs. English had been a guest at the Lucky Clover. She would have heard that Agatha should not bear children. It was not a secret.

"Actually, she is thrilled."

"She can't possibly be. All women want grandchildren."

"What she wants at this moment is to come here and give us a lavish wedding reception."

All of a sudden a mere cat in the window did not seem so horrific.

"She'll act as hostess, but you will also be called upon." He touched her hand, ran his long thumb over the ridges of her knuckles. "Is this something you can do? Shall I forbid her to come?"

Agatha Marigold Magee could not do it. Not in a thousand years.

But Mrs. William English? That woman could do nothing but try. Perhaps if she showed herself to be an extraordinary hostess, confident to her bones, maybe then her husband would not see her as a virgin in need of safekeeping.

"Of course I can do it."

She stood up because she really did need the privacy of her bedroom. So many things had happened tonight that she could scarcely wrap her emotions around them.

Slowly coming out of his chair he reached for her, ran

his hands up her arms then cupped her chin in the fingers of one hand. His thumb stroked her cheek, made her want to close her eyes with the pleasure of it.

"Thank you, Agatha. I know this isn't an easy thing for you."

She'd seen a cat, imagined an enemy and been informed that she would be hostess to a party to celebrate her marriage.

She shouldn't be, but she was ill at ease.

The temptation to lean into William, to allow him to make it all go away for a time was beguiling.

Temptation pushed its seductive fingers at her spine. In the end, doing so would only postpone her agitation.

"It's been a long day, William. Sleep well."

She hesitated only a second beside his door before she turned to her own room.

She hated that the distance felt like a hundred cold miles.

The midmorning sun shone down bright as a new penny. In William's opinion, there was nothing quite as lovely as a summer morning. Those few hours before the sun wilted everything and everyone were something to make a man feel good.

Evidently Miss Valentine felt the same because as soon as he opened the front door she rushed out to accompany him on his stroll to the telegraph office.

"No more limp, little miss. Looks like all that time on the couch has done you good."

She'd also put on a bit of weight with all the indulging Miss Fitz did.

"Good morning, Mayor." Tom Baynor greeted him with a broad smile when he entered the office. "Who is that you have with you this morning?"

The light inside the office seemed dim, as he had come in from the bright sunshine. He heard Miss Valentine's nails tapping around in the small office while she smelled the doorway then the corner of the counter.

"She's my wife's dog. Miss Valentine is her name."

Tom came around the counter and stooped down. "And a fetching little thing she is."

The fetching thing lived in his house, slept on his furniture and probably scratched his floors, but yes, she was endearing.

And she did make Agatha smile. In fact, the only happiness he'd seen from her this morning was when she fastened the pink bow between Miss Valentine's ears.

He'd hoped to be the one to make her smile, so he'd asked Agatha to come walking with him. She had declined, claiming to have another engagement.

All he could hope for was that her engagement was not with a chair in deep shadow.

She had to feel that he had rebuffed her affection and he worried that she would withdraw into herself. Take a step back toward the person she had been when her nurse was in control of her.

While William did like to be in control of what happened around him, he did not want to be in control of his wife.

After nuzzling the dog behind her fluffy ears, Tom stood up and walked to the business side of the counter.

"What can I do for you, Mayor English?"

"I'd like to send a telegram to my mother."

He needed to know when his mother was planning her party. It could be a lavish gala with all the eminent folks of Cheyenne invited, or an intimate affair involving a hundred of her closest friends.

The celebration was being planned with his future in

mind. His mother was supportive of his political ambition. He'd been all of fifteen years old when she realized he would be content with nothing else.

Whatever she had in mind, he would need to prepare Agatha for it.

It was true that many grand events had been held at the Lucky Clover, but Agatha had always been peering out from the shadows, not the one to greet and welcome guests, to make sure they were comfortable, to solve any issues that arose.

"You might not need to." Tom turned, reached into a cubby in the polished wood shelf behind him and plucked out a telegram. "It came first thing this morning. Looks like she'll be here day after tomorrow."

He felt gut-punched. It was not that he didn't want to see his mother, he did. But he'd need to warn Agatha that their quiet time with just the two of them, Miss Fitz and Mrs. Bea was at an end already.

Life spun around his mother. Wherever she was, a whirlwind of activity swirled about her.

"There you are!" The door slammed against the wall. Henry Beal charged inside, his breath puffing like one of his bellows.

Miss Valentine wagged her tail, jumped up to greet him. If the man noticed, he didn't show it.

"Good day, Henry."

"I'm not so sure about that." The blacksmith's heavy eyebrows dipped low, his mustache traced the downward slant of his lips. "Last night folks heard moaning and crying coming from the Bascomb. I figured you ought to know."

"I'm not sure why I need to know about it more than anyone else." Except that the moaner might be the person who had been peering in his window.

"It needs to be investigated." Henry stared at him without blinking.

"That's a job for a lawman."

"I'd tell him if we had one."

If he didn't need the position of mayor as a stepping-stone to governor, he'd quit. After he punched Henry in the nose.

"That's the town's doing, Henry. I've presented you many good candidates."

"That don't change the fact that some old woman is keeping folks up at night with her wailing. It's downright eerie if you ask me, the way she keeps keening. Mrs. Peabody says then she isn't crying, she's singing lullabies."

So, it was a woman. He'd thought so.

That would account for the small footprints leading away from the garden window.

What he couldn't understand was why she would be peering in his window. He'd invited her to come to his office and she hadn't.

"I'll check the hotel, Henry. I doubt the woman is a threat."

"Figured we could count on you." All of a sudden Henry's lips tipped up under his mustache. The severe line of his eyebrows softened. He appeared to notice the dog for the first time. "Why, what a sweet pup."

Even though Miss Valentine was not a working dog like the ones on his ranch, he realized that she was useful for something other than leaving fur on his furniture.

Unless he missed his guess, the dog had just earned him two votes.

By the time Agatha walked the short distance from town to the cliff, she was winded. But not as winded as she had been yesterday.

Morning sunshine warmed her shoulders, made her want to stretch out on the big rock to her right, act like a lazy cat with nothing to do but purr and soak up warmth.

She might do that one day, but right now that indulgence was not her goal.

Down below, she spotted the horses galloping the same as they had done before. And just there—she was certain she saw right—a newborn foal ran on spindly legs beside its mother.

Removing her bonnet, she set it on the rock. She plucked the pins from her hair, shook it loose and free, the same as she'd seen the horses do with their manes.

She ran until she was winded, rested then ran again.

Last time she had run a shorter distance. Tomorrow she would run farther than she did today.

Because someone was counting on her. Someone she did not yet know. But a small, sweet someone who belonged to her—and to William.

In its own way, the great full moon shone down as brightly as the sun had this morning.

Not that he could appreciate the beauty of light and shadow glazing Main Street. He was far too weary for that.

Even though he'd hired a crew for the day to prepare six extra bedrooms for his mother and some of the guests she was bringing, he'd done much of the work himself.

Mrs. Bea had been helping Mrs. Fitz in the kitchen. Agatha, having convinced them that she had some experience with feeding large crowds, spent much of the day and evening elbow-deep in bread dough and other things that kept them dusted in flour.

It had been near 10:00 p.m. when the ladies emerged

from the kitchen, smeared with what looked to be purple juice.

With all the hard work they had been doing, he hoped they would not be offended if his mother brought her own cook from home.

Another hour had passed before Agatha had gone to her room and another forty minutes before he heard the creak of her bedsprings.

He was going to investigate the Bascomb later than he had planned on. He would have preferred doing it in daylight hours. What sane person would not?

But besides not having the time to do it then, he didn't want Agatha to know what he was doing. He'd told her there had been a cat at the window the other night. That was all she needed to know.

Finally, at twelve thirty he'd put his ear to her door and heard the slow, even breathing of sleep.

At last he had been able to creep from the house with no one knowing.

No one but Miss Valentine who trotted happily out the door behind him. He'd tried to make her go back inside but she wagged her tail, scrambled down the stairs then sat to wait for him.

Truth to tell, at this time of night he didn't mind the company.

Confronting the woman in the hotel was not a thing he looked forward to, but it had to be done. Perhaps the presence of the dog would make him seem friendlier, more approachable.

With the moon bright, he decided there was no need to light the lantern until he was inside the hotel.

Looking at the abandoned building a block ahead, he thought it looked foreboding.

Better empty and foreboding than the den of malignancy he feared it would be turning into soon.

An image bloomed in his mind while he stared at the darkened windows. The once elegant hotel turned tawdry, with red lights in the windows, bawdy music spilling out of open doors and inebriated men lounging on the boardwalk. Rouge-cheeked, half-dressed women calling out from upper-floor windows for them to come back inside.

Even if it wasn't as bad as his imagination painted, it was not going to be a place fit for Tanners Ridge.

As before, he entered through an unlocked back door. Miss Valentine's nails tip-tapped on the dusty wood floor.

Something was different than the last time he was here. Cigarette smoke lay heavy on the air. That was odd since he hadn't gotten the impression that the shy woman was a smoker. There had been no lingering residue.

Glancing up and down the hallway, he saw no light creeping from under doors. But the further along he went, the stronger the smoke scent became.

Miss Valentine stopped at a door to his right, growled softly.

This had to be the room. Would the woman flee again before he had a chance to speak with her? He hoped not. It ate at his gut, wondering why she had been spying on him and Agatha.

Slowly, he opened the door.

Two people sat at a table beside the window that overlooked Main Street, their shapes black silhouettes due to the moonlight streaming in from behind.

The glowing tip of a cigarette rose, fell, then traced a circle in the air.

"Welcome," said the deep voice of the larger figure.

A chair scraped, the smaller form flipped up the hood

of her cloak then stood up. William could see nothing of her face, which was cast in deep shadow.

Sure was strange for someone to be wearing a cloak in July.

She limped from the room going out a door at the other end of the space, the head of her cane striking a regular rhythm on the floor.

"I'll miss that one's charming company," the man said with a half laugh that sat uneasy on William's nerves. "Won't you join me and explain what you are doing in my establishment?"

William lit the wick of the lantern, adjusted it to low then set it on the table.

The man sitting across from him had a long face and dark shaggy hair that needed cutting.

"Mr. Lydle?" It could be no one else.

"You have the advantage of me, sir."

"William English." William offered his hand. Pete Lydle accepted his greeting. Even in the soft light given by the lantern he noticed that the man's fingernails were nicotine-stained. "Mayor of Tanners Ridge."

"I must wonder why you are wandering about my place in the middle of the night."

It set William a bit on edge that Miss Valentine leaned against his pant leg, trembling. The dog usually greeted everyone with a wagging tail.

"I was hoping to meet with the woman."

"Why would you want to?"

"I've had complaints about her crying at all hours. I believe she was looking in my window the other night."

"I can't imagine the wretched creature would cause you any harm."

"I imagine not. I am concerned for her well-being, though. Are you acquainted with her?"

"Just met her when I got here a couple of hours ago." Pete Lydle took a long draw, blew out a ring of smoke. "Can I offer you whiskey?"

"Thank you." For friendliness' sake, he accepted the amber liquid.

"Don't worry, it's good quality, not the rot-gut that so many don't mind drinking."

That Lydle didn't mind serving. It was one of the things he'd learned about the fellow.

He finished the drink and had to admit it was fine stuff.

"I'd like to speak to the woman if you know where I might find her."

"She's an old crone is all."

"But possibly mentally unbalanced."

"Might well be, Mayor. But you need not concern yourself over her. I've just hired her to look after my girls. She is now under my protection. I'll see she doesn't bother you."

From all he'd heard, control would be a better word than protection.

"Feel free to visit the Palace anytime you like, Mr. English. But don't bring the dog."

William stood. The expression on Lydle's face was an outright sneer.

"Had a bad experience with a dog that size once. That one was white. Had a bow in its fur, just like your mutt. It was responsible for the ruin of my saloon."

The story of the ruin of Pete's Palace was no secret if one looked into it, and he had. The man had tried to cheat a dead woman, and to enslave a lady piano player. She resisted him and it caused a riot among the patrons who doted upon her.

The woman and the dog escaped with a bounty hunter while the customers left the Palace in splinters.

"I bid you good night, Mr. Lydle."

Pete did not rise to bid him farewell but instead huffed out a smoke ring then snuffed out the cigarette in his whiskey glass.

"I expect we will meet again, Mayor. I believe your office is not far from here. I look forward to a pleasant and profitable relationship with the folks of Tanners Ridge."

"I'd like to hope so—but I'm familiar with your former establishment, Lydle. Folks won't welcome it."

"Won't they?" Lydle tipped back in his chair, propped his boots on the table. "No matter. If they don't come, others will. They will come from far and wide to drink and lose money at my gaming tables and to spend time with my girls."

"Tanners Ridge is not that sort of town."

"Perhaps it wasn't. Who is there to stop me in whatever I do? Unless I've been misinformed, you have no sheriff."

A sad fact that he could not dispute. He took his dog, snagged up the lantern and left the Bascomb.

The walk home was more distressing than the walk into town. All of a sudden an old woman peeking in a window didn't seem so troublesome.

Chapter Nine

Winded from her run, Agatha braced her hands on her knees while she caught her breath.

It was hot, already uncomfortable and it was only nine in the morning.

For the first time since she'd begun her morning run, the horses hadn't come. Gazing down at the valley, she missed them. Watching their sleek muscles strain and stretch, and counting newborns had become a beautiful way to begin her day.

Far in the distance, she saw a cloud of dust rising from the road. No, there were two dust clouds, one about a hundred yards ahead of the other.

As the groups came closer to the ridge she began to hear sounds—see figures more clearly.

The first group was made up of men on horses, brightly dressed women in a buckboard, and three other wagons loaded with supplies.

There was not much doubt about who the first group of travelers were. William had told her how he'd run into Pete Lydle when he was walking Miss Valentine last night.

Over breakfast, he'd revealed all he knew about the man and his ambitions. Even warned her to keep the dog inside or in the yard.

With her breathing now normal, she straightened up, stepped closer to the edge of the bluff to get a look.

She had never seen anything like these people. The women with their low cut, vibrant-colored clothing and hair, the men laughing and cursing and—she squinted her eyes to look more closely—drinking. At this early hour between the cuss words, she saw bottles being tipped.

As if to annoy the party behind them, they hooted, hollered and galloped their horses in circles, raising a great cloud of choking dust.

The second group of travelers appeared to be more refined. Women wearing proper bonnets rode in fringe-bedecked buggies. Gentlemen on well-groomed horses rode sedately beside them, perhaps cursing at the dust, but not drinking.

This group also had buckboards trailing them. But instead of supplies for the saloon, they were heaped with traveling trunks.

A woman on horseback split from the group in the rear and charged her horse toward the group in front.

It was hard to see her face until her bonnet blew off but her shout was easy to hear, given that the commotion was taking place only fifty feet below.

"You uncouth heathens!" She shook her fist at the heathens. "You miserable louts!"

The painted ladies in the buckboard stared at her open-mouthed. The men swept their hats from their head in mock respect.

One of them lifted his bottle in salute. "Beggin' your pardon, ma'am." Clearly, given the sneer in his voice he did not beg anyone's pardon.

Agatha's heart crept halfway up her throat because—if she was not mistaken, the outraged woman was Victoria Mary English—her mother-in-law!

* * *

"She's here!" Rushing into the house, Agatha clutched Mrs. Bea's arm as she placed a flower in a vase on the table beside the door. "Mrs. English! In a few minutes she'll be knocking at our door!"

"How lovely." Mrs. Bea patted her cheek. "The rooms have been ready for hours. I'll just run and tell Mrs. Fitz to put on the coffee and warm the muffins. Don't look so worried, Mrs. English, all is ready."

"I'm not ready!"

Far from it! Her hair drooped about her shoulders, a limp, tangled mass. She'd lost her bonnet on the dash home. Sweat dampened her blouse and the hem of her skirt was dusty.

"Why, of course you are. Just smile and welcome her." Mrs. Bea wiped something off the tip of Agatha's nose with the pad of her thumb.

"I look a mess!" She turned for the stairs, dashed up.

"No one wants her daughter-in-law to look like a china doll."

"They might!"

All at once Mrs. Bea erupted into a coughing fit.

"I've never met Victoria English directly." Agatha called over her shoulder. "Maybe she's always wanted a china doll for her son!"

"Perhaps," came another voice from the bottom of the stairs. "She has never had any use for china dolls."

Agatha turned on the top stair, looked down. It felt like her bones and muscles had dissolved, her face turned to flame. Apparently her voice had also fled because she stared mutely at the woman looking her over from top to toe.

"Welcome, Mrs. English," Mrs. Bea said with a smile

and nod of her head. "Miss Fitz will serve refreshments in the parlor. How many shall she expect to entertain?"

"Only five for the parlor, thank you. But I imagine the help would appreciate a bite in the kitchen if Miss Fitz won't mind."

"Mind?" Mrs. Bea clapped her hands one time under her chin. "She is beside herself to have folks to do for."

With that Mrs. Bea spun about and left her—alone.

"Come down, my dear. Give your new mother a hug."

Somehow she made it down without stumbling, or weeping, because quite without warning, tears stung the backs of her eyes.

Until this moment she had not considered the fact that William's mother would be her mother as well.

She'd had two already. One had abandoned her and the other enslaved her.

But the woman at the bottom of the stairs had called her "my dear" and was smiling with her arms wide open.

"I scarcely recognize you, Agatha."

She would not. Mrs. English would only have seen her from a distance or a secluded corner when she attended parties her father held at the Lucky Clover.

Mother Brunne had made sure of that.

The nurse disliked her infatuation with William and would have prevented a meeting with his mother or anyone whom she might have formed a bond with.

"I'm sorry, I'm hardly presentable, Mrs. English." She did not step into the hug.

"And look at me! All covered in dust and…" She slapped at her skirt, squinted down at it. "What is that? A burr? No. I believe its manure."

William's mother straightened and laughed. "At least we meet as equally soiled! I'd have felt horrid had you spent the morning getting gussied up while I blew in like a tumbleweed."

All of a sudden Agatha found herself wrapped in a tight, swift hug. "From now on you will call me Mother and I will call you Agatha, or my dear, or perhaps my dear sweet girl."

"Mother always longed for a daughter," William said striding into the foyer from the parlor and giving his mother a kiss on the cheek.

"You surprise me at every turn, son," she said then stepped into his hug.

"Oh!" Suddenly incensed, Mother shoved away from him. "I ran afoul of the most horrid ruffians on the way into town. One of their horses flicked dung onto my skirt!"

But, as Agatha had seen firsthand, she'd faced them down with courage. None of the men in her party had done so.

Her mother-in-law was a person to be respected, to be emulated.

"Yes, well—I've been expecting them," William answered with a grunt.

"I suggest you notify the sheriff."

He grunted again—or was that quiet cussing?

His mother did not reprimand him so perhaps it was a grunt after all.

With a hand under each of their elbows, William escorted them into the parlor where the scent of coffee and warm muffins beckoned.

"How many folks have you brought with you this time?"

"Only eleven. Five very close friends and six to help with the extra work."

Mrs. English had five very close friends? The knowledge made her stomach uneasy.

Agatha would be expected to smile, laugh and be witty.

Sadly, the muffins did not smell as good as they had a moment before.

William stood beside Agatha while his mother made introductions. While his bride did smile and nod her head in greeting, she also leaned quite close to him.

A part of him wanted to carry her upstairs, set her in a chair with a book and a snack. That was where she would feel safe.

Of course, he could not do that. She'd made it clear that she did not want to be shut away and protected.

Also, for the sake of his career, he needed her to be socially accomplished.

So, instead of standing between Agatha and the curious glances Dove and Lark Norman were casting at her, he twined his fingers with hers. She held them tight, but she was not trembling as he feared she might be.

"Agatha," Mother placed her hand at Agatha's waist, flanking her on the other side.

His mother was nothing if not perceptive about people, what was in their hearts and minds…what lay behind polite smiles.

"These are my dear friends, Mr. and Mrs. Norman." She indicated the older couple sitting together on the divan with a wave of her hand.

The couple nodded and expressed their thanks for her hospitality.

"And standing behind the chair are their daughters, Dove and Lark."

"Charmed," chirruped Lark.

"Delighted," agreed Dove with a smile.

William did believe they were charmed and delighted, but baffled, too, as their expressions showed.

At thirty and thirty-one years old, the misses Norman had failed to find husbands. No doubt on the ride here the reasons that he had married Agatha so quickly had been discussed incessantly.

"And the gentleman in the chair is Mr. Bert Warble. Mr. Warble is new to Cheyenne and I thought he might like to meet you, William. He's interested in civic-minded things just like you are."

It crossed his mind that his mother might be matchmaking again. She enjoyed putting people together, seeing them find happy endings.

He ought to know. He'd had numerous potential brides set in his path.

Glancing sideways at the bride he had won all on his own, knowing how nervous she was, but seeing how she smiled, commented on the loveliness of Dove's plain travel gown and the pretty colors of the limp feather on Lark's hat, and understanding the courage it took for Agatha to look at ease—he was glad his mother had not succeeded with the other women.

In most ways, he was quite content to have been forced to marry Agatha.

But there were times, deep in the night when he wanted to go to her. Times when his skin tightened in temptation, when his mind could not put away an image of her in her bed, blankets kicked on the floor and red hair tumbling over bare shoulders, sheer gown riding high over smooth, fair thighs—those times he wanted go to her room, scoop her up and carry her to the marriage bed.

"William?" his mother's voice intruded. "Are you feeling well? You look flushed—Miss Lark just inquired if you enjoy being Mayor of Tanners Ridge."

In case his mother's observation of his high color was

not startling enough, Agatha had turned her wide green gaze upon him, her expression inquisitive.

If he were going to tell the truth he would say that, no, he was not all right and might never be. He was becoming exceptionally fond of a woman he could never have even though the woman was his wife.

"I do enjoy it." Much of the time. "The people here are fine, reasonable folks." Usually.

"Not the ones coming into town ahead of us. I certainly hope they do not mean to settle here." His mother flicked at a spot on her skirt.

"They were quite the brutes." Lark wrung her hands at her waist.

"Yes, quite. I'd have gone after them myself, taught them some manners had my stomach not been ailing me." Bert Warble frowned at his muffin, popped it into his mouth.

Apparently the ailment had passed.

Letting go of Agatha's fingers, he slipped his arm about her shoulder, drew her closer and kissed the top of her head.

The scent of roses wafted from her hair. It might not be wise to let the provocative fragrance seep so deeply into his senses, but he did it anyway.

For this one moment he allowed his growing feelings for Agatha take root in his heart. He could weed them out again later, but for now—she was his wife. He was her husband.

Her very proud husband, in fact.

There was every reason to believe that she was unnerved to have the attention of strangers settled upon her, but even so, she was far braver than Mr. Warble.

He suspected that inside of his retiring wife, there was a woman of courage trying to fight her way out.

His mother had set a few outgoing socialites in his path over the years, but the one she had not placed there, the most retiring one, shone the brightest in his heart.

He could not be more pleased to call Agatha Marigold English his wife.

"Come, my sweet girl. Let's walk in your lovely garden and discuss your wedding reception."

Victoria English set her teacup on its saucer with a decided clink.

Tea had been served late today because the visitors had been weary from their travel and napped until the day was nearly gone, so when Agatha and her mother-in-law stepped off the terrace and onto the back lawn, the sun had already begun to dip below the horizon.

And a good thing, too. The day had been a blister. Dim light and cooling temperatures made the garden an ideal place to discuss something pleasant. Too bad for Agatha, it made her anxious.

Hopefully, by the date of the party, two weeks from now, she would feel differently. Day by day she gained strength and with that came confidence.

"You have a lovely home." Victoria was a tall woman, almost regal-looking. But not in an unapproachable way. Not in a stuffy way, either. Manure on her skirt did not over trouble her, nor did rowdy people on the road. Agatha had seen that for herself. "And the garden! I adore how lush and peaceful it is."

While they walked, shadows faded from gray to deep blue. Crickets chirruped and night birds called to one another.

It was a lovely, peaceful place. How odd that William had asked her not to walk here alone.

Even now she saw him at the window, peering out. He waved, smiled, then turned his attention to the shrubbery.

Perhaps he worried that the cat from the other night had gone rabid and was about to pounce.

Strangely, at that very moment the shrubbery rustled and a cat did leap out.

She had wondered if he was being truthful about the cat peering in the window, but now, seeing the creature sit and lick its paws on the middle of the lawn, she could only believe he had been.

Glancing back at the window, she saw him still staring at the hedge.

"I believe we ought to have the party take place in the garden as well as the house." Glancing toward the window, she smiled at her son. "Lanterns all over the yard would be enchanting, don't you think?"

Agatha did think so. In her mind she could see it clearly. It would look like a magical land, lifted from the pages of a book.

"We'll have a dance floor. It might be crowded for everyone who is coming, but I believe there is enough room."

Victoria strode to the west end of the yard. With hands on hips she turned about nodding.

Agatha followed her.

"How many people have you invited, Mother?" It felt strange to call her that, but moment by moment, it began to feel right.

Odd that she could feel a bond with someone she had just met that morning. Perhaps she was vulnerable due to the great gaping hole in her soul left by her mother and Hilda Brunne. Maybe she should not let her affections develop so quickly.

Still, the woman was William's mother and a very engaging person.

"Oh, just a small group of friends and people who will be important to William's future." Victoria snatched at a moth flying past her face and missed it. "Some of these creatures are so lovely! As for guests, we can expect about a hundred people in all."

It was hard to imagine where all those people were going to stay, given that the hotel was turning into a saloon.

William strode onto the terrace.

"Son! I need you to hire someone to build us a dance floor right here in the open. It will be ever so romantic."

"Are you looking for a beau, Mother?"

"Ha! You know I am not. But it will be a romantic spot for anyone who wants to steal a kiss under the stars."

Ignoring the steps, William leapt over the rail, landing on the grass with barely a thud. Doing that made him look playful in a way she hadn't seen before.

Probably being around his mother brought out the boy in him.

"How big do you want it?" he asked.

"Smallish rather than large. Space for ten couples will do."

"I wonder if I might invite my sister and her husband?"

"Oh, my dear!" Victoria took both of her hands, squeezed them. "You must think me horrible not to have mentioned that they are the first people I did invite! Your uncle and his wife as well."

Uncle Patrick! Madame Du Mer? She hadn't expected to look forward to her wedding reception and its one hundred guests with anything less than dread, but all of a sudden she felt half-giddy with anticipation.

"Thank you, Mother!"

A kind of joy that she could not recall having before swelled in her chest, made her twirl about. She felt her skirt flutter around her ankles, then the warm pressure of William's fist when he caught her hand.

"Good night, my dears. I'm for my bed. I'll see you at breakfast."

"Sweet dreams, Mother," William said without lifting his gaze from Agatha's eyes—her lips.

The backdoor screen squealed when Victoria went inside. The tip-tap of Miss Valentine's toenails trotted across the terrace.

"We should go in as well." Still, he didn't lift his gaze from her face.

"Yes, with the cat from the window now watching from the bushes, it might not be safe out here."

"I imagine it's only a neighbor's nosy pet." He slipped his arm about her waist so she leaned into him. "It's early. How about a game of checkers?"

How about a kiss in the moonlight? "I'd like that."

Miss Valentine followed them across the yard, up the stairs and into the house.

While William set up the game in the parlor beside the fireplace, which tonight contained a vase of flowers instead of snapping flames, she gazed out the window.

It was hard not to look at the spot where they had stood a moment ago. What if they hadn't come in the house? What if he'd given her the kiss that had been in his eyes?

What if he had laid her down on the lush cool grass?

"What are you looking at?" his voice murmured past her shoulder.

She turned, felt the heat of his breath skim her hair. He reached behind and loosened the curtain tie back. The panel fell into place across the window.

"Intrusive felines."

He touched the hair at her temple, fingered it between his thumb and finger. He removed one pin. She removed two more. The hard-won loops and whirls fell down her back and over her shoulders.

"You have the prettiest hair, honey."

"So do you." How could she do anything but reach up and stroke the dark wisp that flopped over his forehead.

He caught her hand and kissed her fingers.

"In spite of the way things happened," he murmured then let go of her hands. He touched her cheek with one finger, slid it under her chin. "Of the way they must be between us—I'm not sorry I married you. I care for you, Agatha."

"I care for—"

He cut her off with a kiss—a tender one that heated to a simmer when he pressed her to his chest. She sighed and leaned against his heartbeat. The sweet simmer ignited and smoldered.

Breaking the kiss, he did not push her away but bent his forehead to hers.

"Chess—we were going to play—" His breath beat fast against her face.

"We ought to."

"We will."

And they did. After another kiss.

This one lasted only seconds before William set her away from him at arm's length, both of them breathing heavily. It left her mouth scorched, her heart shaken and her toes curled.

She lost the first game because all she could think of was, one day he was not going to tell her he cared for her.

He was going to say he loved her and she was going to say the same back.

She won the next two games.

When he left her at her bedroom door, he did not kiss her good-night.

William sat on his mattress, legs hanging over the side, hands clenched between his knees and his head bent.

It was useless trying to sleep. At three in the morning he gave up trying.

Every time he closed his eyes he saw the red fall of his wife's hair, felt the silky curls slide under his fingers.

If he lay on his side he imagined her beside him, moonlight caressing her shoulder and the curve of her bare hip. If he lay on his back he could see the contentment in the curve of her smile as she gazed down at him, the beat of her pulse in the slender column of her neck.

That sultry image launched him from his bed.

Going to the window, he braced his hands on the sill. Below, the yard lay in darkness. Nothing stirred except an owl that swooped across the yard then landed in a tree on the far side of the fence.

There was only one way to get impossible images of Agatha out of his mind and that was to look back.

He didn't want to remember the past, but he forced himself to bring up a hurtful time—no, not hurtful—shattering. A time that had left him forever distrustful of the sudden changes life served up.

By force of will he made himself remember his mother's milk-white face on the night he sat at her bedside waiting for her to die.

All of a sudden he was young, he was Billy. The pressure behind his eyes was very real. Even though his mother was safely sleeping in a room above his, emotions from the past cramped his chest.

It was true that his mother had not died. Not on the

outside, but she had grieved so horribly for her lost daughter that she might have on the inside, for a time.

Had his mother not been such a strong woman she might not have survived it.

He wanted Agatha to his bones, but not so much that he would be willing to go through that experience again. He would not see his wife in that bloody bed. Watch their child turn blue after only one breath of life.

Aching to make Agatha his wife in the way God intended was not enough to make him act on it.

He cared for her far too much.

Hell, that was not the truth. His feelings for her were growing stronger than mere caring every time he looked at her, heard her voice or caught a whiff of her rose scent.

Day by day, watching this woman face down her demons and overcome them, seeing her spirit grow stronger with the struggle—he—well, he damn well more than cared for her.

Chapter Ten

This morning while dressing, Agatha noticed a difference in her thighs. Where the skin was once flaccid, weak, there was now a faint shadow that defined her muscle.

Earlier today she'd run a quarter of a mile without becoming winded.

In her opinion, she had become as strong as any other woman her age. Indeed, stronger than some.

She was going to say so to William. Give him proof, professional proof, that she was not one of the china dolls his mother had no use for.

This was how she now found herself staring at a glazed window with the name "Dr. Frederick Connor, MD" etched on it.

It was time to know the truth. If she was fit for motherhood, she would rejoice. If she was not, she needed to know that, too.

She rallied her courage with a prayer, opened the door and went inside.

Moments later she sat in a chair, across from a stranger who might determine her future.

"What brings you here today, Mrs. English?" Doctor Connor asked, his smile friendly as he stroked the stethoscope looped around his neck.

"Proof."

"Proof? Of what?"

"That I'm healthy enough to bear a child." Her heart beat against her ribs, her face felt hot and cold all at once. The future of her marriage, of the family she wished for, depended upon what he had to say. "Am I strong enough?"

"Is there some reason you would think otherwise?"

His bushy gray brows dipped toward his nose. His eyes crinkled at the corners while he listened to her tell about her illness, how the doctor had told her father childbirth would kill her.

Dr. Connor was so understanding about her concerns and professional in his comments and questions, she confided about the laudanum as well.

Until today, the only people who knew about that were Ivy, Travis, and William. And now Dr. Connor knew, too—he had to know everything in order to give her an honest opinion.

He listened to her heart and her breathing, asked her to jump up and down then listened again.

"I see no reason why you should not have a lovely child, nothing I see that tells me otherwise. Before, when your father was given that diagnosis, you were gravely ill. But you've been running, strengthening your heart and your muscles. You are a vision of health, Mrs. English."

"My husband is terrified that he will be responsible for my death," she admitted.

"Ah, the concern of every man. All I can tell you is that you are healthy. I cannot predict the future. Many things can go wrong, even to the stoutest of women. But most give birth with no problem at all."

Leaving the doctor's office, Agatha felt light, buoyant in a way that suggested gravity did not exist.

Ever since the first time she had defied Mother Brunne by eating a forbidden croissant that Ivy had offered, she had been taking small steps toward standing, walking and becoming hardy.

Now, with the sun blistering down upon her shoulders, she wanted to dance home.

She was going to be able to give William what he wanted most. Watching the planks of the boardwalk, all she saw were babies. Some with blue eyes like her husband's, some with green like hers. One was even blond like Ivy.

William's proud smile, newborn cries and toddlers' laughter filled her mind. For a second she saw herself gray-haired, bouncing a grandbaby on each knee.

Life was about to become perfect.

Walking past the Bascomb, another kind of laughter caught her attention. This was not the laughter of people sharing a joke. No, this was the practiced calling card of a fallen woman.

Just because the sound came from a second-story window of the formerly elegant hotel did not mean that it sounded any different than it had at the circus.

Looking up she saw that the Bascomb sign had been replaced with one reading "Pete's Palace."

In Agatha's opinion it wasn't much of a palace when princesses hung out windows calling to passersby with intimate organs swelling out of their underclothes.

Someone dressed in black clothing limped past the window, yanked the princess out of view.

Something about the woman in black—at least she believed it to be a woman—made Agatha miss a step. She stumbled into the grasp of a stout man wearing dirty boots and a travel-stained hat. A gun belt rode low on his hip.

"You envy her? Want her job, maybe?" He spat a wad of tobacco juice at her, missing the hem of her skirt by an inch. "A fine lady like you? The boss would be real interested."

He forced her against the wall by stepping too close, walking her backward to avoid being touched by him.

Leering, he put his face within inches of hers. She wanted to vomit, seeing spittle leak out of the corners of his mouth.

She heard the footsteps of several boots coming out the front door and shuffling about on the porch. Given the position she was in, she couldn't see anyone.

Insulting laughter carried down the block.

She kicked out with her boot, landed a blow to her captor's shin. He grunted, but her assault didn't sway him.

The way the men carried on, laughing and whistling, she might have been a sparrow, locked in the sights of a sparrow hawk.

Still, she did land a blow, which was more than she had managed with Frenchie Brown.

"Let go of me," she insisted, making sure her voice remained calm, assertive.

She balled her fist, swung at the lout. Her knuckles barely grazed his nose, but he went down.

Shiny black boots flashed in her line of sight.

William!

He stood between her and the man on the ground, legs braced, shoulders heaving. Those on the porch jeered at the fellow because it had not been her fist that brought him down, but the swipe of William's boot. The villain had toppled over like a tree felled by a logger's saw.

"Gentlemen, please!" A tall well-dressed man pushed through the onlookers. The cigarette clenched between his lips bounced with his words.

Standing before her he nodded his head, plucked the cigarette from his mouth.

"I do apologize for the rudeness of my employees." His remorse might have been more believable had he not blown a ring of smoke in her face. "Barbarians one and all."

He slid a half-lidded gaze at his men. "In the future you will treat the lady with the deference she deserves."

"Sounds to me like you don't care what they do," William snapped, anchoring his arm around her waist and drawing her away.

"Does it?" He snorted, took another drag on the cigarette then dropped it on the boardwalk.

It took all of half a minute for William to hustle her past the bank, the bakery and the general store.

"Get to work, you fools! We open in two days!" she heard the lank-haired man shout.

Glancing back, she noticed that he had not bothered to snuff out the smoldering butt.

Again that night, William stood beside his open bedroom window. Wind blew the curtain inside, ruffled the lapels of his robe. He looked out at the stars, at the moonlight illuminating the garden below.

Naturally, he thought about Agatha. There was something different about her tonight. There had been all day.

After the way she had been nearly assaulted on the street, he would have expected her to be withdrawn, frightened.

It made his insides edgy wondering what would have happened to her if the office coffeepot hadn't run dry and forced him to go to the bakery for more.

Those men had been leering at Agatha, insulting her. Things had not escalated beyond words, but they might well have. There was little doubt that they would in the future.

She had to be awake, fretful, worried.

It would not be a good idea to go to her now, not given the way his feelings had deepened toward her. The way his body reacted whenever her rose-scented fragrance passed within a foot of his nose.

Even so, he did have a responsibility to comfort her.

Turning from his window, he left his room, went to hers. He would have to be man enough to hold her without the touch going from comfortable to sensual.

Damn, this was risky. He knew how easily it could—had—happened.

Quietly, he entered her unlocked room to discover that she was not pacing, staring out the window, or even weeping.

She was quite peacefully asleep in her bed!

Had she turned to drugs to help her sleep? No, she would not—he would never believe it.

Besides, she didn't have a drugged look about her.

She appeared healthy. Because of the heat she had kicked the covers down about her ankles. Filmy pink fabric bunched high on her thighs.

Moonlight beaming in the window shone softly on her face. When had she gotten freckles on her nose? How?

Perhaps she spent time in the garden while he passed his day in the office. No doubt she had Mrs. Bea carry a chair into the sunshine so she could read her book out of doors.

Very gently so as not to wake her, he sat down on the edge of the bed.

Her hair, glimmering auburn and speckled with hints of copper, fanned out over her pillow. The slender fingers of one hand were tangled in it. Her other hand rested on her belly.

It was hard to believe that given what she had been through today, she smiled in her sleep.

Good. She would be dreaming of puppies, kittens and pretty pink flowers rather than leering, insulting men.

Clearly, she did not need him to comfort her tonight.

He ought to get up and go to his own room, but couldn't quite get his limbs to agree with the idea.

Not when he had the chance to look at her like this. A soft glow touched her face, her throat and her chest. It kissed her bent knee and her trim ankle.

It hit him then that it was not only freckles making her look different. She had put on a bit of weight. She no longer had the gaunt look of a helpless waif but was curved, womanly.

No wonder his reaction toward her had changed. Somewhere along the way he had gone from wanting to protect her—to wanting her.

"Hell," he murmured.

There was no denying that she did look stronger, but that only increased his misery.

Just because she now looked better than she had when the doctor pronounced her unfit to give birth, it did not mean that there was not some other reason she should not risk it.

According to Agatha's father, the doctor had been adamant about it. It was why, before he passed away, Foster Magee had insisted William marry Ivy rather than Agatha.

The doctor had made his decision on Agatha's future for a solid medical reason. Who was William to question his professional opinion?

Bedsprings creaked. She turned to her side, tucked

one hand under her cheek. A hank of hair slid across her face. Carefully, he drew it back, felt the silky fire of it on his fingers.

Where had his lamb of a wife gone?

He'd certainly not seen her today when he had expected to the most.

In spite of what she had been through, she had not found a corner to hide in.

Far from it, she had spent time with his mother, planning the reception and smiling while she did it. At tea she had chatted with Lark and Dove. Played a game of checkers with Bert Warble.

Had he done what he had planned to do and chosen a wife for her social skills, that woman would not have done better this afternoon than the wife that circumstance had given him.

She moved again in her sleep, tucked her free hand between her thighs.

Time to go back to his own room. If she moved her fingers an inch higher, he would become a threat to her safety. There was nothing he wanted more than to slide her hand out from between her thighs and put his own there, to feel the silky glide of her skin beneath his fingers.

The temptation to act on the urge grew more intense the longer he indulged in gazing upon her.

Who was this woman he had married?

In the end, it didn't matter. He had to remember who he was. Her husband, her defender.

Not a man who would harm her.

"I need to soak my head."

Coming down the steps of the Tanners Ridge Library, Agatha looked up at William. She could easily imagine steam coming from under the bowler she had given him.

The day was hot but his temper was hotter. The town meeting had gone much like he'd described earlier meetings, with folks in an uproar over the new saloon and looking for William to do something about it.

"Last meeting, I presented a perfectly experienced candidate and they turned him away." William removed his hat, wiped the sweat from his brow with his sleeve. One drop that he missed slid down his cheek. "I can't believe they just hired a green kid to do the job."

"Well, he is tall and he was wearing a gun. The unmarried ladies are all aflutter." She'd never attended any sort of town meeting before. Were they all this contentious, she had to wonder?

"Yes, and he's like a spring rooster, strutting and crowing." At the bottom step he shook out his hair, no doubt hopeful of a breeze to cool his head. A dark curly lock softened the lines of his frown. "I want to show you something."

He caught her hand and led her down the boardwalk, past the bank and the dress shop. He stopped for a moment to go into the bakery where he purchased two cinnamon rolls to take to wherever they were going.

Walking past Millie's Hat Shop, she spotted a sunny yellow bonnet in the window and came to a dead halt while she stared at it.

She would have gone inside to try it on but clearly William was in a hurry to get to wherever he was taking her.

Two shops further on, he cut into an alley, led her past the dirt road that ran behind them then into a copse of trees.

The temperature dropped by ten degrees in the shade of the small wood.

William took her arm to support her when the earth

turned to a downward slope. Below, she heard the gurgle of rushing water.

"It's the same stream that runs behind the mansion." He led her to a fallen log. If someone had set a plush divan beside the water it could not have been more inviting.

She sat down, breathed a lungful of cool air. William knelt beside the stream, scooped up handful after handful of water and dribbled it over his head.

Coming to his feet he joined her on the bench. His fingers dripped and sparkled in light filtering through the leaves.

Apparently, his mood had cooled as the temperature dipped. Smiling, he stroked his wet fingers on her forehead, down the curve of her cheeks then the column of her throat.

"I find streams soothing." He smiled. All of a sudden she began to heat up again, but this time from the inside out. "I often come here when I've got something I need to gnaw over in my mind—here and the stream behind the house."

Yes, this was a good place to come and think—to settle in her mind when would be a good time to give him the doctor's news.

Agatha was eager to, but this was a sensitive subject and must be brought at the right time and in the right place.

Now perhaps? In this place with the gently lapping water to settle her nerves and give her courage.

"What are you gnawing over, William?"

"The new sheriff, for one. You and I for another."

"I don't suppose there's anything you can do about that young man. The town hired him."

Was this the time to bring up her doctor's visit? For some reason she was nervous to tell him about it.

She was also nervous to talk about the "you and I," because the future of their marriage was involved.

"You and I? William, we do have control over us."

"No. I can't see that we do." He looked up at the leaves, twisting and rustling in a slight but welcome breeze. "Things have changed between us. Become more complicated."

"They don't have to be—I've—"

"Changed? I'm not blind, honey. I see how you have—but it doesn't change the fact that the only love I will make to you is in my dreams."

"You dream of it?" The same as she did?

"Better start locking your doors."

Or leaving it wide open in invitation!

"What if something was different?"

He stood up, shoved his hands in his pockets and walked to the edge of the stream. He gazed down at the water sluicing over rocks and past reeds.

Pivoting, he looked at her, his blue eyes dim, his expression haunted.

"Some things can't change." He shook his head, looking sure of it.

"But some can." Perhaps now was the time to tell him, after all.

"Some can, yes. But not the past things. What has happened will always have happened. Look, Agatha, I saw something when I was little."

Something horrible, judging by the slump of his shoulders and the grim line of his mouth.

"My mother had just given birth to my baby sister. The baby—she died in my arms. Mother took it hard. While my father was in the parlor drinking, I sat by her bed holding her hand and crying. She didn't lift a hand to comfort me, she just seemed to be slipping away. Then, must have been about two in the morning, there came a shadow, or at least my frantic mind thought there was. But I lay down on top of Ma to keep it from taking her.

"The fearful thing came and went for the next two days and every time, I fought it off. One morning I woke up lying across her bed. Her hand was on my head. She was stroking my hair."

The image of him like that stung Agatha's eyes with tears. She felt them slip down her cheeks even though she did not sob out loud.

She went to him, wrapped her arms about his middle and squeezed. "I'm so sorry you went through that, William."

His breath skimmed the top of her head. "I learned something through it all. Life is precious—far too precious to take chances with."

Gripping her shoulders, he held her away from him at arm's length. He cupped her face in his hands. A tremor ran through his fingers.

"I will not take that chance with you."

Four days had passed since the conversation beside the stream. Five since the doctor pronounced her healthy.

The time still did not seem right to bring up her news, but it did feel right to run.

Being pronounced healthy did not mean ending her after-breakfast exercise. If she quit, she feared that she would grow weak again.

Besides, Agatha did love watching the horses. Day by day the newborns grew stronger and more agile. Ellia, Quint and Nellie were nearly as swift as their mothers now.

Some people might think it was silly to name horses

she would never even touch, but why should she worry about that when no one would know she did it? The only one who even knew she came up here was Mrs. Bea.

Today she had picked her way down the ridge and then run back up. Her heart raced, her lungs burned and her legs trembled.

She felt absolutely wonderful. All the while she pushed her body, she wondered how she would go about putting William's fears to rest.

The good news was not something she could boldly blurt out. A seduction would be far more meaningful. Mrs. Bea had given her some creative ideas.

Imagining putting them to use made her breathless, even without the uphill run. Chances were she would need each and every one of the erotic tactics in order to win her husband over.

It was not that he didn't want to take her to his bed. He'd made it clear that he did.

The fact that he had visited her bedroom for the last five nights spoke volumes.

The fact that he sat beside her on the bed to watch her "sleep" told her that he might not be so firm about not touching her as he claimed to be.

Still, she'd turned this way and that, showing herself off to the best advantage, and it hadn't done a lick of good. William was at war with his noble conscience.

Perhaps she should have the doctor write a note giving his consent. Perhaps in black and white, the words would have more force.

No. The thought of it made her shiver. It was hard to imagine anything more desperate-looking—less romantic.

Tying the ribbons of her bonnet under her chin while she walked back to town, she made up her mind. As soon as the moment was perfect she was going to seduce Mr. William English.

Since she would need something especially diaphanous to wear for the occasion, she strolled down the boardwalk toward the dressmaker instead of making the turn toward home.

From two blocks up, she heard a voice raised in outrage.

It could not be! But yes, it clearly was her mother-in-law standing on the front porch of Pete's Palace, one fist curled around some sort of broadsheet and the other gripping the sleeve of the new sheriff.

"This will not happen!" She railed at Pete Lydle. She shook the sheriff. "Tell him it will not. Do your duty."

Lifting her skirt to more quickly manage the stairs, Agatha stood silently behind her mother-in-law.

The sheriff attempted a break for freedom. Victoria cuffed him on the ear with the broadsheet.

"Shall I fetch William?" she whispered.

The sheriff took that instant of distraction to make good on his escape.

Pete Lydle laughed but the humor ended in a coughing fit.

"You ought to quit that nasty habit," Victoria stated.

"You ought to quit giving advice where it's not wanted."

"Perhaps, but shall we face the problem at hand?"

"Ain't got no problem here, lady."

"You've scheduled your gambling tournament on the same day as my son's wedding reception. I insist that you change it."

People inside the Palace wandered past the open front door, pausing to gaze out. Judging by the incredulous looks on their faces, it was a rare thing for someone to cross words with their boss.

A small woman, her body hunched and her shoulders bent at an odd angle, peered out with the others. Agatha could not see her face in the dim light beyond the door. It was further hidden by the hood of her tattered cloak.

While everyone's attention was riveted on Victoria, the disfigured woman seemed to be staring at Agatha. How odd—and unnerving.

A frizzle of dread tingled up the back of her neck.

She would be more alarmed but this unreasonable fear had hit her before and nothing dire had happened.

There had been a couple of times at the circus, at the dress shop, then another when she had foolishly been frightened by the face of a cat looking in the window.

Perhaps it was time to accept the fact that sometimes she would be frightened. The important thing was to act as if she were not.

Digging for a smile she took a step toward the door.

"Excuse me, ma'am?"

In the end it didn't matter that she found a bit of courage. The woman turned and hobbled swiftly away, her cane tapping on the floor.

"Who was that?" her mother-in-law turned to her and asked.

"I don't know." Nor did she want to. Something about that woman made her feel icy inside.

Victoria's gaze narrowed on the saloon owner. "I imagine you do."

"Her?" He took a sip from the shot glass that he balanced between his fingers. "She's nobody—she watches over my girls—sees to their well-being."

One of the girls stepped forward, dressed in a purple corset and red petticoat.

"You're a couple of fine ladies, you are." She swayed to the right. Her employer caught her, balanced her.

"What you need is a bit of fun. Come on inside, I'll share what I've got."

"The clap?" Victoria arched an elegant brow.

"Noooo. Not that." The woman opened her hand revealing a small bottle. "This. It makes all your troubles fly away."

No, the woman could not be more wrong. What it did was make troubles flock to you. It just made a person too subdued to know it.

Chapter Eleven

"Lark Warble? I think not. You may have the man. I'd rather die an old maid than carry that name," William heard Lark whisper to her sister when he passed the ladies in the hallway.

"I'll take him. Dove Warble isn't nearly as bad since doves do not actually warble. Now if his last name was Coo…"

Coming into the parlor he saw Mr. Norman and the unsuspecting Warble sitting before the flameless hearth, heads bent over the checkerboard.

Welcome rain tapped on the parlor window and dropped the temperature by a sudden ten degrees.

Not that the night felt cool, in William's opinion, but it was more bearable than the day had been.

Going to the windows, he drew them open. Air, fresh with the scent of mud and damp grass, carried inside with the fluttering lace curtain.

He took a deep breath, allowing a flood of peace to rush through him. It had been a stressful day.

With the reception only a week away his mother had been a human whirlwind. Approving one plan and disregarding another, making sure the perfect flowers would be in the perfect place, and finding rooms in town for all her guests.

His mother was in a happy state.

At least she had been until this afternoon when she'd discovered that Pete Lydle was planning a poker tournament for the same day as the reception.

Now she sat in a corner, head to head with Mrs. Norman, speaking quietly. It was good to see her resting for the moment.

Dove approached the chess players, made an admiring comment over Warble's last move. The man preened under her praise.

William guessed Dove would make him an adequate wife.

Catching the scent of tea rose, William looked toward the doorway to see Agatha walking toward him.

There had been a time when he would have settled for an adequate wife. Now, gazing down at Agatha's freckled nose, her sun-pinked cheeks, he gave thanks that he had not.

For what, by force, his marriage lacked, he did not regret a thing.

Agatha stood beside him. Turning her back toward the window, she lifted the hair away from her nape. He could not help but steal a glance at the smooth, fair column of her neck.

"Oh, that breeze feels good."

Glancing up she shot him a quick smile. He was relieved to see it. Like his mother, she had been downcast all afternoon.

"Do that again."

"Do what?"

"Smile." A loop of hair slid across her cheek. He wound it about his thumb, taking the moment to appreciate the petal-like texture. He truly did enjoy touching her hair. It was something he could do, a way to touch her, without endangering her with his lust. "I haven't seen many of those today. From anyone."

"Folks are not happy that their new sheriff ran off."

"Can't say I'm surprised he left town, even with the ladies admiring him so."

Agatha turned to face him and the silken loop slipped out of his fingers.

"What is it that's been troubling you? I doubt it's our runaway sheriff."

"Not that." She shook her head.

"Are you worried about the party? About being the center of attention?"

"I might never like being that, but I'm getting better at acting like I do." A sidelong breeze sent a smatter of raindrops inside. A dusting of them settled on her eyelashes. "Did you know that Pete Lydle is keeping the women who work for him drugged?"

"No, but I don't believe it's uncommon for women in their situation to seek escape."

"Escape! It's no escape."

"I know it isn't, but some of them believe it is."

She nodded, clenched her fists in his shirt. "For a time it does create that illusion. Also, there's a creepy old woman at the Palace. She was staring at me earlier and giving me the chills. I'll bet she's the one who gives it to them."

"Because a creepy old woman gave it to you?"

Stepping closer, she leaned her head against his chest. He wrapped her up, drew her to his heart.

Strands of hair tickled his chin when she shook her head. "No. She did not give it to me, she poured it down my throat."

"You're safe now, honey. I won't let anyone hurt you."

She pushed away from his chest with small open palms, but only far enough to look him in the eye. They were still breast to rib. He noticed a raindrop drip from her lashes.

"I know that, William. But they are not safe. I want to do something to help them."

"I forbid you to go over there."

He believed it had been the creepy woman looking through their window that night. It alarmed him that she had focused her attention on Agatha.

Who was she and why would she do it?

"You do what?" Now she did shove away from him.

"Forbid...you...to...go...there."

He must have raised his voice because his mother looked up from her conversation with Mrs. Norman.

For half a second, she frowned. Then she smiled. Winked. But probably not at him. His mother would appreciate having an ally in thinking him overbearing.

Whatever Agatha had opened her mouth to say was cut short by Mrs. Bea hustling into the parlor, flushed and flustered.

"There's someone at the door!" She wagged her finger toward the hall. "Many someones!"

"I do believe it's half the town," said Miss Fitz following in Mrs. Bea's incensed wake. "They'll be here in," she said, glancing over her shoulder. "Now. I told them to wait outside—"

Mrs. Peabody sailed into the parlor waving her cane. "But we said it was raining and since this is the mayor's house and we appointed him, we would be welcome."

"Welcome." He hoped his smile reflected what he said rather than what he felt.

This intrusion—mass intrusion—since more than

thirty people had come into the room with a dozen more in the hall, could not have come at a worse time.

He needed to convince Agatha that it was not safe or proper to go the saloon.

"Pete's Palace has become a menace!" the blacksmith announced loud enough to be heard above the general din of dissatisfaction.

Voices came all at once and from every corner of the parlor.

"My daughter was insulted again today! By two harlots leaning from their windows. I won't have it!"

"My wife was leered at by a drunk."

"Mine, too!"

"Someone stole a ham from my store window."

"I heard a noise outside my bedroom." Mrs. Peabody looked about, engaging her listeners. "When I looked out the window there was a gambler—I could tell he was by the greed in his eye—relieving himself in my geraniums."

For some reason the crowd quieted down when Mrs. Peabody related her horror. Apparently the assault on the geranium was more wicked than the theft of the ham or the disrespect to the ladies.

"We need a new sheriff." Mrs. Peabody pointed her bony finger in a direct line with his nose. "We need him to be you."

"No."

"What she meant was, we're here to ask if you might be willing, for the good of the town," said Aimee Peller with a dimple winking in her cheek.

"No." To his astonishment it was Agatha who spoke up.

"I'm your mayor, not your lawman. How many potential sheriffs have you people turned away?"

"Only one or two who were not qualified," someone said.

"Or too small." A young female voice giggled but it was hard to hear just who it was with everyone murmuring at once.

A woman shoved her way from the hallway into the parlor then through the grumbling crowd.

"Mr. English, Mrs. English, I'm Hattie Smith." She was a widow with young children, he recalled. "We don't know who to turn to. I live near the saloon, only twenty feet away. I can't sleep at night. My little girls are frightened. They won't go outside to play—even to go to school. Please. Won't you help us?"

He remembered that Hattie always attended town meetings. She had also spoken up in favor of the men he presented.

Of all the voices clamoring to be heard, insisting he take the job, her quiet "please" was the one that touched him.

His knowledge of law enforcement would fit in a can of beans. Still, he did know the law, he knew right from wrong.

He looked aside, trying to gauge what Agatha was feeling. Would a change of career, no, not change but addition, be upsetting to her?

She had not agreed to marry someone with a risky job.

Returning his glance, she tipped her head to the side, gave him a slight nod.

The decision was not for her to make, her gesture indicated. But she gave her approval either way.

It felt like a thousand eyes stared at him, waiting for an answer. All he wanted to do was kiss Agatha English for supporting him in whatever he chose to do.

Maybe he didn't have the marriage some men did— but, he thought, he might have more.

"Yes," he said quietly to the widow. "I'll do my best to keep you and your children safe."

The evening had not ended in the way Agatha imagined.

Because who could have envisaged dozens of dripping people invading her home, drafting her husband?

Still, the night was not over yet. There might yet be an opportunity to execute her plan. It would be complicated, given that she was displeased at the way he had forbidden her to help the women at the saloon.

Patience, she repeated in her mind. The man was a protector. And she truly did love that about him. But sometimes, she needed to have her own way.

Over on the couch, William's mother hugged Mrs. Norman good-night, then stood and stretched her back. Lark and her father walked shoulder to shoulder out of the parlor.

Dove and Bert Warble lingered over putting the checkers away.

And the rain beat down harder than it had before. Not that Agatha minded that. She had always found the thrumming of water on the roof to be a sweet lullaby.

"I have to say." Her mother-in-law crossed the room to hug her son about the ribs. "Having sheriff in your resume can only help your chances of being elected governor. It will give you a heroic aura. Given the choice between sheriff or mayor, ladies will vote for sheriff every time. Well played, son."

"Played?" William dragged his long fingers through his hair. "It's no game. I don't know a thing about rounding up criminals."

"You, my darling, are tall, strong and honorable. You

are also a quick learner. And I don't believe I have ever seen a more handsome sheriff, have you Agatha?"

"I'm sure I have not."

With her mind becoming focused—obsessed, truth to tell—on her scheme rather than this discussion, she kissed her mother-in-law on the cheek.

She bid her husband good-night by patting his cheek with her fingertips while yawning.

"I'm sure to be asleep as soon as my head hits the pillow."

She felt his gaze on her back so she swayed her hips, subtly, just enough to make him notice. Mrs. Bea had told her that the line between winsome and wanton was a fine one.

In the privacy of her bedroom, she stripped off her clothes and reapplied a splash of rosewater. She put on the coral-colored sleeping gown she had purchased this afternoon.

It was a pretty thing, the way it fairly floated about her ankles. The way the peekaboo fabric leaned toward wanton rather than winsome.

With a sigh, she climbed onto the bed, tussled the covers then lay her head on the pillow.

This game of seduction would be more fun if she didn't want to punch him as much as kiss him.

Well, she would have to wait and see what developed. In the meantime, she fanned her hair out on the pillow, all except one hank that she used to cover her chest from his view.

She closed her eyes and waited—and waited—and waited some more.

Blame it! Every night he came in precisely ten minutes after her bedsprings creaked.

He must be figuring out a way to apologize for forbidding her to do what she needed to, and for doing the forbidding in the presence of others.

How odd it was that her vexation with him also felt freeing. Until she'd married William she hadn't felt—what? Strong enough—bold enough, to allow that emotion.

Which left her wondering what would happen when he sat down on her bed—if he did. Where was he?

Was it as hot in his bedroom as it was in hers? Sitting up then kneeling upon her pillow, she pushed her window open.

No sooner had she felt the breeze prickle the sweat on her skin than she heard William's bedroom door open.

She lay down and resumed her pose.

When she felt the bed give under his pressure, she turned onto her back, made sure the strand of hair protecting modesty slid away.

She sighed, heard the sudden intake of his breath. As she suspected, the nightgown was only a suggestion of modesty.

Slowly raising one arm, she brought it to rest on the pillow above her head, nestled her shoulders back into the mattress. This was her own idea, not the teaching of Mrs. Bea.

"When did you become so beautiful?" he whispered.

At birth, she assumed, but could hardly say so since she was asleep. And the truth was, what childish beauty she'd possessed had been stolen from her by ill health and Hilda Brunne.

But her husband believed she was beautiful. She had worked hard to regain her health and so felt some pride at his words—more so than had she been born lovely and stayed that way.

Since she'd had to work to get to this point she could

not help but smile because he noticed. Smile in her sleep that is.

"What are you dreaming about, honey?"

If he only knew! Her wide-awake dream was that she wanted him to touch the breast that she had offered to his view.

"Hope it's not about rescuing the doves at Pete's Palace."

Curse the man!

Sitting bolt upright in bed, she used the word waiting on her tongue. It was the foulest term she knew—one that she had never spoken out loud before.

It could not be denied, there was some satisfaction in letting out her frustration that way. Just not enough to make the frustration go away.

"You may not forbid me. I refuse to let you."

"You're awake?"

"Do I look asleep?" She yanked the cover over her chest. The seduction was finished.

"You look angry, and pretty."

"Do not make light of my feelings, William. I have been forbidden to do things all my life. I will not be again."

"I'm only looking out for your good."

"For months I've been looking out for my good. I don't need you for that."

"Then what do you need me for?"

The stricken look on his face cut her to the quick.

"You gave me everything when you married me, Agatha. You saved my reputation and my career. But what did you get from it?"

Her life for one, since she would probably be dead or crippled had she been shot out of the cannon. He'd given her a sweet little dog when he'd rushed back to rescue Miss Valentine.

And he'd given her a home where she would be safe.

There it was. It hit her that she did need his protection.

Without that point of security she would not have been able to go out every morning and run. If it were not for the fact that she loved him and wanted to give him children, she might not have pushed herself to do it.

Without that goal, she might have found a dark corner and moldered in it. Even with Hilda Brunne dead, she might have gone on living in the woman's shadow.

"What can I give you?" He stood up, turned to leave.

She knelt on the bed, caught his hand.

"Yourself." She drew him toward her and he didn't resist. "All of yourself."

"You know I cannot."

She set his hand at the curve of her waist, and once again he did not resist. "I know that you can."

What was it that Mrs. Bea said should happen next? She couldn't recall because her head was abuzz—no, not her head—everything hummed. It radiated from her belly to her toes and fingers. It robbed her brain of logical thought. Her body demanded him, would have him.

She looped her arms around his neck, drew him back to the bed.

Since he resisted lying down, she settled upon his lap. The coral haze of the nightgown rode high on her thighs.

Tangling the hair over his ears in her fingers, she gently tipped his head, gazed hard into his eyes.

A sudden gust of wind blew inside. Raindrops hit her face, neck, and chest. She swore they sizzled against her heated skin.

"Love me, William. It's all I want."

Without warning, he shifted her weight. No longer sitting on his lap, she now lay under him. Muscular thighs pressed her into the mattress.

The dressing robe he wore came loose at the waist. She touched the cords of his chest lightly with her fingertips.

Lowering his head, he licked raindrops from her neck and downward, only pausing at the low-cut neckline of her gown.

He tugged it lower, maybe searching for wayward raindrops but maybe searching for something else, her breasts perhaps and the heart cradled between them.

"I love you, William," she whispered into the dark, damp hair tickling her neck.

If she had slapped him in the face his reaction would not have been so swift.

He leapt from the bed, stalked toward the door then turned to look at her.

"I love you, too."

And then he was gone.

For man who had just made the declaration of a lifetime he looked perfectly miserable.

But he loved her and that was a place to begin.

Since sleep had gone from difficult to impossible, William slid into his rain slicker and left the slumbering house behind.

Chances were, his wife was not sleeping. No doubt he'd left her weeping in confusion. What kind of man was he, nearly seducing her that way?

His act of selfishness might have cost her life.

She wanted his love? She had it.

He would never put her at risk again, no matter how badly he ached for carnal knowledge of her.

What he would do was learn how to be sheriff. He would begin tonight, or this morning depending upon what time it was. He'd long since lost track of the hours.

By the time he unlocked the door to the sheriff's office he was soaked to the skin.

He lit a lamp then glanced about. A gun belt hung on a coat rack but there was no weapon in it. The badge he had so recently given out lay on the desk.

Fool kid sheriff had at least had the good sense to leave it behind before he hightailed it out of town.

At least there was a coffeepot set on top of the stove. There were even coffee beans in one of the cupboards, but judging by the thick layer of dust on the can, they were stale.

Three wanted posters set on the desk. Too bad none of them were of Pete Lydle. But the man was not precisely a criminal, only a lowlife bringing his unwanted business to Tanners Ridge.

Sitting on the desk chair, he opened one drawer, then another. Most of what he found was dust and odd bits of trash. But in the last drawer he came upon what he guessed to be the calling cards of his trade…a gun, bullets and a set of handcuffs.

Lifting the handcuffs from the drawer, he jangled them, locked and unlocked them with the key. Wasn't a whole lot to learn about them.

He knew a bit about guns, having spent most his life on a ranch. But he did have to admit that controlling critters with this weapon would be a great deal different than keeping lawbreakers in line. He wondered if he would even be able to use it on a human if the occasion arose.

He put on the gun belt, loaded the weapon then shoved it in the holster.

It was time to visit the Palace. But with his hand on the doorknob to go out, he paused, bowed his head and prayed that the occasion to use the gun would never arise.

With the saloon only a block down from the sheriff's

office, he couldn't help but hear the piano and the bawdy laughter as soon as he stepped onto the boardwalk.

He thought of the widow and wondered if she and her children were awake and frightened.

The rain had blown away while he'd been inside. Walking down the boardwalk he thought the night looked magical with the moon glinting off wet buildings, even making the mud puddles in the street glimmer.

Too soon he left the fresh beauty behind and climbed the steps to the Palace.

Sure wasn't fresh in here. It was sad to see hints of the elegance that used to be the Bascomb Hotel. Instead of the landscape paintings that used to adorn the walls, there now hung paintings of naked women. Where there had once been vases of fresh flowers on tables, there were empty whisky bottles tipped over and dripping on the floor.

At one time, the piano in the corner of the room had played classical masterpieces. Tonight a man with a lace garter banding his sleeve pounded out tunes that were far from inspiring.

"I wondered how long it would take our fine, upstanding mayor to come enjoy the entertainment." Pete Lydle rounded the corner of the bar and crossed the room a drink in his hand. He shoved it at William.

"On the house." His words were cordial, welcoming, but the curve of his mouth was not.

"Another time," William lied.

Lydle shrugged, downed the drink in a single swallow. "What do you think, Mayor? Fine alcohol, beautiful women, games of chance—all a gentleman could want of an evening."

All the debauchery at least, he decided while he evaded the groping hand of a half-dressed woman strolling past.

"No taste for my sultry Mistymoon?" Pete glanced about, spotted another woman dressed in less than Mistymoon had worn. He waved her over. "I reckon you want someone sweeter, more like your wife. Here, spend an hour with Sugar Blossom, on the house of course."

His gut clenched. Sugar Blossom could barely be out of the schoolroom.

The look in her blue eyes was vacant. She was here, standing next to Pete, but her mind was somewhere else. He wondered where. It seemed to just be—gone.

If these girls wanted help, someone ought to give it to them. But it was not going to be Agatha.

He'd have a word with the preacher about Sugar Blossom.

She left her hand on William's shoulder when Pete placed it there.

"No thank you, ma'am." She stared at him, blinked rapidly but could not seem to focus. "I'm here on business."

"So is she." Lydle turned the woman about then shoved her into the arms of a customer just coming in, dust from a long ride still on his clothes. It was late. William couldn't help but wonder how far the stranger had traveled to get here.

There were a lot of strangers lately. Unsavory-looking fellows like that one, coming to Tanners Ridge for the tournament.

"What business does our gentleman mayor have here tonight, given that you're too fine for my girls—or my liquor. I don't imagine you gamble. So, as I see things you are spurning my hospitality."

"Not here as mayor." He'd neglected to put on the badge before leaving the office. He dug it from his pocket and pinned it to his coat lapel. "I'm sheriff now."

"Well, now, I know we have no business together."

"I've come about a complaint."

"Have you?" Pete waved to the bartender who hustled over with another drink.

"There's a widow who lives close by with her two daughters. Your noise is keeping them awake."

"A widow, you say?" Lydle scratched the scraggly hair on his chin. "The girls got any charms that show yet? I could use some fresh—"

"Don't say it." William stepped close to Lydle, nearly nose to nose. "If I hear that you've even looked at those children I'll arrest you—if I haven't already shot you."

Lydle raised his hands, palm out in a gesture of false capitulation. He might move like someone raising the white flag, but that was not the story his eyes told.

William figured the fact that he was wearing a badge and customers were gaily spending money kept Lydle from acting on his anger.

Young Sweet Blossom tottered behind Lydle, bounced off his back and fell to her knees. She hung onto the legs of his pants to keep from going face first onto the floor.

"Hilda!" he shouted.

The woman's keeper hurried across the floor more quickly than her cane allowed for. Funny that even inside and in this heat she wore her cloak with the hood covering her face.

Something stirred the hairs on the back of his neck. He reminded himself that Hilda was a common name, but the closer the woman limped, the more pronounced the chill became.

She knelt beside the girl. Sweet Blossom struggled against the grip on her arm. She knocked the hood from the woman's face.

"Get her out of here, Brunne, or you're fired," Lydle growled.

Brunne. Hilda Brunne! It could not possibly be the same one. Agatha's nurse was dead.

She swiveled her head, glared sharply at him for half an instant before drawing the hood back over her face.

But an instant was enough. Even though a lightning-shaped scar cut from her left eye to her chin, he recognized the woman who had stood in the shadows glaring while he danced with Agatha that night at the Lucky Clover.

There could be no denying that Hilda Brunne was alive, and that she was as menacing as she had ever been.

Chapter Twelve

Agatha looped the strings of her bonnet through her fingers, deciding to enjoy the sunshine on her hair for as long as she could before proper rules of dress required her to put it back on.

"Come along Miss Valentine."

She patted her thigh to get the dog's attention away from the bush she was sniffing. Even through petticoats and skirt ruffles, she felt how her muscle had grown firm.

After all her hard work, that was something to be proud of. Too bad she could not share her accomplishment with her husband since she doubted he would ever touch her again.

Ivy would be proud, though. She might burst her buttons since it had been her sister who forced her out of her chair and into the sunshine in the first place.

It wouldn't be long now before she could show off her new self. According to the letter Ivy had sent, the whole family would arrive soon.

It had been a relief to read that Ivy was happy with Agatha's unexpected marriage. So were Travis, Uncle Patrick and his new wife, Antie. She could hardly wait to hug each and every one of them—most especially baby Clara Rose.

She sighed. Her joy over her sister's arrival was tempered by what had happened last night.

William had claimed to be happy about their marriage, and to be in love with her.

When he'd made that declaration, he'd looked perfectly miserable. If his heart beat a little more joyfully for loving her, it did not show.

She'd done what she could to seduce him and it hadn't been enough.

Now, it was hard to know what to do about the man given that she was angry with him and wanting him in equal parts.

"What's in that bush that's so interesting?" Tired of waiting for the fascination to pass, Agatha plucked the dog up and tucked her under her arm. "Look at you, full of weeds and dirt. No wonder I don't usually bring you."

"There you are!" William came charging toward her, his hat askew. He'd traded his usual boiler for a Stetson. His coat flared about him and she noticed he was carrying a gun.

Last night she had wanted to urge him not to take the job as sheriff. Of course it was not her place to instruct him on what to do.

No, she was a perfectly reasonable human being who trusted others to know what was best for them—unlike the man she had married.

Since he frowned at her, she frowned back. It was a purely difficult thing to do since he looked dashing in the role of Sheriff English.

"I'm taking the dog for a walk." That was all he needed to know. If he did not recognize the results of her fight to be healthy, she would not point it out or confide in him how it happened.

"I'd rather you stay inside the mansion."

She smiled to help control the steam beginning to cloud her judgment.

Turning in a circle, she gazed at every degree of the horizon. "I don't see a storm gathering, do you?"

"Don't test my patience, Agatha. I know what is best."

Perhaps a storm was coming after all.

Had he any idea how difficult it had been for her to get to the place she was today?

He ought to know it since he'd held her up when she could barely stand on her own.

She had learned confidence since the night he'd kept her from the laudanum. She was not going to cower inside because William Byron English told her to stay in the house.

And, she had to wonder, why did he suddenly want her to stay inside when he had never restricted her goings and comings before.

"Take the dog home and give her a bath." She shoved Miss Valentine into his arms. "I'm going to town for tea and cake."

"Agatha, stop!" she heard him call but pretended she hadn't.

Placing her hat on her head she tied the ribbons under her chin with a yank on the bow loops. Her boots hit the ground with more force than they needed to, her strides long and determined.

Here was one man who was going to learn that Agatha Marigold English had found her backbone.

Half an hour later she realized that lesson was not going to be so easily taught.

Instead of taking the dog home to bathe her, he had followed her, never more than ten steps away.

What on earth had come over him? Had becoming sheriff changed him in some way? Perhaps now that he was acting in that role, he saw villains behind every bush.

Purposefully, she had taken her time getting to the bakery. If she stalled, he might get tired of trailing her and leave her to her sulk over chocolate cake.

She'd turned aside into the milliners' shop and purchased the hat she had admired. In the window of Clara's Fine Apparel she spotted a pair of gloves that she could not do without.

Noticing how dusty her boots had gotten, she spent some time at the shoemaker having them polished.

At last when it became clear that he would follow her about all day, she went into the bakery to try and enjoy her cake and coffee.

It wasn't proving to be an easy thing to do, not with William sitting on the stoop outside and Miss Valentine jumping up and down trying to see her through the window.

Finishing the last inch of coffee in her cup in a single gulp, she got up and went outside.

William stood. He did not smile at her but the dog jumped upon her skirt, unable to contain her joy at the reunion.

"Do you love me?" she asked outright because the question gnawed at her and needed answering. Although he'd said so, he had not convinced her of it last night.

"I told you I did."

"Humph. Your hat is askew." She reached up, straightened it then spun about and went home.

* * *

Once again he had declared his love. Agatha's response had been to straighten his hat.

He hadn't expected a kiss, but a smile would have done.

At least she had finally decided to return home. Following her about in the heat was not on his schedule of things to get done today.

Neither was feeling heartache. Agatha's continued anger hurt him in a way he'd never experienced. Being in love was not the rosy condition poets liked to go on about.

There was one way to deflect her anger away from him. Tell her the truth. Reveal that her former tormentor was not dead but living two blocks away.

No, he would keep that to himself. There was no telling what the knowledge might do to her. What if it plunged her backward to where she had been?

The safest thing would be to deal with Brunne on his own. Since charges had never been filed against the woman, would he be able to arrest her?

A real sheriff would know. For now his plan was to keep Agatha indoors. His gut told him that the witch was not here by accident.

It was hard to imagine how she'd found Agatha. How she'd gone from presumed dead to working at Pete's Palace. In the end the how of it didn't matter. The woman was here.

So he would do what he needed to in order to keep his wife safe, even if she hated him for it.

Which, apparently she did. No matter. Agatha was going to stay indoors unless she was with him.

And he was going to resist the temptation that nearness would create. No matter what, he was going to keep his hands off her.

Yet another thing she was unhappy about where he was concerned.

Didn't she understand that leaving her bed when he'd wanted to stay was the greatest way he knew to express his love and respect for her?

All day she had been acting like he'd tossed dirt in her face.

Now, standing on the patio and gazing into the moonless sky, he dug his fingers into the rail. How could he make this impossible situation right?

"Well, there's my big, handsome sheriff!"

His mother joined him at the rail. He leaned down to kiss her cheek.

"We've hardly seen you tonight, son." She arched a brow at him. "Is something wrong?"

Denying it would do no good. This was the woman who had known him since birth. He did not doubt that she already knew what was wrong and had come to state her opinion about it.

An owl hooted in a tree at the edge of the yard. A block away a dog barked. Miss Valentine, dashing about and sniffing bushes, barked in answer. Seconds passed, he remained silent.

"Son?" She set her hand on top of his. "It's time to share a bed with your bride. It's no wonder she's cranky with you."

Good thing he hadn't been drinking anything. He'd have sputtered it halfway across the yard.

A scolding for his tendency toward bossiness was what he expected.

"That's a private matter, Mother."

"I've known everything about you from the day you were born. Try as you might, you cannot keep anything private from your own mother." She folded her arms across her bosom, tapped her bottom lip in thought. "I know that you love Agatha. Anyone with eyes can see how much. So why won't you bed her? I've given it a great deal of thought."

"You've what?" His mother had been thinking about his intimate life? In lurid detail? His stomach clenched. He wondered if he was going to keel over the rail, hit his head on the ground and never come to.

"Been thinking about you and your sweet wife. I do not believe the reluctance is on her part."

"I wish it was. Life would be easier."

"What do you mean? She's lovely! Any man would be fortunate to have her. You ought to count your lucky stars."

"Believe me, Mother, I do. All those things you said about her are true—but this is Agatha Magee." He looked at the stars he'd recently thanked, wishing there was a moon to fix his attention on. Anything to keep from having this conversation with his mother.

"Of course she is."

"And you'll recall that the doctor warned her father that she could die giving birth."

Mother waved the idea away with a flick of her fingers. "That was a very long time ago. She was ill. I'm sure she is a different person now. Really, son, open your eyes and take an honest look at her."

"All I know is what a doctor told her father. I cannot act as if he had not."

"I've thought about this a lot," she said, patting his hand where he gripped the rail.

"I'm surprised you had time to think about anything but the reception."

"Even the most efficient planner has room to be concerned about her child. And I am concerned about you, William."

"I'll get by." Somehow.

"Yes, once you face what the problem really is." She reached up and ruffled his hair as if he were five years old again.

"I don't want to kill my wife is what the problem is."

"No man does. But William, your fear goes deeper than most men's. You watched me nearly die in childbirth. Your sister left this world while you held her in your arms. As sick to death as I was, don't think I was not aware of the way you knelt by my bedside for a week praying. The reason I did not die was because you needed me. I fought hard to live."

"It would break me to see Agatha like that."

"No doubt, but it would not break her."

"Dying would break her! And me. Look what it did to Father."

"Never mind him. He was always weak. You are not like him in any way. You are strong and honorable, a good man to your bones." She slipped her arm around his waist and leaned her head against the side of his arm. "Do you think that had I known I would die giving birth to you, I would not have done it anyway? Death comes to us all at some point, but how sad to have lived one's life without love."

"Do you think Agatha would survive giving birth?" He wanted to know her opinion, not that her opinion would have any bearing on the situation.

"Very likely, but nothing is guaranteed, dear. But I do believe that she has the right to make her own decision about it. As much as you want to be in control of everything, you are not."

The longer he lived, the more apparent that became.

His plan had been to be appointed to the territorial legislature; instead he was Mayor of Tanners Ridge. His plan had been to serve the town as best he could; now he was sheriff as well.

His plan had been to marry a socialite to advance his career. He'd married a woman who was shy in a crowd.

He'd accepted the fact that his fate would be to merely like his wife. To his everlasting wonder, he loved his wife.

Nothing it seemed was under his control. Especially Agatha Marigold English.

"It's good to see your smile." Mother went up on her toes, kissed his cheek then went back in the house.

Damn, one more thing not under his control. His emotions. Now he was smiling, besotted with Agatha, when a moment ago he wanted to shout his frustration at the non-present moon.

At some point during the day, someone would knock on the front door, wanting her husband's attention.

Given that he was both mayor and sheriff, he was going to be needed. It was only a matter of time before she would see him leave the house and she could make her escape.

Not that she should be required to escape. But William had changed toward her and blamed if she knew why.

The ladies at the saloon needed her help, not tomorrow or next week, but today. This morning!

If she didn't warn them that they were slowly dying, she would be no better than Hilda Brunne was. She had been where these women were, helpless, hopeless.

She wanted to be more like her sister. This was her chance. Just as Ivy had dragged Agatha to freedom, she would do it for the *filles de joie* at Pete's Palace.

Exactly how she was going to help them was another problem altogether.

She'd considered writing letters to each woman, but from all she'd seen Pete was a wicked man. He might punish them if he found the notes.

There seemed to be only one way to go about it. Speak to them face to face.

Perhaps when they were leaning out of their windows recruiting customers. It seemed the safest way to go about it since at this hour of the day Pete Lydle was probably asleep.

Her challenge was a big one. For now all she could do was sit in her chair by the front window and pretend to read.

The clock seemed to tick endlessly but in reality it was only a few moments before the library door opened and her husband strode out, looking far too handsome for her frame of mind.

If he matched her mood, his hair would be disheveled, his shirt ripped. Three days of shaggy beard growth would shadow his chin.

Oh, drat. That image did not suit her mood, either. It was rugged in a way the made her heart stutter.

She needed him to look contrite, his head hung low in regret for forcing her to remain indoors.

But no, here he came, his hair neatly gleaming in the beam of sunlight he crossed through. His jacket was buttoned and his shoes polished. He smelled like shaving soap. The Stetson was just low enough to make him look—drat, she could not think about how it made him look.

Rather than appearing repentant for his high-handed treatment of her, he was smiling.

Oh, the nerve of the—the—king! The ruler of everyone!

Stopping in front of her, he bent at the waist to drop a sweet, light kiss on her forehead.

"I don't believe you love me. No more than you would a bird in a cage," she said.

He straightened up. "I told you I did, twice."

Standing, she still had to look up in order to face him eye to eye. No wonder he was bossy. He was taller than almost anyone else.

"You said the words, but there was no passion, no sincerity in them. There ought to be fire in your eyes when you tell me that."

"Yes, there ought to be." He glanced at the shine on his shoes, or possibly the ivy pattern on the rug.

For some reason he hid his expression from her. He hid his expression but not his heart. In spite of his distant attitude, the pulse in his throat beat hard. She doubted it was because the ivy beneath his shoe was all that interesting.

As naïve as she was, she could tell that he wanted her, knew the reason he would not show it.

They had discussed his need to protect her. It was normal for a man to want that, but she was not going to be sheltered to the sacrifice of her happiness.

In the very instant she was about to leap upon him, plunder his mouth and claim what he was keeping from her, someone pounded on the door.

"Wonder if it's the mayor they're here for or the sheriff."

"Better find out." She sighed.

Going toward the door, he stopped, came back and kissed her cheek, very close to the place where the curve of her lip nearly lifted in a smile.

And there it was, a quick and revealing flash in his eye—a yearning for more.

She waited ten minutes after the door closed before she moved. When he did not return, she put on her bonnet and smoothed her skirt. She was ready for battle. Ready to tell addicted women about a better life.

Opening the door, she was blown back two steps by a great gust of wind. Dust so thick she could not see across the street blew sideways.

The dust storm hadn't been there a moment ago. It was unlikely that William had made it to wherever he was going without losing his new Stetson.

Even worse, the ladies would not be hanging out their windows.

She would have to come to them at night, appeal to them between customers. At least she had the rest of the day to figure a way to do it.

For her adventure into the night Agatha put on her darkest gown. Hopefully she would blend in with the shadows.

Even though it had taken William far too long to retire this evening, and during that time she had made several sincere yawns to help him along, he did at last go up the stairs.

Walking upstairs beside him, she continued to yawn and stretch. She'd declared how she would be sound asleep the instant her head felt the give of her pillow.

Luckily, he had not visited her room last night. She only hoped he would not tonight either.

In spite of the delay because of the wind, luck had been on her side.

As it turned out, both Mrs. Bea and Miss Fitz used to work at the Bascomb Hotel. After spending the afternoon with them discussing its former glory she had a fair idea of the floor plan.

Now all she had to do was step off the front porch and walk the two blocks to the Palace.

If the moon wasn't a bare sliver over the horizon, too low and too small to light her way, she might not hesitate to step off the front porch.

If the wind wasn't racing down the road, whistling around corners and moaning under eaves, she might be halfway to her destination already.

If, if, if! The problem did not lie with elements of nature. The fact could not be denied, she was acting more timidly than Ivy's pet mouse.

Well then! She lifted her skirt and stepped down to the street.

A tumbleweed careened toward her but she stepped out of its way. A large wolflike dog on a front porch saw her and charged the fence. Instead of barking, it wagged its tail.

Hugging a shadow, she stood across the street from the hotel. Red-globed lanterns sat on the sills of upstairs windows. Raunchy laughter spilled out of the front doors. Men lounged on the boardwalk, some smoking and some drinking.

Pete Lydle came out to join them, both smoking and drinking.

Was the man so much worse than Frenchie Brown? Was Pete's Palace more decadent than the circus?

Probably not. Understanding the underbelly of the circus as she did, she knew that perhaps it was worse. At least the saloon was what it was. There was no mistaking what one would find when entering a saloon.

But the circus? Folks brought their families, unaware that beyond the thrills and bright colors lay corruption.

All of a sudden she was grateful for the moon that was too weak to light the street, for the wind that muffled her steps as she dashed across the road and behind the building.

Thanks to Miss Fitz and Mrs. Bea, she knew there was a back stairway. In order to get to it she would need to pass by the kitchen door, which was open and spilling light into the darkness.

Easing along the wall, she heard voices—at least six of them mostly women and at least one man, and he seemed angry that a steak was taking too long to prepare.

If she walked past the door she was sure to be spotted. Glancing about she noticed that the space under the kitchen stairs was open.

She would be able to crawl under it and make it to the back stairway without being seen.

It was a small space, though. She would have to slither on her belly in the dirt for at least ten feet.

The darkness under the stairs was inky black. It was easy to imagine being swallowed by it never to be heard from again. Perhaps she should go home and let her husband protect her every step like he wanted to.

Silently, she went down on her knees only to discover that it was not only dark, but smelly. No doubt they tossed garbage under here—which meant there might be rats.

Small ones though, unlike the one who owned the saloon. Holding her breath, she went down on her belly, entered the black cave-like space.

A rustle of tiny feet skittered into a corner—many tiny feet. She would have squealed but in that moment boots thudded on the wood overhead.

Going still, she held her breath, afraid that even her heartbeat would give her presence away.

The person belched, sighed. A second later a splash

of water hit the dirt and made a sizzling sound. The boot steps went back inside.

Luck was on her side even though she would have sworn a second ago that it was not. Yes, she was spending a moment with unidentified creatures, but she had not been scalded by a pot of boiling water.

Quickly scooting her body forward, she was nearly out when her elbow slid on something slick. She had no idea what it might be other than odorous. Since she had to drag her body over it in order to get out, there would be a trail of stench on her dress.

In the end she made it to the back stairway without being discovered. Inside was a landing with two short sets of stairs, one going left and one going right. She knew that either way would lead to rear hallways with back doors to each room.

It was an odd design with a front and rear door to each room but Mr. Bascomb had designed it that way so the cleaning staff would not be seen. Not only that, Mrs. Bea had confided that some people used the private passage to go from room to room for secret trysts.

No wonder Pete Lydle had purchased the hotel. Hopefully, his customers only used the main hallway.

It was dark here but not like it had been beneath the stairs. A bit of light did seep out from the under the doors.

As far as she could tell there were no vermin creeping about, either. Instead of the scent of garbage, she smelled an odd mingling of tobacco, sweat and lavender.

On tiptoe, she crept along the hallway, listening at doors for the sounds of women who might be alone so that she could speak with them.

This, of course, was a far more intimidating thing to do than slither through refuse. The ladies might not want to hear what she had to say. They might laugh, call her a busybody. No doubt they would alert Mr. Lydle that she was skulking the back hallways.

But if she could help just one woman, it would be worth everything.

Judging by the sounds coming from under the crack of the door she just passed, Agatha could tell the woman was working. Same with the second and the third doors, but not the fourth.

Quiet weeping came from behind that door. The voice sounded young—too young. Then came the tap, tap, tap of a cane across the floor.

Agatha knew very well what was about to happen. The old woman dressed in black was about to douse the girl with laudanum since it would not do for the customers to hear the young prostitute's despair.

She touched the knob, ready to burst in and carry the girl away—somehow. All at once fingers clamped over her mouth. A man's arm banded her waist, lifted her and carried her backward down the hallway.

Chapter Thirteen

Standing on the front porch and staring at the night, William hesitated in going down the stairs.

He felt the weight of the badge on his shirt, the heaviness of the gun on his hip. Even if there had been a real sheriff to turn this problem over to, he would not.

Because this one involved his wife.

Hilda Brunne was hiding out with Pete Lydle. No way in hell did he believe that was by chance.

The insane woman had come for Agatha. As long as he had a breath in his body, he would not let the witch get to her.

Luck was with him tonight, though. Agatha had been especially tired and fallen asleep quickly.

Bounding off the stairs, he strode down the street. The neighbor's large dog rushed the fence, barking its fool head off. He'd been hit by a couple of tumbleweeds taking aim at him but it wasn't long before he stood in front of the saloon.

Lydle and a few other men stood on the porch.

"Evening, gentlemen," he greeted from the boardwalk.

"What brings you out in the wee hours? Sheriff at the

moment, I assume?" Lydle's voice expressed friendliness, but William knew better than to believe it.

"Just making my nightly rounds. Folks are uncomfortable with all the strangers coming to town."

"They oughtn't to be. They're spending money, fattening everyone's bank accounts, not just mine." The men Lydle had been speaking with went back into the saloon. "Come on inside, have a drink with me this time, have a cigar. I don't hold grudges."

"I've got my rounds to finish up." He went down the steps, Pete staring after him.

Hell, not staring so much as shooting glaring hot anger at his back. Oh, he'd be smiling in case anyone noticed, but William felt the prick of imagined daggers through his shirt.

He walked past three buildings then turned down an alley.

As luck would have it, a pack of coyotes had ventured into town and were yipping and carrying on. If he were still watching, Lydle would think William had gone that way to chase the pack back to open land where they belonged.

Since he was not after that sort of predator, he circled back toward the rear of the saloon.

A gunshot cut the night. The coyotes' frenzied yelps stopped at once. Someone must have taken care of the problem on their own.

Walking past the saloon's kitchen door, he looked inside. A woman noticed him and came out on the porch.

"I'll never get used to those vicious beasts," she said, glancing toward the direction the coyotes had been. "The entrance is in the front, mister or—Sheriff, is it?"

She squinted up her eyes, peering through the dark at his badge.

"I'm looking for someone."

"Around the front, like I said."

"It's the old woman with the cane."

"The lunatic?" Wind fluttered the apron tied about the woman's generous waist. A foul smell blew out from under the stairs.

"I'd like to speak with her."

"She'll be tending the girls, I imagine, but talk to Pete first. And go around the front."

"I reckon I'll come back in the morning."

"Suit yourself," she said then went back inside the kitchen.

If the smell wafting from under the porch was any indication of the quality of the food they served, he wouldn't dare to eat it.

Luck was still definitely on his side. If the saloon owner asked around, he would be told that the sheriff had gone home.

William opened the door to the back stairway and silently went inside. If he was going to find Brunne, he could not make a noise that might alert anyone that he was creeping behind the rooms, especially her. From what he'd seen, for all that the woman appeared crippled, she could slip away as easily as a wraith.

Back here in the hallway he heard the noises he expected to, grunts, moans—and from behind the door he was shuffling by, a fellow getting to the point of what he had paid for.

But further down there was a sound that disturbed him. The unhappy weeping of a young prostitute, also the tip-tapping of a cane on the floor.

Rounding the corner, muscles tensed, he was ready to burst into the room and prevent whatever wicked thing was happening.

He came to a sudden halt. A woman stood at the door, her hand on the knob.

Even in the dark he recognized his wife. She was so intent on what she was doing she didn't notice him rushing her.

Until he clapped his hand over her mouth, lifted her and carried her away, she had been unaware of his presence.

What if it had not been him in the hall but one of Pete's customers? What if it had been Pete and not William carrying her away right now?

It could have been! He felt red inside. Anger pulsed in his brain, shot through his arms and legs as he hurried her outside.

He'd always believed Agatha to be a reasonable, intelligent human being. In the moment he did not know who she was.

She was not the person she used to be! It was true that she was being carried away—again, but this time she would not be forced into the mouth of a cannon.

She would not be forced into anything.

She kicked backward, landing a blow on her assailant's shin. He grunted but did not let her loose.

It wouldn't do to scream since that might attract more men of his depravity.

Reaching back, she yanked his hair. Something metal poked her in the back. Suddenly she was in a life-and-death struggle. She bit his fingers.

This time the attacker yelped.

"Agatha, stop!" he hissed in her ear.

She did. A stone dumped on her head would not have stunned her more.

William dropped one arm from her waist. She spun

about, looking smack at the brass badge reading Sheriff. She still felt the imprint of the metal, the terror of it pressed between her shoulder blades when she'd believed it to be a gun.

"You beast!" she mouthed at him.

He proved she was right by hauling her once more along the hallway, then out the back door. Instead of going left past the kitchen, he took her right.

After ten minutes in which she was certain her arm would fall out of its socket from all the tugging he was doing and the resisting she was doing, he stopped abruptly.

She heard the sound of gurgling water. He'd taken her to the stream that ran behind the town shops.

"You're right! For the first time in my life I feel like one. A red-hot-tempered beast!"

He clutched her arm again, this time dragging her downhill past trees and through shrubbery.

A few times, she thought she would fall but he held on to her so she didn't.

The water was close now. Cooler air filled her lungs, brushed her face. The earth turned softer under her boots. It smelled damp and green.

"Do you have any idea how I felt seeing you in that place when you were supposed to be home in bed?"

He pressed her down until her bottom thumped down on the trunk of the fallen tree.

"Well, yes! As a matter of fact, I do." He reached for her hand but she swatted it away. "I also left you asleep in bed. What were you doing prowling about behind those rooms? Hiding? Not wanting your reputation to be ruined if anyone saw you consorting with those women?"

He gripped her shoulders, but gently, considering how angry he was...and completely without cause. "I think you know me better than that. I would never do such a thing to you."

"You were there for some reason."

"Why were you there?"

"You know why! Those women are being drugged. I thought I could help one of them—and I was about to when you carried me off. Perhaps if you hadn't been riding so high on your white horse you could have helped me."

His arms fell away from her shoulders, moved down her arms in a caress. He cupped both of her hands in his. This time she did not pull away.

Probably because even in the inky dark she saw his expression change. With a blink, the anger faded from his eyes, the tension in his jaw softened.

"You have no idea what you were walking into, honey."

She did. "Of course I did. I know exactly what was going to happen in that room."

"You didn't know. The reason I was there is to make sure you never did."

"Might I point out that even though you are my husband and honor-bound to watch over my every little step, that was a high-handed thing to do—even for you."

Shaking his head, he touched her jaw, traced the outline of it, then pressed her head to his shoulder, stroked her hair where it had come undone. As if he could soothe away her well-earned resentment!

"That little step you were about to take? Honey, Hilda Brunne was in that room."

Her mind exploded, white lightning splintering her thoughts.

No! "She's dead."

The denial turned fuzzy in her brain.

When she next became aware of the world, William

was holding her on his lap, rocking her. She found that she had one hand clamped onto his badge, the sensation in her fingers gone numb.

For once, for this moment at least, she was very glad to have a protector who watched over her every little step.

The fact that Hilda Brunne was alive did not want to penetrate her brain.

Huddling against William's side while he led the way home, she knew what he'd told her but the idea would take some time to accept. At some point she expected she might cry and tremble.

She was shocked and afraid, but the emotion of it refused to lodge in her heart. She must be too unnerved to allow it in.

How long would it be before she ran home to the Lucky Clover?

She could not do that of course, not without drawing Brunne back to the ranch—to Ivy.

With the shock beginning to wear off, her emotions hit hard. Her stomach twisted and she felt nauseous. Pictures of doom rolled over her, one after another, until she had to stop and take a deep breath.

"I might be sick," she warned.

Instead of moving to safety, William patted her back, drew her hair away from her face.

"Don't be afraid. I'm here."

As he had been the last time Brunne plotted evil. That awful, horrible night when the sky opened up and the land shook with violent lightning. He'd held her close then, just as he was doing now.

The house was silent, everyone asleep, when she and William climbed the stairs to their bedrooms.

"Stay with me tonight, Agatha."

It was what she wanted, what she had been praying for but—

"I can't." She shook her head, pushed out of the safe circle of his arms.

Immediately everything grew colder, more frightening.

"I can't," she repeated, not because she thought he didn't hear but because she had to convince herself that going to her room alone was the right thing to do.

It had to be. It was not what she wanted, but if she went to William's bed, hid from reality in his embrace, how would she know what her true reaction to the news that Brunne was alive would be?

Would she crumble at the fear of being stalked? Or had she grown in strength as she believed she had? The only way to know for sure was to go to her room alone.

"I want to know that you are all right."

"I'll call out if I need you." She kissed him on the cheek. "You're only a door away."

And if she knew him at all he would be awake and listening, maybe even with his ear to the wall.

Closing the door, she sagged against it. A full minute later she heard the quiet click of William's door shutting.

Unless she missed her guess, during that minute he had been listening, waiting to see if she fell apart.

As she well might. The trembling began as a quivering in her belly but soon moved outward, making her hands quake, her knees weak.

Tears welled in her eyes.

Brunne was not dead as everyone had believed. Not dead—and she knew where Agatha was. She'd no doubt hatched a plan in her deranged brain to enslave her again.

Brunne would be watching, waiting. But no! She had been watching all along. Remembering the times at the circus when she thought she was imagining shadows, she grew dizzy. And the time she saw the cat in the window— it had not been a cat at all.

Sick to her stomach, Agatha sank down on the chair beside her bedroom window. The window was open, the wind whistling inside.

She ought to close it up. What if Brunne got inside and made her drink laudanum? In her mind she saw it happen, felt herself drift away without really caring that she did.

Reaching for the blanket that had slipped onto the floor, wanting to cover up, hide in it even though it had to be eighty degrees inside, she stopped and kicked it away with her foot.

Did she really think that an old woman, a crippled old woman now, would be able to climb to the second-story window, burst inside and pour drugs down her throat?

Even if she did sprout wings, fly inside like a rabid bat, William was in the next room.

The threat of Brunne assaulting her tonight was imagined.

Something else was not.

For as much as she wanted to applaud herself for gaining strength and independence, she would not have managed it without William.

She was brought to mind of a baby learning to walk. The child did it all on her own, but right behind were a pair of protective arms, not interfering but there just in case.

This was who William was to her.

Oh, she'd gone on about how high-handed he was, how bossy and wanting to be in charge of everything.

Somehow, she found in the moment that she didn't mind it so much. If it weren't for him, she would have walked in on Hilda Brunne and been taken by surprise—no, not surprise so much as complete and utter shock. This evening would have turned out much differently had her husband not interfered.

She did owe him quite a lot. He must think her the most ungrateful wretch.

If one looked at things in a certain way, she partly owed him the new vigor in her body. Had it not been for her determination to give him children, she would not have gone running every morning.

Gazing down at the yard, feeling the wind on her face and hearing the crack of a falling branch—peering into a deep shadow and not fearing Mother Brunne would materialize out of it, she knew she was not going to fall apart.

She was free—nearly. The woman was still here, still had evil intentions. But rather than cower under the blanket on the floor, Agatha would face the woman.

Hilda Brunne would never drug her again.

Never again would she be reduced to an oppressed, quivering child.

She was a woman, able and grown.

Spinning away from the window, she crossed the room and went into the hall. Raising her hand to knock on William's door, she drew it back, clenched her fingers.

Instead, she turned the knob, opened the door. As she'd thought, he stood near the wall, listening.

"I'm not going to fall apart," she told him. "You can move away from the wall."

He did. He rushed her, grabbed her about the waist and twirled her inside his bedroom.

Hugging her to him he whispered in her ear. "I love you, Agatha. You don't think so but I do." He tangled his fingers in the back of her hair, tipped her head back, gazing hard into her eyes. Slowly, deliberately, he lowered his mouth and kissed her. "I love you."

Then his arms went slack, and he set her away from him.

He didn't need to urge her toward the doorway because she was already there, on her way out.

As much as she wanted to cross the room, leap onto his bed, this was not the time for seduction for either him or her.

But he had declared his love with passion and she believed him.

It was enough for tonight.

Victoria English swept through the doorway. Standing on the carpet set out for stormy days, she brushed raindrops off the shoulders of her wrap then removed her bonnet and shook it out.

"It doesn't rain this much in Cheyenne!" she announced. "Twenty-five miles should not make such a difference."

"I imagine it's raining in Cheyenne, too, Mother," William said, coming out of the parlor and stopping to kiss her cheek on his way to the library.

"That may be, but my guests are arriving here, not there. How many bedrooms can you spare, dear?" She snagged his sleeve when he would have continued on his way. "I'm having the devil of a time finding places for our guests with all those gamblers arriving at the same time. The folks in town say they would rather rent to me. I believe the problem is that Pete Lydle is blinding them with cash."

"We'll offer more. Don't worry, the weather wouldn't dare ruin your plans. The saloon owner wouldn't, either, if he knew you better."

"Well, he's a greedy fool. I doubt a dressing-down will sway him."

"I imagine Ivy and her family will be arriving soon, so all I can spare are two rooms."

"I'll need one more at the least."

"I suppose we could put a bed or two in the library. Someone could have the couch."

Mother handed him her coat so he hung it on the rack.

"You could share a room with your wife."

"You know why I can't."

"Actually, I do not." She patted his cheek then walked into the parlor.

He followed her, his work in the library forgotten.

Mrs. Bea stood up from the hearth where she had just laid a new bouquet of flowers. The scent of roses washed the room.

"Good day to you both," she said with a sunny smile. "I'll send in tea if you're ready."

"I'll wait for my daughter-in-law if she's not too long. I passed her dodging raindrops half an hour ago."

He sat down on the couch. His mother joined him.

"I wonder how she will do," his mother said.

"With what?" Childbirth, did she mean? He did not want to have this conversation with her again.

While Agatha did appear stronger there might be things regarding her health that were not apparent.

"Playing hostess for your guests. She is a dear girl, but shy. I wonder if she will be happy doing it."

"I don't know. I won't force her, but I believe she will shine."

"You ought to count your lucky stars, son. For a man who was ready to wed for political gain you have been very fortunate."

"Aren't you the one who set a few prospects in my path?"

"They were lovely women and I'm glad you did not choose them."

"So am I. Political gain isn't what I value most any longer."

Ever since he'd carried a frail waif dressed in red underwear into his house he had not seen his life in the same way.

"I could not be more pleased—"

The front door blew open. He smelled damp air and wet clothing when Agatha washed inside.

"It's a wicked one out there!" she exclaimed. "Have I missed tea?"

Water cascaded from her bonnet, dripped off her eyelashes. Apparently she hadn't worn a coat when she went out because her white blouse was stuck to her skin.

She ran her hands down the front, sluicing water from her chest. "I ran halfway home."

From where? He ought to have known she'd gone out.

She did look invigorated. Her chest heaved with the exertion of her outing. Her eyes had never looked such a bright emerald color.

Still, it was her smile that made his insides grow warm—no, not warm but hot—pulsing hot. He shouldn't be feeling like he wanted to haul his wife upstairs and toss her upon his bed with his mother sitting shoulder to shoulder with him.

It was indecent.

"Oh, no," Mother declared with a sly turn of her lips. "I believe you are right on time."

Agatha dashed upstairs, shed her wet clothes for dry ones then hurried back down.

"Where's Mother?"

Three steaming teacups sat on the side table along

with half a dozen oatmeal cookies but William sat by himself on the couch.

"Napping, she said."

Since she hadn't taken time to dry her hair, droplets fell on her fresh bodice. She rubbed the damp spots with her fingertips.

Sensing William's gaze intent on the movement of her fingers, she rubbed more vigorously. Parts of her shimmied that were fit for only a husband's eyes to see.

Glancing up quickly, she had the satisfaction of watching his face flush, his chest heave on a held breath.

"Will you pass me a cookie, William?" she asked with the most innocent smile she could imagine, but all the while thanking Mrs. Bea for the lessons in seduction.

She most definitely had his attention now. The question remained, could she convince him to do more than gawk at her, to set aside his fear of killing her and make her his wife in every way.

Taking a nibble of the cookie he handed her, she sighed in exaggerated pleasure before she dropped a crumb on her breast.

"I'm such a mess." Once again she made a great show of brushing her bosom.

William caught her hand, his expression tense. "Where were you?"

"Walking in the rain." He could hardly argue since she'd come in soaked to the skin.

He needn't know she'd been to see Dr. Connor and gotten a letter informing William that he was no more likely to kill her than any other woman he might have married.

"I love the rain, don't you?"

"You didn't go to the saloon?" His brows lowered, and his gaze narrowed upon her.

"I did not!" she vowed because she hadn't.

That did not mean she wouldn't. A time was coming when she would have to. She could not know that Brunne was in Tanners Ridge and not confront her.

If not for the way she had treated Agatha all her life, then because of Ivy.

Sometime within the next couple of days, her sister would be here and her new baby with her. If Hilda discovered there was a child and believed her to be the missing Maggie, who knew what insanity might be triggered?

"Good," he said.

Another crumb fell on her chest. She ignored it because William did not. He followed the descent of the oatmeal-crusted raisin with his eyes.

"I'll deal with Hilda Brunne."

She nodded, but the truth was Agatha needed to be the one to deal with her. As her victim, it was Agatha's right.

Silence fell while William stared at the crumb and she stared at his face.

Slowly, he lifted his hand. Covered the piece of cookie with his palm. Quickly, she raised her hand to cover his... pressed it closer to her heart.

As if moving through warm, languid water he bent his head toward her. She lifted her lips to him.

"Oh! Tea!" came Dove's voice from the hall. "I was afraid we had missed it. Hurry, Bert, before it cools."

"At least someone looks flushed with pleasure," she grumbled so silently that she doubted even William heard it.

Or maybe he did. His eye twinkled, right in the corner like a tiny star winking at midnight.

She flicked the crumb away with her own finger at the same time as the lovebirds hurried hand in hand into the parlor.

Chapter Fourteen

William awoke to sunlight poking his eyelids, to the slam of hammers pounding wood in the yard.

This was going to be a hot day. The workers would be getting an early start on building the dance floor.

"Hey!" he heard a deep voice shout. "Bring back my hammer!"

Miss Valentine must be helping.

He sat up, scrubbed his hand across his face.

He'd spent a restless night knowing that Agatha was only a thin wall away. He could not help but wonder if she had turned and flopped about on her mattress the way he had…or worse, if she had not.

He could not recall ever being so unsettled when he ought to be sleeping. Every time he'd drifted off, he dreamed of cookie crumbs…thousands of them. Sometimes he'd struggle to get to Agatha through waist-deep crumbs, other times he'd tried to cross a road to get to her but was blinded by oatmeal and raisin chunks falling from a clear blue sky.

Grabbing his robe from the foot of the bed, he shrugged into it, but left it hanging open because of the heat.

Walking to the window, he gazed down below to check on the transformation of the yard.

In the far right corner tables were set up. The dance floor was about halfway finished. Only a few boards were in place for the musicians' platform.

The roses were beginning to wilt.

All but the one named Agatha.

His wife stood on the center of the incomplete dance floor seemingly untroubled by the carpenters working madly around the hem of her skirt.

Her attention was caught up in reading a letter she gripped in one small fist. She seemed to be smiling at it.

All of a sudden she glanced up at his window. Seeing him, she shoved the note behind her back. It was as though she did not want him to see what it was, as though he might be able to read it from the second-story window.

While he studied the expression on her face trying to judge what she was up to, he noticed that she was not looking at his face but his bare chest where the robe gaped away.

"At least someone is flushed with pleasure," he mumbled, repeating her lament of yesterday.

The thing was, he wasn't sure which of them was more agitated by pleasure.

A knock rapped on his door. His mother marched in, dressed and ready for a long day of party preparations. No doubt she had risen well before dawn.

"There's a man at the door. He wants to complain about the saloon."

"To the sheriff or the mayor?"

"I doubt he's that particular. The woman in the parlor, though, is demanding to see the sheriff. What are you doing lying abed so late, young man?"

"It's only six thirty."

"Yes, and the sun has been up for forty-five minutes."

"Beg a cup of coffee for me from Miss Fitz and I'll be right down."

Ten minutes later he was in the parlor with his coffee, dressed in his suit for those who wanted to complain to the mayor, and wearing his badge, gun, and Stetson for those needing the help of the sheriff.

From the way things were beginning, it was going to be an interesting day.

The sooner he went to his office and got out of her way, the happier his mother would be.

Glancing about, he didn't see his wife. She must still be in the yard supervising the building of the dance floor, or reading the mysterious note.

He'd better not take time to find her. He could only imagine that if people were searching him out at home, they must be ten thick at both his offices.

He opened the front door to go out. Sunshine in a bright yellow dress filled the doorway.

"Gosh almighty, Bill! This is some grand house you've got here!" Ivy stepped inside, holding her baby in her arms. The child gave him a quick smile then buried her face into her mother's shoulder.

"I don't believe I've seen anything so elegant since the last time I was on the *Queen*," Ivy declared while turning in a circle to take in the foyer and all its fancy trimmings.

Travis came in behind her, shook William's hand, patted him on the back.

It struck him suddenly that this man was his brother. He'd always wanted a brother and was glad it was Travis Murphy.

Behind Travis came Agatha's uncle Patrick and his wife, Antoinette. Antie had been Ivy's social instructor when it had been necessary, for the sake of the Lucky

Clover, to transform her from a riverboat pilot in train-
ing into a lady.

It was good to see that she was still as much river
queen as she was social belle.

"Say! Where've you stashed my sister?" Ivy placed
the baby girl in Travis's arms. "Hope you've been watching over her good."

"I've done what I could."

"She isn't sick, is she? Stuck in a chair somewhere?"

"Ivy!" came a shriek from the top of the stairs.

He turned, saw a flood of blue fly down the steps.

Yellow and blue mingled then broke apart when Ag-
atha dashed over to hug Travis and kiss the baby's cheek.
Next she stepped into her uncle's embrace, then Mrs.
Malone's.

Love given and received, Agatha went back to Ivy to
hug her again.

"I can hardly believe what these old eyes are telling
me." Patrick Malone snatched the pipe from between his
lips, grinning.

"*Mais oui, mon mari.* This is our poor sweet girl." Antoinette hugged her husband's arm, tugged on his sleeve
until he bent his ear down to her. "But, she has fallen in
love, has she not?"

She said this while looking at William, sending him
a wink.

That little wink went straight to his heart. It touched
him that the woman approved of his marriage to Agatha.

Within five seconds, the parlor overflowed with the
guests who followed his mother to greet the new arrivals.

Miss Valentine rushed past them all, jumped on Ivy's
skirt, then on Travis, and at last upon the Malones.

Agatha scooped the dog up. "Have you brought Little Mouse?"

With a grin Ivy drew a pouch from between the folds of her skirt.

"Knew you wouldn't mind it, Bill. We did discuss it once as I recall."

They had, and he'd said he wouldn't mind. It was hard to imagine his mother feeling the same about having a rodent in the house, pet or not.

"Here, let me hold her." Agatha shoved Miss Valentine at her sister, took the pouch and opened it.

A small white nose emerged, sniffing the air. Lifting the bag, his wife stroked the mouse between its black eyes.

Apparently Miss Valentine liked the rodent, too, just not in the same way.

The dog lunged, the mouse leapt off Agatha's hand. Several female voices screeched.

Agatha turned to run after the animals but Ivy caught her hand.

"No need to worry. There's no creature on God's great earth quicker than Little Mouse. Better at hiding, either."

William had never seen his mother pale or speechless. Right now she was both.

"I need to take off these fancy shoes before my toes fall off," said Ivy. "Reckon I'll loosen the corset, too, if we're just going to be home."

Lark and Dove watched Ivy walk past them, their mouths twin circles of astonishment.

Ivy grasped her sister's arm, "You know, sister, I didn't want you to leave home—then I got the letter telling me you married Bill! And now—look at you!"

His wife looked so very pleased at her sister's approval. He couldn't help but be pleased as well.

"Tomorrow morning I'll show you where I run with the horses—well, near them anyway."

Horses! What horses?

Miss Valentine pressed her nose to the edge of the couch, huffing and snorting.

It seemed that Mother, watching the dog, was about to do the same.

Looking up, she caught his eye, crooked her finger and waggled it at him. Answering the summons, he crossed the room.

"A word please, William."

He kissed her cheek. "Got to go, Mother. Folks will be waiting at my offices by now."

Going out the front door he heard the murmur of many voices, but one stood out among the rest.

Agatha's. She mentioned Mrs. Bea, her instructor in everything carnal.

Hell, Ivy was going to discover his failure as a husband.

That didn't mean she would disapprove. There wasn't a whole lot she put ahead of her sister's well-being.

He carried that thought, felt vindicated by it all the way to town.

William longed for the month of October when the weather would cool off. For that more pleasant time when sweat would not dampen his shirt even while he sat in the shade.

He'd begun the day by spending an hour in the sheriff's office then an hour in the mayor's office. By eleven o'clock frustrated folks had gathered at both places, becoming more irritated than they already were.

In the end, he'd taken the sheriff's shingle and the mayor's shingle then nailed them to the wall of the general store. He set a pair of chairs on the boardwalk.

It only took a couple of hours for his ears and his

voice to become worn out by all the listening and talking he'd done.

People did a lot of complaining about the saloon and the gamblers drifting in for the big tournament. Some of them looked decent and others, like criminals.

Since there was not enough lodging for his mother's guests and the gamblers, many of the gamblers had taken to sleeping behind buildings, or even in private yards.

Mrs. Peabody had rattled on for half an hour because the man sleeping in her flowers had returned and brought a friend with him. Now, not only were the pansies ruined but the petunias as well.

Most of the complaints were trivial, but not all of them.

Decent women were being mistaken for Pete's girls. Not that they looked like they were, but because Pete's customers tended to be so drunk they could not tell the difference. A woman was a woman and therefore fair game.

Which led to fisticuffs between the town's men and the drunks.

It couldn't be long before his mother marched over to the saloon, pitchfork in hand to present her own grievance.

Of which there were many. Today she was worried that the saloon's bawdy music would be so loud that the musicians she hired for the reception would be drowned out.

"Good afternoon, Mayor English, Sheriff."

Dr. Connor sat down in the chair beside him and wiped his brow on his sleeve.

"I didn't come to complain. Just needed a place to sit in the shade for a spell. Mrs. Parson is in labor and it's awfully hot upstairs." He indicated a house on the other side of the blacksmith shop with a nod.

"It's going well, I hope." William prayed.

"She's not as strapping as your young wife. But I believe she'll come through it fine. Not sure about her husband, though. I trust that he's going to faint a few times before the baby comes."

"What do you mean 'as strapping as my wife'?" The doctor really did need a rest in the shade.

"Mrs. Parson is not as healthy. When the time comes for your wife she'll do quite well, barring the unexpected."

"How do you know she will?"

Bushy gray eyebrows arched. "Why, because of the results of her examination."

"Of course," he said, not wanting the doctor to know he was ignorant of the visit.

"Yes! I've seen her twice now. The second time only to give her the letter verifying her excellent health. I imagine you were relieved to hear the good news."

The day had been hot before the doctor sat down, but now he felt blistered from the inside out.

Agatha had sought the doctor's advice without telling him? Blatantly ignored how he felt about her bearing children?

"She confided in me about her life before. If you are worried that she might take up drug use again, rest assured that I find it unlikely. I imagine this time next year you'll be calling upon me to help your own child come into the world."

"Do you?" His voice sounded clipped, nearly rude when it was not the doctor's fault.

A scream came from the upstairs room of the house across the street. It sounded like Mrs. Parson was dying. Oddly, the doctor smiled.

"I better get going. It appears I'll be needed soon."

Less than an hour later, a newborn's cry cut the afternoon. He lost track of what his current grumbler, a gambler with a black eye, was going on about.

Something having to do with Pete running a crooked game, he thought.

William could not keep his gaze off the window. Had Mrs. Parson survived? Had Mr. Parson?

The child clearly had: its lusty wails went on and on.

"Watered-down liquor…"

Then there he was. The new father stood in front of the window rocking back and forth with the squealing bundle in his arms. Judging by the width of his grin William guessed everyone had come through the ordeal.

"And the women are too medicated for a man to get his money's worth."

His attention snapped back to the speaker so fast he felt his neck creak.

"Drugged?" he asked stupidly. Hilda Brunne was there. Of course they were being drugged.

"That's not what the old woman calls it. 'Course, if you ask me she's touched." The gambler pointed to his bald head, tapped his finger on it. "She's looking all over the place for someone named Maggie. Must be a fairy or something since she's always searching under pillows, or behind chairs. Once she even tipped over someone's straight flush, thinking that Maggie was under the cards."

"What happened?" There had been shootings over lesser offenses.

"We all got a free drink. Ole Pete, he just laughed it off. Said the old lady didn't mean any harm."

She did mean harm—to Agatha.

Luckily, his wife was a sensible woman. Knowing what Brunne was capable of, she would keep to the house.

Wouldn't she?

Certainly, with all the guests about, Brunne would not dare come to the mansion again.

He needn't worry. If anyone knew better than to confront the witch, it was Agatha.

No, he need not worry—much.

The guests were napping.

Mrs. Bea, Miss Fitz and her mother-in-law hummed about like busy bees while they prepared for a casual dinner tonight.

If Victoria English was wilting under the heat, it only showed by a misting of sweat on her brow and upper lip.

Industriously, she swept the couch with a broom on the hunt for fine white fur.

"I do hope that rodent will stay confined for the rest of the visit." Apparently satisfied that she had found every strand, she set the broom aside and settled her full attention on Agatha. "You look done in, dear. Go up to your room and rest."

"I should help."

"You can, by looking refreshed for your guests. It's one of the secrets of entertaining. The hostess must appear invigorated, otherwise the guests will feel bad... like they've put her to too much trouble."

"Then you should rest, too."

"This is what refreshes me. Now scoot. Up to your room with you."

She hadn't known her mother-in-law long, but long enough to realize that she got her way most of the time.

In truth, Agatha did not mind going to her room for respite. It had been a long day meeting new people, smiling at them and looking poised.

However, to her surprise, it had not been the agony she'd expected it to be.

Plucking the dress away from her skin, she wondered if she would do as a politician's wife. Given enough time, she might.

Peeled down to her shift, she flopped backward on the bed, fanned her face and chest with her hands. It would be pure torture later when she had to put her gown on again.

Her door creaked open. William stepped inside. It did not escape her that he hadn't knocked first. For some reason that struck her as intimate.

"What are you doing, Agatha?"

Looking at the ceiling, she flopped her arms wide on the mattress. "Waiting for the sun to go down so I can breathe. Your mother says I must look refreshed."

"That's not what I mean."

Drawing her arms back in, she eased up on her elbows. "What do you mean?"

Judging by the master-of-all look on his face she had done something he did not approve of.

There soon would be something he did not approve of, but she hadn't done it yet.

"You went to see the doctor."

"It's not against the law, Sheriff."

"I made it clear that we would not have children."

"Do you really think that if you act like a tyrant I will bow down to your wishes?"

Slowly, she rose to her knees, got off the bed. It was hard not to notice the pulse ticking madly in his neck.

She brushed by him.

"I know who you are," she said, passing within an inch of his chest.

Snatching the letter written by Dr. Connor off the dresser, she shoved it at him.

"Do you?" His eyes narrowed upon her.

Having an argument with him in sheer underwear

made her feel at a disadvantage. She walked to the wardrobe, opened the door to snatch out her robe.

"You are a blind man," she stated, glancing back over her shoulder.

The look he gave her was heated, but not, she thought, because of the weather or even his rising temper.

"Not so blind," he muttered defensively.

Of course, his blindness had nothing to do with eyesight. His gaze grazed the curve of her hip, swept over the twirl of her hair where it fell down her back, and watched while she shifted her weight from one foot to the other.

She closed the door without taking out the robe. It seemed that she was not at as much of a disadvantage as she believed.

"Good." Crossing the room, she stood in front of him, near enough that looking up she noticed the hair growing at his temples glistening with sweat. "Tell me what you see."

He stared down at her mutely, so she took his hand and placed it on her arm, slid it down to her wrist.

Bending her knee, she lifted her leg, pressed it against his trousers. Her chemise slid along her skin, a whisper of pink lace.

Clasping his other hand, she pressed it on her thigh, drew his fingers down to her knee, then her ankle.

"What do you feel?"

"Seduced."

"No!" Was the man really that unaware? She set her foot on the floor with a thump. "Strength!"

Stooping down she picked up Doctor Connor's letter from the floor where William had dropped it when she shoved it at him.

She uncurled his fingers—she had to since he had

clamped them into fists at his sides—then squeezed the note into his palm.

"This is who I am—not who I used to be at the Lucky Clover, not even who I was when we married. This is who I am now."

A fine way to make her statement would be to open the door, walk away from him without a backward glance. Since she wasn't dressed, she could not do that.

Instead she paced to the window, anchored her arms across her chest.

"Yes, to all appearances." He stood behind her, his hand on her shoulder, but she was determined not to be moved by his touch. "Do you know how happy I am, how proud I am of you? Coming back from where you were— not everyone could. Honey, never think I don't see you. The thing is, what if the first doctor was right? What if he noticed something that Dr. Connor does not see?"

"I'm willing to risk that possibility."

"And I am not."

"I think you should go now, William."

In her heart, she hoped he wouldn't, that he would come to her, wrap his arms about her and tell her she was right, that he saw everything clearly now.

It was what she wished, but it was no surprise to hear the door quietly closing as he left.

Chapter Fifteen

With dinner finished and the sun gone down, William left the mansion to make his rounds on the streets of Tanners Ridge.

If luck was with him, troublemakers both from town and the saloon would be too hot to do anything but fan themselves.

The big tournament was tomorrow. It would begin at noon and end the next day at noon. Twenty-four hours. William figured after only eight hours, men would be tired, quick-tempered and remorseful over money lost.

He'd attempted to hire a deputy to help out so that he wouldn't be called away from the reception but no one wanted the job.

The boardwalk was deserted this time of night with the shops closed and folks in their homes.

Everything was peaceful except for the occasional shout that erupted from the saloon a block over.

Walking past the Parson home, he heard the baby crying and Mrs. Parson singing a lullaby.

It was one of the sweetest sounds he had ever heard. Children were a great blessing.

This afternoon while watching Ivy, Travis and their

little one together, he'd nearly wept. He wasn't sure what the emotion behind the withheld tears was.

Joy at seeing Ivy so happy—watching with longing while Agatha tickled the round little belly—sorrow that he would never tickle the belly of his own child—all these things probably.

And hope—it poked its improbable head up through his angst. He quashed it as soon as he noticed a smile tugging his mouth. Not once but several times since he'd left Agatha in her lacy shift he'd had to deny hope.

He'd accepted the fact that his marriage would be barren of intimacy and children. When he demanded that Agatha marry him, in spite of what he had hoped for, he'd accepted the fact his career would be satisfaction enough.

For the sake of his aspirations he had denied what he wanted and reconciled himself to the reality that he would marry an appropriate woman—be fond of her, but not fall in love with her.

Before he had decided to marry Agatha, he'd believed he would feel respect and affection for his wife and love for his children.

The opposite had happened. He loved his wife and would have no children.

There was nothing he could do about that—the situation was beyond his control.

If there was one thing he disliked, it was a situation out of his control.

So here he was, walking along under a canopy of sparkling stars, feeling like he might spin away like a top wound too tight.

Nothing seemed under his control. Certainly not life—not death.

Yes, he had Dr. Connor's assurance that all would probably be well for Agatha bearing a child.

And yes, she was no longer the weak girl he had felt protective of that stormy night when he'd danced with her at the Lucky Clover. That night he'd felt like he had been holding a porcelain doll in his arms.

One thing he had learned about his wife was that she was not a glass doll.

Damn! All the reassurance in the world would do no good because giving birth was a risky thing to do.

He had no control over it. The only thing he could do was make sure he never put his wife in that sort of danger.

From half a block away, he still heard the baby's faint cry. He remembered seeing Mr. Parson standing in his window looking like he had been given the most precious treasure of his life.

He and Agatha might have that treasure, too. If only he could let go. Be willing to accept that it was all right for things to happen that were beyond his right to control.

All those gamblers at Pete's knew about risks, were eagerly looking forward to them, even though all they would win was money.

He stood to gain far more—or lose it.

A gunshot cracked, ruining the peace of the sleepy town. It might have been fired by someone chasing off coyotes.

More likely it came from the saloon.

He meant to go there anyway. His business with Hilda Brunne was urgent.

It was also tricky. He wondered again whether a crazy woman who had never been charged with a crime could be arrested? Did he have any grounds to put her away? He'd know that if he were a real sheriff, not a politician with a badge pinned to his chest.

Brunne had been deceitful when she'd lured Ivy into

a storm. Left her in the path of stampeding cattle by running off with the only horse.

He couldn't imagine a judge charging her with attempted murder, though. Ivy was the only witness and in the end, she had not been harmed.

For a long time, everyone assumed justice had been served, believing Brunne to be dead.

Crossing the street, he climbed the porch stairs, went inside.

Men were drinking, dallying with women, but not gambling much. Must be saving their luck for tomorrow.

Lounging at a table, his boot propped on it, Pete waggled his cigar, inviting William over.

"What do you want this time? Paying a visit as sheriff I assume?" Pete snuffed out his cigar. Rings of smoke twirled toward the ceiling.

He nodded. "Folks don't like your business."

"Now that's a downright shame. But no matter. Don't see why you and I can't be sociable. Perhaps come to an understanding about how to keep peace in our fine town."

"You don't break the law. We have peace."

"I am a law-abiding man." Lydle traced the rim of a shot glass with his long, slender finger. "But things do happen that are beyond my control. I'm sure you understand. I do my best but sometimes when men drink, things happen."

"I heard a gunshot. Sounded like it came from here."

"Might have. Like I said, things do happen. What I suggest is monetary compensation. You hear a noise and ignore it, I give you money every week."

"No thanks."

"Suit yourself, then." Lifting his leg off the table he thumped it on the floor then slid a glance at a burly-looking man standing at the bar. The patch over his eye made him seem like a pirate. Some sort of understanding passed between them. He didn't have to be a lifelong sheriff to understand the saber rattling going on. "Have a drink, play some cards. Oh, wait… I bet you'd like a woman."

"That's what I came for."

Lydle's brows shot up. The curve of his smile brought to mind a snake's unhurried, sinuous slither.

With a flick of his fingers he summoned a bareshouldered harlot standing beside the man with the eye patch.

"Send out Hilda Brunne," William said.

That made Lydle laugh, slap his open palm on the table.

"She's the one I want."

"Ain't here. She went out."

"Where to?"

"Couldn't say, but don't go getting any ideas about finding her and cheating me of my money. My women belong to me. Even that dried-out old hag is under my protection—so to speak. The Palace does not give anything away for free."

Whether the man was telling the truth or not about Brunne going out was a coin toss.

With the odds even, he'd better get home.

William arrived home to find the guests who were staying in the mansion gathered in the ballroom.

The large space had been used for the town's Christmas gatherings, for weddings or any event that required a big, festive room.

This evening Mother had gathered her guests for a performance by the orchestra she'd hired for the reception.

After the dirty feeling he had leaving the saloon, he

wouldn't mind sitting and listening to the orchestra, letting beautiful melodies wash away the ugliness.

First he had to check the backyard, make sure that Brunne was not in hiding in the shrubbery or peeking in windows. It was unlikely, with so many people who might see her, but he did need to satisfy himself.

It turned out there was only one person in the yard.

Agatha.

She sat on the wood dance floor with her back toward him. Her legs were folded under her while she swayed slightly to the music drifting out of the open ballroom doors.

Eyes closed, she tilted her face toward the star-spangled sky. Was she seeing something behind her eyelids that was more wondrous than the show overhead?

It was hard to imagine what that could be until it occurred to him that he was not looking at the sky, either.

Nothing in that moment could be as enchanting as watching the play of lamplight in her hair. She'd left it loose with only a green ribbon to tie the wavy mass at her nape.

Not wanting to disturb her peace like he had earlier in the day when he'd invaded her bedroom and given her good cause to be angry with him, he approached the dance floor silently.

After the women he'd seen at the saloon, she was a cleansing breath, the same way the music was. The one and only thing he wanted—needed desperately, was to stand and watch her upturned face while she swayed to the melody.

Until she lifted her hand, that was. It was as though an invisible partner had asked her to dance. She smiled, accepting the invitation.

All of a sudden, watching was not enough.

Stepping silently onto the dance floor, he clasped her fingers. Her eyes opened, growing round in surprise.

"Good evening, Miss Magee," he said the same as he had the night of the barbecue at the Lucky Clover when he'd asked Ivy's weakling sister for a dance. "You look fetching this evening."

Funny how the moment came back to his mind so clearly. He heard the drum of rain on the roof and the distant rumble of thunder. He recalled how her eyes suddenly sparkled when he spoke to her. He remembered the way she'd resisted for a moment but then given herself to him in trust.

Like that night, the ghost of a tremor shook her hand when he touched her.

"I believe this dance was meant for us."

He had felt tenderness for her even then. His intention that night had been to bring a moment of joy into a life that seemed subdued.

He'd promised that he would not let her fall.

Tonight, she rose gracefully from the floor, poetry in motion, really. She did not need to grip his hand for leverage or balance.

In spite of the fact that she had every right to be angry with him for the way he had acted earlier, she smiled.

In the flash of a second, as quickly as the star that just shot across the sky, he saw the truth—accepted it deep in his heart.

Agatha Marigold Magee, the girl he had danced with that night, was a different person than Agatha Marigold English.

Or rather, she was the same, but the lovely woman she had been meant to be had been suppressed, forced into submission by the very one who should have nurtured her.

The Agatha he held in his arms now was free. He would like to think he had something to do with that, but he hadn't.

It had been all her from the time she took her first step in order to please her sister, to the moment she walked away from the security of home, to right now, when she stepped into his arms, smiling and self-assured.

"I'm sorry," he whispered against her hair and tugged her tight to his chest. Clearly, she held no grudge but the words needed to be said. She deserved to hear them.

"Forgiven."

Just like that she put his high-handedness behind her. No lingering resentment, no wanting to make him grovel. She just forgave him.

He buried his face into the side of her neck. "I never expected you."

"I always dreamed of you."

He felt the swish of her skirts brush his boots when he twirled her slowly about the dance floor, breathed deeply of the fragrance of roses in her hair.

Looking up he saw his mother standing in the doorway, smiling. She blew him a kiss, turned and went back to her guests.

"Will you walk with me?" He had some things to say and wanted privacy for it.

He led her to the stream that ran through the yard on the other side of the fence.

It was a pretty place during the day, but magical at night.

"It sounds refreshing." She touched his arm while he led her down the bank.

"Sure does, especially right now."

Agatha let go of his arm and sat beside the water.

"Can you imagine the coolness running between your toes? I'm taking off my shoes."

His mind burst to life imagining things that might happen in this private spot.

Gathering her skirt into her lap, she bent to roll down her stockings.

As soon as her feet slid into the water she sighed, twice.

Settling down beside her, he found it hard not to imagine water lapping at more than his wife's feet.

She leaned back on her arms, gazing up. "It looks beautiful with the stars peeking in and out of the branches. And the way the leaves rustle together, it's so peaceful I could drift off to sleep."

She was right. It was peaceful, with nature's song melding with music from the house, floating across the water and among the branches.

Since he could think of no casual way to bring up what he wanted to say he blurted out, "I read Dr. Connor's letter."

He wasn't sure what he had expected her to say, but it wasn't nothing. She glanced at him without a frown, without a smile, then lay back on the wild grass. Folding her hands across her ribs, she looked up at the leaves twisting in the warm breeze.

A raccoon wandering by on the opposite bank in search of fish stopped to look at them. He washed his hands in the stream them scurried through the brush, going further upstream.

"You did also speak with him."

Easing down on his elbow, he lay his hand across her ribs, feeling the rise and fall of her breathing.

"Yes. But it was reading the letter a dozen times that made me realize something."

"That I'm no more at risk than any other woman?"

He shook his head. As he moved his hand up, his finger skimmed the swell of her breast. He twisted the pearl button on her blouse. She was dressed casually for an evening at home. He could strip her bare, lay her down in the cool water without much effort.

He ought to do it. The question was, would she allow it, given that he had spent their brief marriage forbidding a physical bond with her?

"Only God knows that. No, what I discovered was about myself." The button was smooth. It slipped open easily.

"I'm fascinated. What did you discover?"

That he liked pearl buttons. The rest of them slid open to her waist with a whisper.

"Some things are beyond my control." He drew the blouse from the waistband of her skirt and found that she had not worn a corset tonight.

She sat up, shrugged out of the blouse. "Some things are not."

While he lay gazing up at her she whisked her camisole off.

"But I wonder if some things are in my control," she murmured while she slowly flipped open the buttons on his shirt.

"Yes." Everything was in her control. It was what he wanted to tell her, but more eloquently. The problem was, watching her undress stole his ability to put words together.

The desire to reach up and cup her, run his palm over her pink nipples made his hands ache. He would not do it until he'd had his say.

A damn hard thing to do when emotion squeezed his throat until it ached.

"It's too hot," she whispered, with a sidelong glance at the water.

"I do believe that's under our control."

With a quick grin she stood, shimmed out of her skirt and everything else.

Standing naked in the stream, she bent over, scooped up a handful of water then dribbled it down her neck, her chest. It ran in rivulets over her firm belly.

She had tried to show him that she was fit, forced him to touch her arms and legs. But his mind had been closed to accepting the fact.

If he had been blind to her earlier, it was impossible to be so now.

Stooping once more she caught up another handful of water, dribbled it on her head then rose with ease. She kicked up a spray of water with her toes. Cool sprinkles hit his face.

Laughing, he shed his clothes, dashed into the stream splashing, kicking up waves of water at her.

Catching her about the waist he picked her up and spun her around. Damp hair tickled his nose. Her smooth, round backside slid against his belly when she wriggled and kicked, pretending she wanted to get loose. His grip about her waist slipped up. He felt the ripple of her ribs. The weight of her breasts jiggled on top of his arms, tickling the coarse hair that grew there.

By playing in the water, they did have some control over the heat on the surface of their skin.

Inside, he felt like a simmering teapot ready to scream.

Reluctantly, he set her feet back into the stream, but it was hard to quit laughing because—because it felt so damn good.

On the other side of the fence was a mad woman, a

gambling tournament, a town with no real sheriff and his mother's perfect party.

He'd rather stand in the stream, shaking with laughter in the arms of a naked woman—his naked woman.

She turned, flung her arms about his middle.

"I—I—can't stop—giggling. I don't even—know what's so funny."

"Me, either, but I think we should stand here just like this until we figure it out."

He pressed her back with open fingers, slid them down the firm dip of her waist, the flare of her hips.

If she had been frail at one time she was no longer.

"I truly cannot remember when I've had such a good time," he said, slowly gaining control over the hilarity of nothing. Although, he didn't really want to.

At the same time he noticed Agatha's giggles slowing.

She tipped her face up to him. He traced the water drops on her face with one finger, down her nose, and circled her cheeks then the curve of her smile.

"I want to tell you something, Agatha."

"All right." She kissed his finger then sat down in the slow-running stream, cross-legged. "I need to cool off while you do."

He did the same, his knees brushing hers. It did not make him cool off any. In fact he thought it might be a very long time before he did—years, decades, never maybe.

"That thing I discovered about myself—that I cannot be in control of everything. Well, I haven't the right to think I can. Things will happen in life. Because of them I might grieve or I might laugh. I can't do anything about that. But I can love. That's the one thing I can do, Agatha."

He reached across, cupped her cheek. Maybe she would

think the moisture gathering in his eyes was water from splashing, but if she did not, he didn't care.

"I can love you. I do love you."

"That's all I want."

"Will you come to my bedroom?"

"Well—it's a long walk and Mrs. Bea says—"

Chapter Sixteen

"Please, honey, don't start me laughing again."

William went up on his hands and knees, shifted toward her...over her. He brought to mind a sleek and powerful predator. For all that she leaned backward, she would not flee from him.

"But she has some interesting ideas."

Water rushed over her chest, down her belly—between her legs—tickling and caressing. It was impossible not to picture some of those ideas in her mind.

William lowered himself until his mouth hovered over her only inches away. Her heart beat triple time wondering what he was going to do with it. Nip? Lick? Caress?

"What do you want from our marriage?"

This was too big a question to answer with newly awakened sensations demanding her utter and complete attention.

Too bad—or luckily—sitting up did not dispel them. Corralling thoughts was not possible, but her heart spoke up, quite loudly.

"Fun." It was the very thing that had been lacking in her life.

"Fun?" He sat back on his heels, brows arched. Perhaps he had been expecting something more profound.

"Exactly."

Now it was her turn to play the predator. She touched his shoulder, crawled over him until he had no choice to lie back in the water. She watched it wash over his strong, muscled body. Did it caress him with cool, lusty fingers the way it had done to her?

"I want to wake up in the morning to a kiss and a smile. I want to see you in a hallway and touch you in passing. At the end of the day I want to lie beside you and hear the funny things that happened to you, laugh over them."

Lowering herself, she let her breasts brush his chest, felt the masculine hairs catch her nipples when the current gently brushed them across his skin.

"Fun, William. It's what I've been missing all my life."

This time he was the one to scoot to a sitting position, but he set her on top of his lap. She felt his intentions toward her against her nether cheek.

"For me, too." He nuzzled her neck with kisses. "For years all I've thought about was what people would think of me. How would they vote if I cursed in public, or laughed too loud or didn't laugh at all? If I acted inappropriate in any way, how would they vote? It's why I forced you to marry me."

"I wasn't forced. Just so you know, I chose to do it."

"Did you? I'm glad." Leaning forward, he lowered his head to the tip of her breast, nipped and suckled it. "From now on, my sweet wife, let's have fun."

All of a sudden he stood up, swept her up with him and carried her to the bank.

"I thought that is what we were doing."

"It is." He grinned and set her down. Even in the dark she saw a twinkle flash in his eye. "Lift up your arms."

She did. He yanked her camisole back over her head, quickly kissing each breast before he tucked them out of sight.

He held the bloomers for her to step into. While he pulled them over her thighs, he stroked and caressed them. Just before he slid them over her hips, he stopped, looked her in the eye and smiled. Then he touched her where she had never been touched—caressed, petted— then stepped away to yank on his pants.

"Fun?" His brows arched over his grin.

All she could do was nod because for some reason when he touched her there, he'd stolen her voice.

Stooping, he gathered the rest of their clothes and tucked them under his arm.

"Let's go," he said.

"Where?"

He grabbed her hand, leading her toward the gate in the fence.

"To our bedroom. I won't take you among the weeds."

"But we have to cross the yard—we aren't dressed."

He winked, drew the gate open. "We'll have to be quick. They're still in the ballroom."

"We should get dressed first."

"You wanted fun? This is fun."

"It's daring."

"Fun." It only took the slightest yank of her hand to convince her it was true.

"Let's go!" She felt laughter building in her chest again but held it back lest anyone hear.

Hand in hand they dashed across the yard, she in her camisole and bloomers, William bare-chested with a bundle of clothes tucked under his arm.

Grass sprung up between her toes, warm air rushed past her ears. Halfway across, someone noticed them. Bert Warble's mouth sagged open to his collar.

William nodded, laughed out loud, then hurried her past the rose garden and into the house through the kitchen.

There was someone standing at the counter. Luckily it was only Mrs. Bea who turned with a wink then went back to whatever she was placing on a tray.

William opened his bedroom door, winded. From exertion, laughter, or lust, he couldn't tell which—probably all.

Shutting the door with his bare foot, he hustled Agatha across the room with both arms clenched about her waist.

In a leap he launched them both upon the bed.

"Finally where you belong, Mrs. English. I hope you approve."

He rolled from on top of her, keeping her hand and bringing it to his lips.

"Oh, I do." She turned on her side, touched his chest and traced the shape of a heart just under his throat.

"Is my bed good enough to meet Mrs. Bea's requirements?"

"I think so." She patted the mattress with the palm of her hand. We will need to try it out in order to be sure."

He caught her face in his hands and at the same time rolled on top of her.

His fingers trembled imperceptibly when he gathered her camisole in his hands then eased it over her head and arms.

When she lifted her hips and allowed him the right to slide off her drawers, he was like a beast ready to roar in triumph. She might have removed them herself, but because she hadn't, it made him feel like he was well and truly claiming his mate.

The beast wanted to take her quickly, with wild intensity, but now that she was naked beneath him, he wanted to savor the moment.

He sat up, shucked out of his pants then lay on top of her again.

Touching his lips to her chest, he felt her heartbeat under his mouth. He trailed kisses down her ribs, over her belly. He felt a quiver thrum under her skin. Felt his own heart tremble.

Here was where his children would begin life. Perhaps one would begin tonight. The power of what they were about to do stole his breath. If it did happen, he would rejoice at the blessing.

No matter what came later, he would love, he would live.

"I do love you," he whispered the words up her body.

"I love you, William."

He nudged her thighs apart with his knee. She whispered his name when he pressed inside her, claimed her with tenderness—with his heart bursting.

She arched her neck, her back, cried out. He plunged deeply, this time letting the wildness, the primal beast inside of him lead the way.

When the world became solid, when his body cooled, he went up on an elbow to peer down at her face.

He's always thought her pretty, but now? Innocent, seductive loveliness—she touched his soul with her beauty.

Her fast, heavy breathing slowed to a bare rise of her chest. He wondered if she might have drifted into a pleasure doze.

He took the moment to appreciate the way her lashes

curled at the tips, the way her fair skin had become dotted with freckles. The way her pink mouth tipped up at both corners.

This woman was his to cherish and protect, but discreetly, very discreetly.

"I never expected you, Agatha. Not even in my dreams." He traced the curve of her eyebrow with his finger, kissed her mouth lightly.

"No? I dreamed of you all the time."

Ah, not asleep, then.

"I hope I lived up to your dreams, and to Mrs. Bea's expectations."

"It's clear that she didn't tell me everything."

She caught his hair, drew his mouth down for a kiss.

"Oh, what did she miss?"

"The part about my heart swelling with love so strong I thought it might burst open."

"Ah, well that's because only I can show you that. And I will, every day for the rest of our lives."

In fact, he decided, drawing his hand up the length of her thigh, he was going to show her again—right now.

The next morning Agatha went to the ridge, but not to run. Not even to watch the horses frolicking below.

With her skirt spread out like a blanket on the ground, she gazed at the sweet face of Clara Rose Murphy.

"You sure have changed, little miss." She tickled Clara's rosebud-pink cheek.

"So have you," Ivy said, standing nearby and watching the horses run. "I was so worried when you left home. Travis had to tie me to the bed to keep me from fetching you home."

"That must have been interesting."

"Now that you're a married woman, I guess I can tell you it was."

Ivy sat beside her, leaned down and nuzzled her baby's hair.

Someday, with luck and God's blessing, Agatha would do that to her own child. After last night, that day might not be too far off.

"Even though I was worried, I'd have been wrong to wrangle you back. You don't look much like the Agatha who left to go adventuring."

"Looking for life more than adventuring. Truly, that old Agatha seems like someone else."

"I do admire you—" Clara began to fuss and shove her hand into her mouth. "Reckon she's hungry."

Ivy freed her blouse from her riding pants and set the baby to her breast.

Her sister liked to dress with the least restriction possible to her person. In this they were different. Agatha liked feeling pretty in frills and bouncy ruffles. If it came at the price of a pinching corset, she didn't mind.

"Like I started to say, I admire you, sister. You've had to scrap and fight for your freedom. That old Brunne had you under her boot heel." Ivy shook her head, her lips thinned to a grim line. "I don't mind saying, I'm glad she's dead."

And dead she would stay to Ivy. The very last thing Agatha wanted was for Ivy to encounter the woman who'd tried to kill her.

"You were the one. If it weren't for you—I hate to think—"

All of a sudden she was overwhelmed, horrified at what her life would be like now if Ivy had decided not to come home and take over the Lucky Clover.

William would still be a dream. A dream she would

only recall during moments of lucidity, when the drug had worn off.

Ivy touched her cheek, smiled. "Where you are now is all of your own doing. You look as happy as a lark in a clear blue sky."

"Guess I am. And more than grateful you turned William down."

"I had to, I reckon, since I was flat-out in love with Travis. I'm bustin' with happiness for the both of you." Ivy set Clara to her other breast. "Bill's a lucky man."

"He will be tonight, after the party's over." It was a wonderful thing to be able to say that to her sister and not even blush.

"Reckon he'll need some luck after spending the day keeping peace at the gambling tournament." Clara's breathing turned to contented coos. Ivy removed her from the breast and set her over her shoulder for burping. "Wouldn't mind giving my luck a try."

No! That was the last place her sister should go.

"It's a wicked place, Ivy. You ought to stay clear of it. Besides, William will forbid you to set foot in there."

"He still thinks he's the boss of everything?"

"Not everything." She took the baby while Ivy put her clothes back in order. "But he is in charge of keeping peace around here. It will make things easier on him if you don't go to Pete's Palace."

It would make it easier on him if Agatha didn't go, either, but of course, she had to.

Tonight, she would use the distraction of the party to sneak away then use the distraction of the gambling tournament to face her tormentor.

She would be gone and back so quickly that William would never miss her.

"I'll stay home. Sure would have enjoyed the challenge of outwitting those gaming men, though."

Agatha stood in the foyer between her mother-in-law and her husband, greeting guests as they came in the front door.

Perhaps being bolstered between the two of them made her not as nervous as she might have been.

Even so, shaking the hands of the first five guests to arrive made her feel sick to her stomach. Had William and Victoria not been there she might have run back upstairs.

It didn't matter that she wore the most beautiful gown she had ever seen. She still wondered what they thought of her. In their eyes did the blue ruffle fluttering on the bodice make her look too daring—too shy? Did the sweet bustle on the back of the dress make her look fashionable or overdone?

Did her smile look welcoming or like she wanted them to turn around and go home? Which she wouldn't mind horribly if they did.

Things changed a bit by the time the tenth guest arrived. The woman told her she looked lovely and seemed sincere in the compliment. Agatha began to feel comfortable with the fluff of the ruffle on her chest, the sway of the bustle.

Somehow, after half an hour of welcoming guests, she no longer hoped they would leave.

When the time came to go into the parlor and mingle with them, she held to William's sleeve without her hands sweating.

She remembered names. Which gentleman was married to which lady. Who lived in Cheyenne and who had come from places even farther away to celebrate her marriage.

After an hour, William kissed her on the cheek then walked away to speak with a group of men in the corner. Every minute or so he glanced at her, no doubt checking to see how she was holding up.

To her complete surprise, she was holding up fine. She laughed with a Miss Brown and a Mrs. Glenbye. A nervous laugh at first, she had to admit, but when Mrs. French, an old woman with lines on her face etched by a lifetime of laughter, told her a joke meant only for married ladies and widows, Agatha's laugh was genuine.

By the time William detached from the men and returned to her she felt warm and not jittery.

"You look like the perfect hostess. How are you feeling?"

"It's your mother who is the hostess, I'm just speaking with people."

He hadn't come to her empty-handed. She was glad when he pressed a glass of something pink and bubbly in her fingers.

"Are you feeling all right? Would you like some time alone? Mother would understand."

Time alone was exactly what she needed, but not for the reason he thought—and she didn't need it yet.

"It's the strangest thing." She glanced around the room then back into his eyes.

He leaned down and kissed her cheek. "What is the strangest thing?"

"It's just that half of the people in this room no longer feel like strangers, they feel like friends. Did you know that the Berdmans traveled three days to get here?"

"They've been friends of my mother's since before I was born. Looks like they are friends of yours, too."

"Yes they are—and Mrs. French."

William laughed quietly. "Did she tell you the joke about—" he whispered in her ear, repeating it word for word.

"You know it well."

"Oh, I've heard it from my mother. Any married lady that Mrs. French counts as a friend will hear it at every gathering. Look, she's sent Dove and Lark off to fetch punch. She's telling the joke to Mrs. Norman."

"It's a relief to know she counts me as a friend. I wonder if, maybe, I might make it as a politician's wife after all."

"There's every indication. But will it make you happy?"

"I could not be any happier, no matter if you become governor or decide to go back to the ranch and become a cowhand.

"Do you mind if I take a few moments alone after dinner? Just to refresh before the dancing?"

"I'll help you refresh," he suggested with a lopsided grin.

"You'll leave me boneless, rather."

The other side of his grin lit up. A part of her wanted to run upstairs with him now, push him down on the bed and leap upon him, see if Mrs. French's joke would work in real life.

Before she could wonder further about it, Mr. and Mrs. Watkins walked up, going on about what a lovely couple they made and how much in love they looked.

It was an odd thing when an event she dreaded was about to become a cherished memory.

A crowd of gamblers, mostly men but a few women among them, gathered on the front porch of Pete's Palace. A dozen more escaped the heat by standing about on the boardwalk.

Nodding and smiling in order to give the appearance of being one of them, Agatha wove her way down the boardwalk toward the rear of the saloon.

So far, it seemed that she would have an easier time sneaking inside than she had last time. With so many people mulling about no one paid attention to one more.

Rounding the corner, she found another group of people gathered near the back door to the kitchen.

This time she would not have to crawl under the back porch steps.

She would not have, even at the risk of being noticed. Her fluffy blue gown was far too lovely to become streaked with dirt and mysterious smelly things.

If she returned home smelling ripe, William would know where she had been. She would rather he didn't find that out since it would only make him worry. If he worried, he might forbid her to do things in the future that she wanted to do.

With any luck, she would confront Hilda Brunne and be home before her husband noticed.

And confront her she must. Hilda had to be made to understand that Agatha was no longer a weakling to be controlled. Until she did that, the demented woman would always be hiding in the shadows, waiting for her chance to make things the way they used to be.

The problem was, could someone in her mental state be convinced of anything?

In the event that she could not be convinced, she would call William. With a badge pinned on his shirt, he could do things she was unable to.

"It's hot enough to toast bread on my hat," she heard one man declare as she passed by the kitchen.

"It's hot enough to wilt a straight flush right out of my fingers." A sudden gust of wind blew the hat off of the head of the man speaking, tumbled it away into the dark.

It might be a blister outside but entering the rear of the saloon she found the heat even more smothering.

Stepping quietly along the hallway, she listened to muted conversations seeping through the walls.

From what she was hearing, she could tell that some of the rooms had been set up with tables allowing for more gambling space.

Clearly, some remained for the purpose of paid pleasure.

Tonight the private hallway was dimly lit with lanterns set thirty feet apart.

She was forced to maneuver around boxes of whiskey, beer and other alcohol stored in the hallway.

Stopping, she put her ear to a door of a room that had neither gambling nor pleasure sounds coming from it.

"Here there, miss!" A gangly adolescent stepped into the hallway from one of the rooms a few doors down. "Only employees back here."

"I lost my way."

The young man stooped, filled a lantern with kerosene then set the container beside the lantern.

"I'd show you the way out," he offered while lifting a case labeled Bourbon. "But Pete's got us all busy. Wouldn't want to be found out dawdling. Just follow the lanterns. You'll find your way back."

"Wait!" she called before he closed the door. "I was looking for someone when I became lost—an old woman who sells calming medicine for ladies."

"She sells it? Pete won't like it if he doesn't get some of the money."

"Will I find her back here? I hate to walk all the way

around—have to make my way through those men. They can be rather rough."

He studied her for a moment, then inclined his head. "Three doors down. Just make sure you leave right away after—and let her know to give Pete his share."

There was nothing she would like better than to give Pete Lydle his share but couldn't imagine how to go about it.

On tiptoe she walked to the third door, put her ear to the wood and listened.

Someone was weeping.

"Open your mouth, girl. Mr. Lydle is tired of your prissiness. What's so special about you that you can't serve the men like the others do?"

The familiar voice hissed through her, the insistent tone a snake coiling around her chest, squeezing the breath out of her.

"No!" the young voice sobbed. "Don't make me drink it."

"Now, now, I know what's best for you. Mr. Pete wants you to be nice to his gentlemen. Sweet and docile, not bite them, you wicked child. Now open your mouth."

Docile. Run away and be docile. It was the reasonable thing to do.

But the girl began to weep. There was the slap of a palm on soft skin.

"Spit it out all you want to. I've got more."

Agatha turned the doorknob. It was locked. She banged on the wood, her fist clamped in anger.

"Don't be so impatient," Mrs. Brunne's voice snapped. "If you want Sweet Blossom now you'd better watch out for your wil—"

The door jerked open.

"It's you!" Hilda Brunne snagged the sleeve of her

dress and dragged her inside. Whatever had happened to her, the strength that Agatha remembered her having hadn't lessened. "I wonder what took you so long. You knew I was here, my arms aching for the want of you, Maggie. You should not have made me wait."

The musicians picked up their instruments, began the first piece of music. Poor fellows had to be sweating under their jackets.

William shed his an hour ago, the moment dinner was finished. He'd removed his jacket and put the sheriff's badge in his pocket.

The last thing he wanted to do was steal away from his reception and go to the saloon.

But he was sheriff, as well as a husband. Hilda Brunne had to be dealt with. Not only for Agatha's sake, but now for Ivy's and Clara's.

If the crazed woman saw her babies in adult women, what might she believe of Clara Rose when she learned of her—which she would.

Brunne might look like a bent and shriveled crone, but the image of vulnerability made her even more dangerous.

Standing on the porch, he scanned the crowd below looking for Agatha. He thought it would be a good idea to dance with her so that when he left, she would assume he was simply out of sight among the guests.

If she suspected he had gone after Brunne, she would insist on going with him. That was something he would not allow. No matter if she called him a bully or worse, she was not getting near the woman who had enslaved her.

He hadn't seen Agatha in the house. Couldn't see her among the guests in the yard, either. She would be impossible to miss, the way she looked like an angel in blue froth skimming over the ground.

If he lived to be an absentminded old man, he would never forget the way she looked tonight.

She wasn't in the yard, but he hadn't seen Ivy, either. No doubt they were huddled in a quiet corner, laughing over things that sisters laughed over.

Seeing his mother below, he went down the steps and crossed the grass to where she stood beside the dance floor, watching her guests and tapping her foot.

He kissed her cheek. "This might be your best party yet."

"Of course. It's for you and my sweet daughter."

"If you see Agatha, will you tell her I'm looking for her?"

Only a small lie since he had been looking for her, but it was one that would prevent Agatha from believing he had gone anywhere.

"Tell her yourself, dear. She was on the front porch no more than a quarter of an hour ago."

Something about that was wrong, but blamed if he knew why. No doubt Agatha and Ivy simply found it a quiet place to visit. It made sense, but the itch in his belly didn't ease.

"Was she alone?"

"Yes, I believe she was."

Rushing across the house he burst onto the porch to find it empty.

Where was Agatha? Ivy was nowhere to be found. Something was not right.

They might be together. But where?

The moment that his boot turned to go back inside, he recalled that Agatha had wanted time alone after dinner.

In his gut he knew she was not resting in their bedroom. That had been an excuse to keep him from looking for her.

Hell, he ought to know since he'd also made up a story to cover his absence.

Agatha had gone to face Brunne alone. She had a fifteen-minute head start on him.

Chapter Seventeen

Rushing past Brunne, Agatha knelt beside the girl lying on the bed. And really that was all she was—probably no more than sixteen years old.

"Are you hurt?"

"Some, but…" The girl turned her inner arm toward Agatha. It was bruised above the elbow. "This is what shows."

"How old are you?" She was too thin. Her shift sagged, revealing a bony shoulder.

"Old enough for my ma to think she could sell me off to Pete."

Hilda clamped her hand hard on the back of Agatha's neck, her fingers biting.

Agatha squeezed her wrist, slung the hand away then stood up. She looked down on Brunne. That was not how she remembered it being. As she recalled, her nurse had always glowered down at her.

"Is this how you greet your mother?"

The girl tugged on the back of Agatha's gown. "Don't rile her, she's crazy as a loon."

"We thought you were dead. How—?" Agatha had so many things to say to the woman but this question pressed forward.

"A tinker man found me and patched me up as best he knew. The fool didn't know much. You see how he left me bound to this cane. Of course, I blame it all on your sister, the devil take her as I'm sure he did."

"Whatever happened to you was of your own doing." Perhaps if Agatha spoke reason, reminded Hilda of the truth, she would be able to convince the woman to leave her alone. "Ivy's not to blame for any of it. You're the one who left her to die."

"I did." Her smile lifted in a rare show of teeth. One in front was broken. It hadn't been the last time she had seen her. "Because she took Maggie and Bethy. She was trying to take you, too. Silly girl that you are, you never saw it. I had good reason to trick her into coming out in the storm. I meant to lock her away—probably to die. I'd not have gone back to give her food or water. That would have been foolish of me. Doesn't matter. She deserved what happened to her. I always knew Bethy would be the evil one of my twins—there's always an evil one."

"Ivy is not Bethy."

"I didn't mind a bit when she got trampled in the stampede."

If Hilda thought Ivy was dead, so much the better.

"We minded. We missed her, Mrs. Brunne."

The woman lifted her cane and struck Agatha on the backside. Layers of fabric prevented the blow from causing pain, but still, the strength of the swing was surprising.

"You will call me Mother."

Time and adversity had not been a friend to Hilda Brunne. It had only made her more insane.

As much as Agatha wanted to convince her former nurse that she was not the submissive girl she had tried to make her, there was one thing more urgent at the moment.

Getting the young woman cowering on the bed to safety.

Turning, she touched the girl's hand, picked it up and held it tight. The poor thing was trembling badly.

Kneeling beside her, Agatha whispered in her ear. "The door's no longer locked. I'll keep the old woman distracted long enough for you to run."

She shook her head, tangled black hair shimmying about her face.

"What are you saying to her?" Brunne demanded.

"I'm convincing her to take her medicine, Mother."

"I can't go." The girl yanked her hand away. "I belong to Pete. All us girls do. If I run, he'll come after me."

"Trust me. I'll hide you. My husband is the mayor and the sheriff."

"Yes, I know who you are. I've watched you from my window. Pete's got a sore spot when it comes to your man. I've heard him talking. Mr. English needs to watch out."

"What's that?" Hilda's cane struck the floor.

"It's for your own good, I promise," Agatha said in a louder voice. Then back to a whisper, "Run to the mansion. Find Mr. English or his mother. They'll protect you."

"You don't convince! You ought to know that. You just pour it down the harlot's throat."

Brunne nudged Agatha aside with a whack of her cane.

The old witch must have big pockets filled with laudanum bottles because she seemed to produce one from nowhere.

"Let me, Mother Brunne. I know how." She took the vial of poison, hating the way the blue glass felt so smooth and seductive in her fingers—so feared, so hated.

"Run. Now!"

In one move, Agatha turned, shoved the old woman backward and threw the bottle against the wall.

Glass shattered, tinkled on the floor. The door slammed against the bed in the wake of the girl's flight.

Agatha's heart sank. The girl ran toward the casino, not toward the back hallway and freedom.

"You did that." Brunne shrugged from her place on the floor. "I tried to help her but you—you've insured her a good beating. Someone will pay Pete extra for the pleasure of bringing that willful child to heel."

If only she had run to the mansion! Agatha should have gone with her, made sure she made it to safety.

She could not have gone, though. She was not finished here. Ivy and Clara's safety depended upon convincing Hilda Brunne to go away for good.

"You naughty, naughty girl!" Brunne launched to her feet quicker than her crippled-looking body would account for.

Pure wickedness must be what powered her.

"What will I do with you?"

Slap, slap, slap went her cane across the floor. Clearly the sharp sound was meant to intimidate Agatha.

"Not a single thing." The truth was, she did feel intimidated. A bigger truth was, she did not feel like running.

"As willful as you always were, I see."

Clearly, Hilda Brunne did not perceive reality. Agatha had never been willful. Not until Ivy came home and freed her.

"Sit on the bed, you ungrateful wretch. I'll give you your medicine. Everything will be as it was."

"You need to understand that you no longer have the power to make me do anything."

"And take off that dress. It's far too cheerful. It doesn't suit a girl like you."

"This dress is exactly who I am. Happy—and fluffy—

fun! I've changed since you knew me. I will not allow you to drug me again."

"I blame it on that man. You thought he was your prince and all the while he wanted to marry your sister. I've told you over and over he is worthless. I thought your silly brain understood. You are not good enough for him—not for any man." Brunne tapped her cane on the floor, slowly—no more than a light click. "But no mind, he doesn't matter."

"He's my husband. He will always matter."

"A man will always betray you in the end. Trust your mother, Agatha. There is no one else you can trust." The cane tapped harder, faster.

"The fact is, I can trust everyone but you!"

"He's filled your head with lies. I knew he would."

"He loves me—Ivy love—loved me."

"Oh, my, you have grown willful. I'll have to punish you."

Brunne swung the cane at her head. Agatha ducked, felt a whoosh of air skim across the top of her hair.

Before she could straighten, Brunne landed a heavy blow on her back. The air rushed out of her lungs. She struggled to catch a breath.

"Who is going to protect you, now? Your husband?"

"I am."

The scent of kerosene lanterns drifted in the open door along with Ivy, her yellow skirt settling about her in a swirl of outrage.

"Put down the cane, you low-down, mad dog."

"Bethy? I thought I killed you. I never meant to—" Brunne blinked, stared, then her eyes flew wide open. "Ivy Magee! I did mean to kill you."

"Gull-durned lunatic."

"Ivy!" Agatha rushed forward, took her sister's elbow

and tried to steer her back out the door. "You shouldn't be here."

"Here I am, though." And clearly here she would stay.

"I knew you were up to something, sister. Nearly smelt it." Ivy reached for Brunne's cane but got smacked on the hand. "So I followed you."

"Stop talking to my girl, luring her away from me again."

"I'm not your girl. Look at me!" Lunacy blazing in her eyes, Hilda struck out at her, the same way she had at Ivy. Agatha caught the tip of the cane, held tight to it. "Your girl was weak-hearted and frightened of you. Is that who you see now?"

"You were a sweet baby, Maggie. I'd have drowned Bethy if I knew she would turn you on me."

"Must be why your husband took your babies away," Ivy spat.

Suddenly enraged, Brunne yanked the cane from Agatha's grasp. She slammed it against Ivy's chest.

Grasping her breasts, her sister went down on her knees.

"That little thump shouldn't have hurt so much—unless? You're feeding. I wonder..."

Agatha leapt for Brunne's back, but Brunne turned. Taking the brunt of the fall on her shoulder, Agatha sat up, the pain sharp as a hot blade.

Brunne's lips peeled back from her teeth. "You've taken my Maggie to your own breast!"

"My teats are as dry as yours, you old hag."

"Where have you taken my baby?" Brunne screeched.

She dropped the cane, curled her fingers into claws, raking at Ivy with long, pointed fingernails.

Agatha stooped to pick up the cane but Hilda stomped on her hand.

Momentarily, she focused her attention on Agatha. "You are no longer my child. I disown you."

In that instant, Ivy lunged for Brunne's skirt and yanked it in an attempt to knock her off balance.

She and Ivy should have had no trouble overpowering Brunne, but being crazed with hate gave the old woman unusual strength.

Hate was not her sole advantage, as it turned out. Her large pocket contained more than laudanum.

She drew out a wicked-looking knife. Sliced the air near Ivy's face.

"Put it down, Mother. If you kill Ivy and go to jail, what will I do?" Agatha eased slowly to her feet. "You are the only one I can trust, remember?"

"Sweet Agatha, come to me, child. We'll be together and your sister can go home." Apparently she had forgotten baby Maggie, kidnapped to Ivy's breasts.

"You must give me the knife. I'll be too overwrought to take my medicine if you don't."

"Here, my obedient child." Brunne held out her arms. "I'll give you the knife and the medicine."

"No!" Ivy warned. "Don't trust her. Back away!"

Ivy scrambled to her feet but Agatha had already entered the spider's web.

Brunne lifted the knife to her throat. She felt the sting when the blade pricked the pulse in her vein.

"You must think I'm mad, Agatha English, if you think I'll believe your pretty words." From the corner of her eye Agatha watched a pearl of red drip down the blade. "You told me to look at you? Well, I did. You've become a stranger—no, not that—a deceiver. An enemy."

"You won't hurt me, Mother?" Of course she would. Hate had been her guiding motive all Agatha's life.

"Do you think I will, Ivy? Will I cut her throat open in order to get my Maggie back from you?"

"Let her go or I'll skin you alive, you hateful besom."

Brunne reached into the pocket again. "Take this."

What other horrid thing might she have hidden in there?

It was a ball of twine. She tossed it at Ivy. "Wrap one of your hands to the bedpost."

She had never seen her sister back down from anything, but she did now. Hands trembling, Ivy picked the twine off the floor then tethered one of her hands to the bedpost.

Inch by slow inch, Brunne lowered the knife from Agatha's throat.

Before she could spin about, wrest the blade from her hand, the maniac moved, pressed the blade to Ivy's temple.

"Wrap your hand to the other post, Agatha—no, not that one. At the other end. I'm going to get my child and I won't have you interfering."

Swiftly, she sliced the twine and tossed it to Agatha. Ivy took that instant to clout the nurse in the head. She wrestled for the knife but all she got was a cut on her inner arm.

Terrified, Agatha bound her wrist to the post. That blasted blade was only inches from her sister's heart now.

Brunne slit the twine then secured her other hand.

Setting the knife on the floor beside her boot, Brunne secured Ivy's free hand.

"Oh, you are both bleeding," she cooed. "You do understand it's what you get for keeping my baby from me all these years."

"Clara is not your baby, Hilda!" Agatha said, not really believing the voice of truth would have any sway. "She's Ivy's baby."

"Perhaps she is. Maybe you are right when you say I'm mad." She spun her glare to Ivy. "It doesn't matter to me. You took my babies. I'll take yours."

"I'll gnaw through this binding before you have the chance!" Ivy's dark look back at Brunne should have made the woman quake.

"I imagine you could, given time." Brunne giggled. The depraved sound was like nothing Agatha had heard before. "Oh, but you don't have time."

Glancing about for her cane, she spotted it and hobbled toward it, crippled once again. Picking it up she went into the hallway.

Her skirt hadn't cleared the doorway before both she and Ivy began to pick at the twine with their teeth.

It would take a while, but it could be bitten through.

The scent of kerosene grew stronger in the hallway.

"Hey! Are you crazy?" It was the voice of the young man who had directed Agatha to Brunne. "Put that down."

There was a thump, the sound of a body slumping to the floor.

Hilda returned dribbling lantern fuel across room.

"Poor boy slipped in the hallway. I hope he comes to before the fire reaches him."

Hilda Brunne set the can of fuel on the floor only feet from the bed.

She struck a match, tossed it into the hallway.

On a run toward the saloon, William made a mental list of the ways he would chastise—no, not that, *remind*— his wife of how she needed to be more careful.

Confronting Brunne on her own was a foolish thing to

do. He never should have admitted that the woman was in town and working for Pete.

From a block away, he heard the sounds of revelry. Laughter, cursing, the pounding of piano keys. It was a far thing from the elegant event he'd just walked out of.

And somewhere in that debauchery, Agatha was confronting the devil. Did she think she would be able to reason with her? Was she seeking revenge for all Brunne had done to her and her family?

Retribution didn't seem likely. Agatha was not the type of person for it.

That meant she had to be trying to talk an insane woman into sanity.

He wasn't much of a husband, letting her face this on her own. Hell, he hadn't meant for her to deal with it at all.

Images of what might be happening made him pick up his step. He heard his boots thudding faster on the boardwalk, the air rushing out of his lungs with the exertion of pushing himself to his limit.

He was brought up short when he saw a young woman running toward him wearing only a shift. She waved her arms, cried out his name.

She thumped into him, grasping him tight about his ribs. She pivoted until she was under the crook of his arm.

"Don't let him catch me! Your wife promised you wouldn't let him have me."

It was the girl from the saloon, the one who was drugged until she was barely conscious.

"Whoa, there. It's all right." He held her at arm's length, feeling bones under thin muscles. The poor girl was far too frail. He couldn't help but remember when Agatha was the same way. "Who is trying to catch you?"

She pointed up the boardwalk.

The answer to his question jogged toward them, past the bank and the general store, the tip of his cigarette bobbing red in the dark.

"Pete, he says he owns me," she whispered.

Gently, he placed her behind him.

"I see you've caught my runaway." Pete had to bend, brace hands on knees to catch his breath. "I'll take her now."

"I get the impression she doesn't want to go with you."

A gust of wind whistled down the middle of the road, twirling up a dust cloud. It ruffled his sleeves and twisted the badge pinned to his shirt.

"What difference does that make?"

"Every difference. She stays with me."

Lydle dropped his cigarette. The fiery tip rolled away with the wind to be snuffed out in the dust ten yards down.

"I don't think you understand, Mayor. This girl is my property. I paid her mother good money for her services."

"Are you admitting to purchasing a human being, Lydle?" That right there was reason to apprehend him. "To kidnapping?"

"Her mother signed her away into my custody, so to speak."

"She's under my protection, now." Impatience to get to Agatha made his nerves jump, twitch under the surface of his skin. But before he could do anything, he had to take care of the young woman she'd sent to him.

"Let's go." He turned toward home, keeping his back between her and Pete Lydle's glare.

The faster he got the young woman into the care of his mother, the sooner he could bring Agatha home and arrest Lydle.

"Expect a visit from my—" Lydle shrugged, slowly

closing his hands into fists. "My employees. They'll come around and collect her directly."

"Is that a threat, Lydle? Directed at this child?"

He curled his fist, anger beating hot in his brain. He longed to punch the sneer off the saloon owner's face. But he was the law, not free to lash out in anger.

Another figure strode out of the dark. As the man came closer he recognized Travis Murphy.

This was a bit of good luck. He could send his charge back to the mansion under his protection.

If he was lucky, he'd have Agatha back home and still have a few minutes to figure out what to do about Lydle's hired thugs.

"Howdy, miss," Travis said with a curious nod at the mostly undressed girl. He didn't acknowledge the saloon owner. "I figure my wife must be with yours, William. I hope you know where they are. Clara's hungry and raising the roof."

The girl startled them all with a sudden scream. She wagged her finger in the direction of the saloon. "Fire!"

In the instant, all else was forgotten. The four of them dashed for the saloon.

William's heart slammed against his ribs at the sight of flames scratching the sky.

Agatha twisted her hand in the twine, pulling and tugging. Thankfully, Hilda Brunne hadn't noticed that she had only loosely bound it.

Still she would have to reach the knife that Brunne had left on the floor in order to cut her hands free.

"Rotten witch." Ivy spit out a piece of twine then resumed gnawing the binding on her wrists.

Smoke from the hallway billowed into the room. Agatha couldn't see the flames yet but she felt the heat and heard its crackle-snap.

She stretched her foot toward the knife but the unconscious bulk of Brunne's body lay half on top of it. While she stretched, groped with her boot toe, she sent up a prayer for the young man lying in the hallway.

"Too bad she didn't slip and hit her head somewhere else. I've almost got it—I think."

Drat! Her toe hit the tip and pushed it free of Brunne, but an inch away from her foot. Glancing at the hallway she spotted flames. It could only be seconds before they followed the fuel trail into the room.

"If I can kick the knife toward you will you be able to shove it back closer to me? I might be able to reach it if I can just get my hand…" She groaned and yanked. The bite of yarn dug into her wrist. "It's out! Quick Ivy!"

Stretching, reaching until she felt her shoulder joint would pop, she brushed her fingers on the floor. The knife slid into her hand as though it had been guided.

Agatha sliced her bonds, then Ivy's.

Smoke became thicker, swirling around their heads with deadly intent.

Faintly, over the roar of feeding flames she heard screams coming from the casino. The fire must be spreading with deadly speed.

Brunne groaned, thrashed about on the floor. Agatha knelt beside her.

"Hilda! You must wake up!" She patted the flaccid cheek.

"I'll see to the boy." Ivy rounded the corner into the hallway.

Hilda Brunne sat up with a start, her eyes bulging.

"We're going to die!" she pushed to her feet, limped toward the door leading to the casino.

Agatha caught her skirt. "No! You won't make it that way."

Banshee-eyed, shrieking, she kicked Agatha's hand. Grabbing up the can of kerosene, she dashed for the door and flung it open.

Overcome with panic, she must not have seen the wall of flame that she raced toward.

"Stop!" Agatha shouted, even knowing Brunne could not hear her.

Agatha shut the door against the smoke swirling into the room. Clearly, there was only death that way.

With the fire spreading so fast, there might not be a way out of here at all.

Crawling into the hallway, she took hold of a worn brown boot. Fighting a coughing fit, she helped Ivy pull the boy out of the hallway.

It might not matter that they dragged him back into the bedroom. Fire was everywhere.

The entire block looked red with reflected flames pulsing on walls and windows.

By the time William reached the saloon, more than half of it was engulfed. The heat was fierce enough to make his shirt smell like it was being ironed.

Folks fled the building, crying, tripping down the stairs while dropping money and chips on the road.

Over the sounds of panic and Pete Lydle's loud cursing, he heard the church bell clanging.

Within moments townsfolk rushed toward the scene in their nightclothes, carrying buckets and shovels.

William's gaze skipped from person to person, searching for the one wearing a frilly blue dress.

"Go around back!" The girl tugged on his sleeve. "Your wife was in a rear room last I saw her."

On a run, elbow to elbow with Travis, he dashed around the back.

The girl didn't follow, but remained across the street with a group of stunned onlookers.

Timber from the roof exploded in a spray of sparks then crashed to the rooms below.

Beside him a window exploded outward. A piece of glass cut his shirt. From the corner of his eye, he noticed a cut on Travis's cheek.

The hallway along the back rooms was not yet engulfed. Not that it mattered a great deal since halfway down the path was blocked by a wall of fire. It curled up the walls and lapped the ceiling.

"I see something!" Travis covered his nose and mouth with his arm, coughing violently. "Our wives!"

William saw them, too. They looked wavy, as though he was viewing them through a sheet of undulating orange water.

From what he could tell, they had removed their gowns, were using them to beat back the flames. They were on their knees, dragging something—no—dragging someone along with them.

He could not recall ever seeing a situation so hopeless. Yes, they did manage to snuff out fire. But for every inch they gained, the ceiling rained cinders.

How many feet of fiery floor would he have to cross to get to Agatha? Five? Ten? Fifteen? It was impossible to tell with waves of heat distorting reality.

From the looks of it she would watch him incinerate before he reached her.

"Everyone! Form a line!" His mother was suddenly beside him. "Pass the buckets! Here's one for you, son."

The bucket did not contain water, but dirt. He dashed

it at the blaze. Six inches of flame smothered beneath the grit.

Beside him Travis dumped another pail. Looking back to get the next one, William spotted the Normans, Bert Warble, Uncle Patrick, Antie, Aimee Peller, Preacher Wilson and a line of people from town passing buckets forward, hand over hand. Even Mrs. Peabody was there to urge them along.

Within a minute they had crushed two feet of flame. The trouble was, the roof was beginning to break apart.

"Everyone get out!" he called. The risk was much too great for them to remain.

Buckets kept coming.

Looking up, he saw his wife clearly. Her hair hung about her shoulders, her face was smudged with smoke and sweat. On her knees she beat at the fire with what was left of her gown. In rhythm, she and Ivy slapped, slapped, slapped again, then pulled a man after them by his boots.

Overhead, boards creaked. Under his feet the floor quivered, just a slight tremble coming up through his boots.

"Get out, now!" This time it was Travis who shouted the order.

Glancing back, he saw his mother pushing the rescuers down the smoking hallway.

The building was coming down with only a few impossible feet between him and Agatha.

She must have heard the structure falling as well, for she stopped batting the flames, reached for her sister's hand then looked at him through the flames.

Touching her lips with a kiss, she turned her fingers toward him.

"Come, William," his mother's voice caught, sobbed on his name. She yanked his sleeve hard.

He kissed her cheek, then dove headfirst through a foot-wide thicket of fire. He heard a thump, looked up to see Travis on the floor beside him.

"What the hell, Travis? You've got a child to raise."

"Yeah, she's hungry and needs her mother."

The last barrier of flame between them and their wives was four feet high. Travis leapt. William followed. Heat seared his chest, belly and legs.

He rolled to a stop against Agatha's knees. She patted the cuff of his pants where a flame had caught.

With no time to talk he picked her up, intending to dash across hell to get her out.

"No!" She wriggled down. "Carry him."

He'd argue about it if there was time. If there was no time, he didn't want his last words with her to be harsh.

"I love you," he said instead.

He and Travis supported the man between them. Ivy and Agatha slapped at the fire ahead.

They needed a miracle.

The building groaned. A portion of the second floor fell in a whoosh, landing with a noise like thunder between them and the exit.

Incredibly, a bed fell down with the floor. The mattress formed a bridge across the flames.

Agatha and Ivy ran ahead, clutching hands. He and Travis bore the unconscious boy between them.

Sounds of hades chased them: ceilings crashed, and the inferno screamed in a voice that sounded nearly human.

Within seconds they were free of the building, not the danger. A flying board hit him in the shoulder. He heard Travis yelp, but not lose stride.

He gave himself a focus point, Agatha sprinting away.

No matter the distraction, he did not allow his attention to settle on anything else.

Cooler air hit his face. The boy groaned but did not wake up. A couple of men wearing nightshirts rushed over to take him.

Glancing quickly about, he spotted Agatha, bloomers singed and camisole black with ash, leaning against a hitching post to catch her breath.

Dodging half a dozen people rushing in all directions, he hurried to her, caught her up in an embrace.

"Your mother." She pointed toward the bank.

A hundred feet up the boardwalk, his mother knelt on the ash-dusted wood, weeping. Lark and Dove patted her back but he doubted that she felt the comfort in her grief.

There was no reason for his mother to believe they had not perished in the fire. She'd been there, witnessed the hopeless situation. Watched her son choose to die with his wife.

None of them should have made it out of there. Had it not been for part of the upper floor falling, delivering the miracle of the bed bridge, they would not have.

Seeing his indomitable mother on her knees, her face buried in her hands, broke him. A single sob clenched his lungs. After everything that had happened within the last half hour, this was what finally left him staggered.

But Agatha was there to take his hand. "Let's go to her."

He drew upon her strength. It was all he needed to get his legs back under him.

Together, they hurried toward her.

Kneeling, he drew his mother's hands away from her face. "Ma, I'm alive. So is Agatha."

"Of course you are!" She swiped her face with the

back of her hand. Tears and ashes streaked her cheeks. He lifted her to her feet. "I never doubted—"

She hugged him tight then reached out her arm and drew in Agatha. "I thought I'd never see you again. Ivy and Travis? The boy?"

"Over there." He pointed a building up. "A bit toasted, but fine. I'm not sure about the boy. He was unconscious last I saw, but alive."

"I'd better see what I can do to help." His mother patted each of them on the cheek then spun about to hustle down the boardwalk.

William grabbed his wife by the hand and pulled her into the privacy of the alley.

He skimmed her arms, touched her neck and ribs, making sure she was as whole as she seemed. Cupping her cheeks he looked at her, accepting the fact that she was alive and unharmed. Then he kissed her long and hard with a full and thankful heart.

"I've got to get to work. Will you be all right?"

"As right as anyone else." She touched him in the same probing way as he had done to her. Apparently satisfied, she squeezed him about the ribs.

Coming out of the alley with his arm around her shoulder, pulling her close, he watched the chaos he would need to deal with. People ran about crying, wailing, huddling on the boardwalk and staring while the formerly elegant hotel collapsed, spraying sparks and flames into the night sky.

"I see your uncle and his wife. Will you go with them while I deal with this?"

She kissed his cheek. "You taste like smoke. I'll be helping your mother."

Watching her go, he was so damn grateful. He only hoped everyone had been as lucky. That no one was watching the collapsing saloon, fearing for loved ones who might still be trapped inside.

One man didn't seem concerned about survivors, or about those who might not have.

Pete Lydle.

He crawled about in the dirt grabbing money that folks had lost while fleeing the saloon. Seemed he couldn't stuff it into his pockets fast enough.

The greedy fool didn't notice William's approach. It was no wonder, with his focus on his lost wealth and not the people in need of help.

"Lydle!" He looked up, seeming surprised to see William. Twisting flickers of crimson from the dying saloon reflected in his eyes. "I'm arresting you."

"On what grounds?"

"More grounds than I know about yet. For now it's false imprisonment and theft."

"That woman was only a whore. It hardly matters. All this cash came from the Palace. It's mine by rights."

William yanked him up and found he had help from three of Lydle's "girls." One by one they kicked him in the rump.

"Did all of you make it out?" he asked.

"I believe so," said one with ash dulling the orange hue of her hair.

"Not that crazy old woman, though," said the last one to kick Pete. "I saw her. I think she was already dead when the beam from the second floor fell on her."

Chapter Eighteen

Clean.

Agatha trailed her chipped fingernails down one arm and then the other while she sat at her dressing table. She studied her face in the mirror, looking at it from one side then the other.

She had doubted for a time that the ashy residue on her skin would ever wash off.

There was that one last speck on the tip of her nose. She scraped it off then picked up a brush and tugged it through her damp hair.

If only the memories that haunted her mind could be scrubbed away. No amount of rosewater was going to make her forget the scent of kerosene and burning wood; of fear and the certainty of death.

Not just her death—worse—Ivy's and Travis's, her own dear William's.

And the grief that death would have left! That is what tore at her. No matter how hard she scrubbed her mind, she could not wash away the image of Victoria weeping on the boardwalk.

If they had all perished, what would have become of baby Clara?

She hadn't heard yet if anyone had died in the fire besides Hilda Brunne. There was no way she could have survived, running into the flames like she had.

Setting her brush aside, she dumped the pail of water she had been warming over a low fire into the bathtub.

Heat and flame were not things she appreciated right now, even if safely contained in the fireplace. But she wanted a warm bath for William when he finally came home.

Going out into the hallway, she listened to the quiet sounds of the sleeping household. No one who lived here or any of the guests had been injured.

At three in the morning, they had all yielded to exhausted slumber.

All except William—he was still in town dealing with it all, either as mayor or sheriff.

Walking to the window at the end of the hallway, she drew the curtain aside. Flames no longer twisted toward the stars but had given way to an orange glow that eerily shifted over rooftops between the mansion and the saloon. It was a wonder that no other buildings had burned.

It must be because the wind had quit as quickly as it had begun. The still air kept the embers from blowing and setting other blazes.

Down below, she heard the doorknob quietly turn. Heavy footsteps crossed the foyer.

Agatha dashed down the steps and would have welcomed William home with a big hug but he held her away from him, indicating with a quick nod how dirty he was.

"Come upstairs. There's a bath waiting."

"I feel like you just told me a bit of heaven slipped into the bedroom."

"Something like that."

Coming into his room, their room now, she closed the door softly. She had no intention of staying apart from him ever again.

William stood beside the tub, gazing at the water. He seemed too exhausted to take off his clothes.

"Let me help," she said while unbuttoning his shirt. She peeled it carefully off his shoulders, the fabric being stuck to his skin by sweat and ash. He winced when the shirt sucked over a beet-colored welt on his shoulder. "You're hurt."

"That's the worst of it," he assured her. "Not too bad."

With his clothes shed, he stepped into the tub. She understood his sigh of surrender when his body relaxed into the bath.

Cupping her hands, she dribbled warm water over his cheeks and nose. He closed his eyes. With dripping fingertips, she rinsed and stroked until the grime was gone.

His lips tugged up at the corners. He kissed her hand.

"The saloon is gone, but I reckon you guessed it would be."

"I've heard it was a beautiful building at one time."

She pushed his shoulders further down into the short tub. His knees poked out of the water like twin mountain peaks.

"It was. Sure isn't how it ended up, though. No one will miss it."

She massaged his scalp, washed his hair and watched rivulets of ash drip into the water.

"Were there many injuries? Did everyone survive?"

Her heart felt like it stopped while she waited for him to answer.

"The last patient left the doctor's office half an hour ago. There were burns and broken bones, but nothing critical."

He caught her hand, opened his eyes. "One person died. Hilda Brunne."

"I thought she had."

With a nod, she resumed washing his hair. She didn't need to, it was black and glossy now, but it was a comfort to touch it.

"Did anyone see her body?"

She had been presumed dead once before.

"One of Pete's employees saw her unconscious. She also saw a beam fall on her. So I assume she's gone, but it will be a while before the fire cools enough to know for sure."

"How is the boy we brought out?"

"He came to with a big lump on his head. The doctor says he'll recover in a few days."

"It was Hilda who hit him in the head when he tried to stop her from lighting the fire. She left him to die without a thought, not a single sign of remorse."

"Everyone's been wondering how the fire began."

"She tied me and Ivy to the bed. She poured kerosene in the hall and some in the room, but she lit the match in the hallway."

"I do love you, Agatha. I'll be grateful to God for every day I get to spend with you."

"Yes, I won't begin a day without being thankful. Or go to sleep not loving you."

They sat silently for a moment. She couldn't tell what William was feeling in the moment. Strangely enough, in spite of all that had gone on, she was simply happy.

"Odd," he said at last, "how the fire burned faster in main part of the saloon than where you were."

"Hilda took the can of kerosene with her when she ran into the main area. That might have had something to do with it."

"Plenty of alcohol for fuel, too. Once those drapes lit, it would have burned in a hurry."

She became silent again, listening to sound of his breathing and the whisper of the water swishing through his fingers.

"Oh! I sent you a young woman! Did she find you?"

He laughed, just a little, but somehow it made the horror of the night lose its chokehold.

Not a single innocent person had perished. The saloon was gone. After a while the nightmare would fade, folks would go on with their lives.

"You could send me a hundred women and I'd never even notice them." With a hand at the back of her neck, he tipped her face down to his, kissed her. "But, yes. She found me. Actually, she led me to you. And because of her, Pete Lydle is in jail. In his way he is as crazy as Brunne was. So greedy he thinks he can own people."

He squeezed her hand and kissed it once more.

"It was dangerous going to the saloon on your own. I wish you hadn't, honey. I was on my way over there to deal with Brunne when the fire began. I wish you could have trusted me to take care of you."

"There's no one I trust more. It's just that I hoped to convince her to go away. I thought if she saw me she would understand that I was no longer vulnerable to her, she would realize she could not make things the way they were before. If you were with me, she would have seen you as the strong one. She might—probably would—have believed that if she got rid of you, she would have me again."

He nodded, sighed deeply. "I understand. I see the logic of it. But still, I'm your husband and in the future when you need protecting, I'll do it. As much as I respect your right to watch out for yourself, I have the right to do it, too."

She rested her chin on the top of his head, crossed her arms over is chest. "I always did think of you as my brave prince. The truth is, I don't mind you watching out for me on occasion."

"I know how strong you are, in your body, your mind, your heart. I'm in awe of you, wife. I can be overbearing sometimes, but it's not out of disrespect for you, because I respect you more than anyone I've ever met. It's just who I am."

"And I love who you are. I don't want you to change. I saw something tonight, William. It made something clear to me that I'd never understood."

He turned his head to kiss the crook of her elbow. The brush of his lips and beard stubble tickled her skin. "What?"

"Grief. I never knew how crushing it could be until I saw your mother crying because she thought you were dead. I was sad when my father died, but he was distant from me and I guess that made the grief distant, too. Growing up, I never even had a pet to cry over.

"What I'm trying to say is that it would kill me to lose you. Life would be desolate—life would be death."

Sitting up in the water, he pivoted as best he could in the cramped tub to look at her.

"I understand, now, why you wouldn't risk my life by taking me to bed. If that is still what you want, I will accept it."

Slowly, he stood up. Water dripped down his tall muscular body. Looking up, she watched a drop slide swiftly down his neck, over his chest until it caught on a dark hair near his nipple. It hung there for an instant then slowly traced the defined shape of his belly. She lost track of it when it slipped into the shadow of his private hair.

Her throat gone dry, she swallowed hard. She would accept whatever he decided, but it was going to be difficult.

In the end, she loved him far too much to be the cause of his heartache.

Stepping out of the tub, he lifted her, carried her to the bed. Laying her down, he stretched out beside her, traced a line from her throat to her belly with his finger.

"I've learned something, too." Leaning down, he kissed her tenderly. "Life is precious, beautiful. Love is worth the risk."

"It's a shame about the old woman," Roy Backley, the banker, declared while staring at the heap of ash and debris that used to be the saloon.

It had taken ten days for the rubble to cool enough to allow the town coroner to retrieve the body and determine how Brunne died.

No matter how he felt about Hilda Brunne, William was glad to discover that it had been by a blow to the head and not by fire.

Agatha and Ivy wanted to see her buried in a proper way because there was no one else to do it. No matter that she was deranged, she had been an employee of the Lucky Clover for many years.

"She was a crazy old besom." Mrs. Peabody wagged her cane at the debris pile. "I, for one, will sleep more peacefully in my bed now that the saloon is gone, and those gamblers in my posies with it."

"Yes, I won't miss the saloon one little bit." Aimee Peller put up her parasol to block the glare of the sun.

"I'm so very grateful that our sheriff put nasty Mr. Lydle in jail."

Not that William knew quite what to do with him now that he had. A circuit judge was coming in a couple of weeks. He'd let His Honor deal whatever justice required.

Miss Valentine whined in his arms. The mouse was out, crawling up Ivy's sleeve and across her shoulder. For as much as Ivy and Agatha loved the rodent, William shared the dog's point of view.

Of course he would not whine his opinion like Miss Valentine was free to do. He set the dog on the ground.

Standing beside him, his mother held baby Clara, rocking and cooing to her. She was rewarded with a giggle.

"You sweet, sweet, girl," his mother answered.

That was an opinion he would gladly express.

"She sure is. Pass her over."

Her weight settled into his arms. He tickled her belly. "I'm your uncle, little darlin'. Your daddy and I will protect you from every danger."

No matter what she might say about it when she got older.

The odor of burned wood lingered all over town, a reminder of what had happened. In case a reminder was needed.

Every day people visited the ruin, standing, staring, feeling grateful that no other buildings had burned as they might have.

A few gamblers remained in town, waiting on the judge. They believed that during the fire Pete had taken money that was rightfully theirs. They were hopeful the judge would see things their way. They were the only folks who were saddened by the loss of the saloon.

"Hello pretty baby." Agatha kissed Clara's cheek,

slipped her hand in the crook of William's arm and squeezed. She glanced up at him with a wink.

It was not impossible that this time next year he would be making his own child giggle. In fact, given that he and his wife spent nearly as much time in bed as out, it seemed likely.

Joyful, that was what he felt about it. If the future held something else, that was for then. He was living now, in a time of gladness.

Leaning down, he answered Agatha's wink with a kiss—a promise.

During the kiss he became aware of a horse's hooves galloping up the dirt street.

He broke the kiss reluctantly. Horses didn't normally gallop unless their riders needed something. Probably something of the sheriff, but hopefully only the mayor.

Circumstances had proven to him that he was far better suited for being mayor than sheriff, even if a few folks—his mother for one—thought otherwise.

The man stirring up the dust looked familiar. Bringing his mount up short, he slid off the saddle then wound the reins about a watering trough.

Striding forward, he tipped his Stetson back from his face.

"Mayor," he stated, hand on hip, his stance self-assured. "I've a matter to discuss."

The man was the candidate for sheriff that the town's people had dismissed as being too short.

William handed Clara to her auntie Agatha.

People turned away from the fascination of the ruins and gathered closer to hear what the fellow wanted to discuss.

"Did you ever hear of the Potter gang? They robbed

the train near Cheyenne last winter. Or Millard Creed, the bank robber who terrorized three states?"

"Everyone's heard of them." Mrs. Peabody shivered visibly.

"I'm the one who arrested them." He handed William a bunch of papers folded up in twine. "It's verified in the letters of commendation I brought with me last time."

"I read them. It was my opinion that you were highly qualified."

"If your only reason for rejecting me is that you all," he said with a quick glance at the people who had turned him away the first time, "thought I'm short, I assure you I am more than qualified for the position."

"I agree. Always have."

"In that case, if you haven't already hired someone, I'd like the job."

"The job is yours, Sheriff."

He slipped the badge from his own shirt and plunked it in the lawman's hand.

"Welcome to Tanners Ridge."

The horse snorted in the silence that followed.

If any man objected to his hiring a sheriff without the counsel's approval, he would appoint him to the job instead.

Aimee Peller twirled her pink parasol, strode forward, her skirt swaying flirtatiously.

"Welcome to Tanners Ridge, Sheriff." Her smile at him was every bit of welcoming. "I'd so love to hear of your adventures."

"Your mother is right," Agatha said moments later, after Aimee latched onto the new sheriff's arm and led him down the street for coffee. "You were a much more handsome sheriff."

"At least he knows what he's doing."

"You were brilliant and brave," she said because he was.

Still, she knew how relieved he must be to have the responsibility for Pete Lydle transferred to a genuine lawman.

"I'm glad to see that matter settled," declared Uncle Patrick, walking up and hugging her shoulder. "I've another thing I'd like to discuss with all of you. Can I treat you to pastries at the bakery?"

Fifteen minutes later they sat at an oval-shaped table, a plate of chocolate cookies centered on the lace tablecloth.

Victoria rocked Clara who had fallen asleep in her arms. It was hard to know which of them was more content.

Seeing it, William reached for Agatha's hand under the table, squeezed it gently. The expression in his glance spoke something more fervid than gentle.

Uncle Patrick sure was taking a long time building up to what he wanted to discuss.

Antie nudged him in the ribs. Whatever it was must be important. All of a sudden her heart froze. Was he ill, beginning his goodbyes?

"The *Queen* is for sale again." His grin shot so wide it looked like it might split his face. "I want to purchase her."

Antie must want that, too. Her smile was nearly as wide as Uncle Patrick's.

"What do you mean?" Ivy's brows dipped low, her gaze at their uncle dubious. "You told me the river trade was dying."

"And so it is." He patted Ivy's hand across the table. "I told you the truth about that."

"You planning on dry docking her until she rots?"

He shook his head, laughing. "You know I love that old boat. I wouldn't do that to her."

"*Tiens! Mon mari*, you have kept the suspense too long. Tell them!"

"Yes!" Agatha leaned forward, eager to hear.

"Tanners Ridge now needs a hotel so I propose to bring the *Queen* here and turn her into one that's more grand and elegant than the Bascomb ever was."

What? How?

Everyone looked back and forth at each other, at Uncle Patrick. He appeared confident, so he must have a plan.

"I can't do it on my own."

"Gosh almighty, Uncle. More help than we can give, I reckon. Do you figure on sailing her in on a cloud?"

"That's where I'll need your help, Ivy. I plan to take her apart, bring her here by train then put her back together. You know every stick of that riverboat. There's no one knows her better."

"Will you keep her as she is?" Ivy asked, her eyebrows creeping up.

"As much as I can and still make her a landlubber."

"I'm so happy I could dance a jig."

"Hold on to your feet a minute, my girl. I've made an offer on the land. Had a wire this morning that it's been accepted. But I'll need a financial partner."

Agatha nudged William's boot, letting him know she wanted this, but he was already extending his hand to her uncle.

"What about the *Queen*? Did you already offer for her?" Agatha had heard so much about the *River Queen* and wanted badly to see it.

"Aye, and it's been accepted as well."

Under the table, Agatha felt her sister's feet move. Sitting in her chair Ivy discreetly danced her jig.

"We shall have a toast to our success and the bright future of Patrick's *Queen*." Antie lifted her teacup.

The rest of them lifted coffee mugs.

"To the future," William stood to say, circling his drink to include each of them.

While he spoke the words to them all, his gaze was upon Agatha.

"To the future," she answered.

Whatever lay ahead, no one knew for sure. But today the future shone bright with hope and love.

Lots and lots of love.

Epilogue

September 1889, Cheyenne, Wyoming

Fifty-five men had been elected to draft the new State of Wyoming's constitution. Forty-five of them gathered with their friends and families for a photograph on the capitol steps.

William stood proudly among them. On July 8 he had been elected a delegate.

The moment that he and Agatha had worked so hard toward was happening.

His mother and forty of her closest acquaintances stood at the foot of the stairs cheering along with many others.

Statehood for Wyoming was something to wave flags for—to cheer about. There was a lot of work to be done to make the new state a place folks wanted to come to and call home, and he couldn't wait to get to it.

He wasn't running for governor, not yet anyway. But drafting the constitution was important work.

It was a task they had only twenty-five days to complete.

For all the work that lay ahead, today was a time for celebration.

Patriotic tunes lifted on the same breeze that ruffled brand-new flags bearing forty-two stars.

Down below, he watched people in the crowd proudly pointing out their relatives on the stairs.

The photographer readied her equipment.

One person was missing from the hoopla. His wife.

He scanned the assemblage for her. Perhaps she had changed her mind about climbing the steps for the photo.

Climbing the steps in her condition was something they had discussed. Depending upon how she felt, she would either stand with him or his mother.

Since she was not standing beside him, she ought to be with his mother.

She was not.

A knot of worry tickled his belly. But perhaps she was with Ivy and Travis who were apparently running late.

As soon as he saw Agatha he would remind her about the importance of staying close by—or maybe he wouldn't.

A blue feather fluttering on a woman's hat caught his attention. He watched it bob across the back of the crowd.

After a moment the wearer, his beautiful Agatha, strode into view. She was walking fast, carrying their eighteen-month-old son Matthew in her arms. Trailing behind like a row of ducklings were five-year-old Billy and three-year-old twins Mary and Ellen.

Spotting him, Agatha waved her hand, shot him an excited smile.

He was proud of standing here with the other men eager to draft the constitution. He and Agatha had worked so hard to get here.

He had stayed on, serving as mayor of Tanners Ridge for four years after the saloon burned. It had been a good time, with the children beginning to come and watching Uncle Patrick and Ivy bring the *River Queen* back to life.

The folks of Tanners Ridge were proud of having a steamboat in their town.

For the English family, life in Tanners Ridge could not go on forever. The time came when he moved them home to the ranch to prepare for the run for delegate.

Yes, he was proud of being here on the capitol steps, for everything he and his wife had accomplished to be standing here.

But down below, lined up in a row in front of his mother, were his children.

Nothing he would ever achieve in his life would make him more proud than they did. Billy was learning to ride a horse. Mary wanted to be a mommy. Ellen hoped to be gubernor, same as her daddy wanted. Peter had gone from walking to running.

Agatha, his heart, approached the bottom of the steps. She had blossomed into a hostess to rival his mother.

He had a few things to be proud of, but mostly it was his wife, his children.

Leaving his spot, he hurried down the steps. Agatha placed her small hand in his. He could not help but be reminded of how reluctantly she had placed it there when they wed.

Of how far they had come since that windy night.

"How are you feeling? Can you make it up?"

"Of course I can."

"We can stand down here for the photo."

"Not unless we want one of the children running to us and making the picture blur."

"If you're certain."

Glancing at the swell of her belly, he wasn't so sure. From the looks of things her time could come at any moment. He scanned the crowd, spotted the family doctor nearby his mother and felt the tension ease from his shoulders.

"After all this time, you still worry."

"Because you are my heart walking around outside of my body. You and our little one in there." Placing his hand on her belly, he felt the child heave, stretch. "I'll never get used to the idea there's a live person in there, even though I know it."

"I wonder who it is."

Lifting her face with one finger, he kissed her.

The photographer ducked under the cloth that covered the camera. She counted down, lowering her fingers one by one to indicate the exact moment she would take the photo.

Five…the crowd cheered. Four…he readied his smile. Three…he felt Agatha gasp. Two… "My water broke," she stated, her smile wide as forever. One…he smiled back at her.

And there it was, their gaze of love for each other, forever preserved in black and white. The moment when the future held its breath, when the promise of new life lived in the smile of its parents.

* * * * *

If you enjoyed this story, you won't want to miss these other great WESTERN stories from Carol Arens:

Get 2 Free Books,
Plus 2 Free Gifts—
just for trying the Reader Service!

HARLEQUIN *Presents*

Get 2 Free Books,
Plus 2 Free Gifts—
just for trying the Reader Service!

♦HARLEQUIN

SPECIAL EDITION